The Long Arm of the Law

He finished scribbling a ticket and handed her a small board so she could sign. Reluctantly, she did so, stuffing the ticket into her purse without looking at it. "What have I done that's so awful? I was only trying out my new car, and no one's even passed us since we've been sitting here." She got out of the car. She didn't like the way he towered over her, so when he moved to put the cuffs on her, she stuck her hands behind her back. "Let me go. Please? I promise not to exceed the limit again." *Until I make it out of this Podunk state . . .*

"Lady, I have a feeling you exceed every limit there is, but that's the judge's problem. You've already made me write my first speeding ticket in at least ten years." He pulled a cigar out of his shirt pocket and stuck it in his mouth, chewing on it as if he badly wanted to light it.

"We all have our temptations," she said pointedly, eyeing the vivid label, which she recognized as a very expensive brand because her Rothschild grandfather, Edgar, smoked the same one. When she tilted her head curiously, eyeing him with bright blue intelligence, he took the unlighted cigar out of his mouth, put it back in his pocket, and continued calmly, "Your hands, please."

Also by Colleen Shannon

Foster Justice

Sinclair Justice

Colleen Shannon

LYRICAL PRESS
Kensington Publishing Corp.
www.kensingtonbooks.com

LYRICAL PRESS BOOKS are published by

Kensington Publishing Corp.
119 West 40th Street
New York, NY 10018

All Kensington titles, imprints, and distributed lines are available at special quantity discounts for bulk purchases for sales promotion, premiums, fund-raising, educational, or institutional use.

Special book excerpts or customized printings can also be created to fit specific needs. For details, write or phone the office of the Kensington Sales Manager: Kensington Publishing Corp., 119 West 40th Street, New York, NY 10018. Attn. Sales Department. Phone: 1-800-221-2647.

Lyrical and the L logo are trademarks of Kensington Publishing Corp.

First Electronic Edition: July 2015
eISBN-13: 978-1-60183-295-5
eISBN-10: 1-60183-295-8

First Print Edition: July 2015
ISBN-13: 978-1-60183-296-2
ISBN-10: 1-60183-296-6

Printed in the United States of America

To my critique buddies: Majorie, Judy and Veronique. It was fun, gals, here's some of your handiwork.
Miss you.

CHAPTER 1

The sign said: "Amarillo: 50 miles. Beaumont to El Paso: 1046. Welcome to Texas."

Managing not to yawn at the needless reminder of how large this state really was, Mercy Magdalena Rothschild pressed slightly on the accelerator, impatient to finish this interminable trip. A new BMW M4 convertible was a great way to cover the miles, but it was still a huge distance from Washington, DC, to the booming metropolis of Amarillo, Texas.

Emm, as her best friends called her, was not looking forward to her destination, or to the tasks ahead, though as soon as she'd seen the job posting for historic preservation trust officer, she knew she had to apply. But the fact that she had another mission in coming to this border state never left the back of her mind. An unapproved mission even her parents didn't know about. But there was one skill she now excelled in after ten very expensive years of higher education: how to do research.

Even of the criminal variety.

Even of the missing persons variety.

But thinking about Yancy and Jennifer would only bring the tears, never at bay very long, back to her tired eyes, and on this long and winding road, she couldn't afford that. Trying to distract herself, she shuffled to the Beatles tune of the same name on the iPhone connected to the car's onboard computer system.

The song, one of her favorites, still wasn't distraction enough even when she sang the lyrics about a long and winding road leading to someone special's door. She broke off in midrefrain. Yeah, like she'd meet someone in Texas. To say men didn't get her was putting it mildly, but their reaction was consistent, as different as all five of her prior boyfriends had been.

One of them had even declared plaintively, "You're just weird, you know? And why do you use such big words?"

Because words are the font of knowledge and life, you dullard, learn a few, she'd wanted to say but had held her tongue as the door closed behind him.

As her song list cycled into another optimistic tune, Emm sighed, doubly depressed now. Her eyes burned behind her sunglasses, but the ache had nothing to do with the bright spring light. Yancy had been missing for six months, nine days—she glanced at her watch—and thirteen hours. Jennifer longer than that. She'd never forget the knock on her door at her tiny efficiency after eleven p.m. almost six months ago.

The Baltimore detectives who'd taken the missing persons report stood there, looking uneasy. "Ma'am, we have news about your sister and her daughter. May we come in?"

In her matchbox living room, they laid it out to her. The reward she and Yancy had posted for information leading to Yancy's missing daughter Jennifer had finally yielded a clue. Yancy had, as usual, been hell-bent and determined to follow up on her own because her younger sister Emm was embroiled in oral exams for her PhD. Then Yancy had disappeared, too. . . .

Of her own volition, before she even completed her orals, Emm had canvassed the downtown Baltimore bars Yancy favored, handing out and posting flyers for both women. Mother and daughter strikingly resembled each other: both naturally slim blondes. Yancy had been twenty-one when she'd had Jennifer, so she was only in her late thirties and looked a decade younger.

Finally, three months after Yancy's disappearance, nine months after Jennifer had been taken, one of the flyers yielded a tip. The night cook at a seedy little café in downtown Baltimore remembered coming off duty at one in the morning, and he'd seen a woman who matched the picture of Yancy being forced into a big black sports truck with Texas plates. Her scream was choked off as she was jammed into the front seat between the man who'd snatched her and the driver. He gave the detectives a description of the man who'd grabbed her but never saw the driver.

When the detectives asked why he hadn't come forward earlier, he gave the usual spiel about being afraid of being deported, but when the señorita—"that was you, Ms. Rothschild," they'd told her—had pleaded for information, he overheard and felt guilty. Besides, he wanted the reward to send back to his family in Mexico.

"But what exactly does this mean?" Emm had asked. "Yancy was taken to Texas? What about Jennifer?"

The detectives seemed uneasy. The younger one looked away, but finally the older detective, Sergeant Ruiz, answered quietly. "Three months ago we had an urgent message from your sister asking us to call, saying she had a lead on her daughter's whereabouts. We were working a dual homicide and by the time we called her back, her phone went straight to voice mail."

Emm wearily rubbed her tired eyes. "So? I was preparing for my orals, so she didn't even call me to tell me she was going after Jennifer. What does the phone call have to do with her being missing?"

"We think she got too close, that she must have stumbled across the northeastern source of the human trafficking ring. And they . . . took her, too."

Or worse. Emm heard what he didn't say.

He seemed oblivious to her doubts, going on calmly, "At least that's what we think if the eye witness is correct. So we combed surveillance footage all over DC's major arteries for a similar truck with Texas plates. The cook didn't recall the number. We found several matches heading south on the interstate, but none of the registered owners match the physical description given by the witness. In the meantime we informed the Texas authorities and were told there's a high-end snatch-and-grab ring with national reach culminating in West Texas. They bring in the . . . their . . . their . . ." He cleared his throat.

Emm inserted quietly, "I think the term is merchandise."

He looked relieved and nodded. "Anyway, they bring them from all over the nation through Texas to the border. We still haven't figured out how they smuggle them across. The Texas Rangers are heading the task force along with the Border Patrol. We've given them all the information we have but will work the case from this end as well."

Emm had to clear her throat because as she asked the question, she dreaded the answer. "What is the . . . the merchandise used for? Surely Yancy is too old for, for . . ."

He opened his mouth, swallowed, and then looked away, for the first time showing some genuine regret. The younger detective reached out to pat her shoulder, but under a sharp look from his partner, he froze and his hand dropped back to his side.

Emm closed her eyes, biting her lip to stifle a moan. She was a trivia and science buff. The average American citizen might not be aware that slavery was worse now, in the technological age, partly because of the anonymity of the Internet, than ever before in human history, but she knew the statistics. Recent UN estimates pegged the worldwide trade in human flesh at $32 billion and rising.

She also knew the vast majority of the kidnapped women were forced into prostitution. Yancy was beautiful, and though she was thirty-nine, looked twenty-five. After being taken more than nine months ago, Jennifer was probably nothing like the vibrant young seventeen-year-old she'd once been. But she was probably too valuable to greatly mistreat.

But Yancy? Emm's wild, irrepressible one year older half sister wouldn't tolerate boundaries, or orders. Once on the inside, assuming she'd been taken by the same people, she'd risk her life to find her daughter. And she would not take well to captivity.

"What can I do?" she whispered over the tears she was restraining.

"I know this is difficult, but keep handing out flyers," Ruiz suggested. "Try maybe to find out why she was in that part of Baltimore. We'll let you know if we get any more leads. Inform us immediately if you get any new information, no matter how insignificant."

"And you'll apprise me of any new leads?"

Ruiz's smile didn't reach his eyes. "Of course." Both men gave her sympathetic nods and left.

And that had been that. Three months passed, but neither detective had called her, even when her old friend Curt Tupperman, a freelance investigative reporter for several well-known papers, wrote a follow up article on the kidnappings. He broke the story, saying that various agencies believed the Baltimore area to be the East Coast beginning of the pipeline they speculated ended in the border town of El Paso or Del Rio, with stops in Dallas and Amarillo.

When Emm called Ruiz to ask for more information about the pipeline, he didn't call her back. Wondering why he'd stonewall her, Emm finished her demanding doctorate. In her spare time, she talked to everyone she could think of: classmates, friends, acquaintances, tenants in her sister's apartment building, old bosses, old boyfriends, including Curt, who had dated Yancy for two years and seemed upset when Yancy broke it off about six months before she was taken.

No one knew why Yancy had been in downtown Baltimore or of anyone who drove a macho Texas truck. The detectives were obviously off on another big case. Yancy was just another missing woman, and since she was Emm's half sister, she wasn't even a Rothschild.

Now, three months later, on a long lonely road to nowhere, Emm glared around at the sere landscape too tough to yield more than mesquite and cactus. Maybe Yancy was already dead. Maybe Emm was on another foolish crusade, as her father had scolded her. Maybe her sister was buried in this wasteland. . . .

Emm removed her sunglasses to swipe angrily at her eyes, pressing harder on the accelerator.

So far, despite all the pressure she was under, she'd been good, exceeding the speed limit only when she could see for miles or had another speeder to follow. She looked around, even over her shoulder, and the landscape was so open she could see from horizon to horizon. Nothing. She was dying to try this new baby out. She knew the effort and expense her father had expended to give his only natural daughter this hundred thousand dollar–plus vehicle, partly his way of voicing his regret that his wife was a self-absorbed alcoholic who had long ago lost interest in her older daughter's fate. As sales manager for a BMW dealership, her father made good money and had been able to get a screaming deal on this car, but the only Rothschild inheritance he had was a silver dollar collection given to him by a remote relative. And the name, all too often, had been more of a burden to Emm than a boon. People assumed she had money and that she was cold and snooty because of her unusual grasp of the English language. Wrong on both counts.

Yancy had even less money; her own father had passed when she was a child, and their social-climbing mother was not happy about her willful older daughter, who refused to get a steady job or go to college. But Yancy and Emm, only a year apart, had always been close. And Jennifer . . . the tears threatened again as she remembered her beautiful, blonde, blue-eyed niece. She tried to picture her as she likely was now, a dead look in her eyes, forced into short, tight dresses and hooker makeup.

Emm's foot twitched at her unhappy thoughts, pushing down until the speedometer passed the conservative eighty, only five over the limit, the speed she'd tried very hard to maintain since she'd hit the Texas state line. She knew the expensive red sports car and her Maryland plates made her a delectable morsel to the typical Texas highway patrolman's ravenous appetite for revenue.

She looked around again. Clear. What was the harm in letting her hair down a bit? She was properly dressed in a sensible gray suit, sensible shoes, with her hair sensibly tied back, her usual camouflage for fieldwork. She was a female in a world of men, and she'd learned long ago to downplay her considerable good looks. Especially in a place as conservative as Texas. West Texas was the most conservative part of the state, the last bastion of the rugged individualist.

Badly needing her usual stress reliever, Emm gave up her battle. Speed was her only vice. Not the oral stimulant, but the automotive version, which was almost as addictive. She had twelve speeding tickets to prove it and had already lost her license twice, getting it back at great cost. Her insurance was astronomical, but nothing invigorated her as much as the wind howling through her hair and the roar of a powerful exhaust cheering her on.

Besides, she reasoned to herself, this car was meant for speed and she only had about thirty miles left to her destination. . . . She'd earned her favorite high after twelve years of tough academic work.

The needle hovered at a mere eighty-five now, ten over the limit. She took a last careful look around, but this section of road was too open for a speed trap. The needle on her M4 convertible didn't bobble when she pressed on the gas—in one gentle arc it went from eighty to one hundred in about two seconds. The engine was so smooth, the throaty growl entirely too civilized. The sleek German machine wasn't even challenged. Feeling one of her hairpins fly free and not caring, Emm pressed harder on the accelerator.

Finally the engine roared back, as if to say, *That all you got?*

Laughing, having the best time since graduation, Emm pressed harder still: 110, 120, man, this baby could fly. . . .

The wail of the siren was faint at first.

She'd glimpsed something black and big and shiny out of the corner of her eye as she streaked past a gate in a long row of white fencing, but she'd discounted it as a rancher's truck. She looked in her rearview mirror and stifled a groan, immediately taking her foot off the gas pedal. A siren wailed and she saw a blue and white light flash from a side of the SUV's roof. The light had obviously been attached only when the driver saw her zip past, so this cop was not a typical highway patrolman.

The neat little speech about how big Texas was, and no, she really didn't know she was going that fast, her Beamer was a new graduation present, went out the window with her deep breath. "Good going, Emm," she said to herself. "No one's more hard-nosed than an under-cover cop." She pulled to the side of the road, got the registration from the glove box, and took her insurance card and her Maryland driver's license from her purse.

In her side mirror, she watched the man approach. He was tall, over six feet, with iron gray hair she could just glimpse under his ex-pensive Stetson. Black, of course, to match his black jeans. His shirt was white, a dress shirt crisp with starch, sort of like his spine. His eyes were covered in mirrored shades, but there was no mistaking his glacial tone. "If you want to race that fancy little import, I can give you the address of a racetrack in Lubbock. Do you have any idea how fast you were going and all the lives you endangered, including mine, as I was about to pull out of my driveway, by driving like that?"

"I'm sorry, Officer, I was just in a hurry to get to Amarillo. You know, I'm like that bumper sticker: 'I'm not from Texas, but I got here as fast as I could.'" He'd stopped at her open window now and perused her documents, glancing between her driver's license photo and her flushed face. Her hairpins had long ago lost the battle, and her brown mane, shot through with blonde and red highlights, was tangled. She took off her sunshades so he could see her eyes. She blinked. "See, blue? Just like it says. I promise I'm not here to com-mit murder or fraud. . . ." So far her attempt at charm had been an abysmal failure, so she tried her original approach. "This car was a graduation present after I got my PhD. I'm still learning all the bells and whistles. I truly didn't know how fast I was going."

He didn't buy it, obviously. His mouth was beautifully shaped, meant for laughing, but she couldn't get it to even twitch. She'd been out of the dating scene too long.

With a curt, "Don't move," he stalked back to his SUV to run her ID. She stifled another groan. It had almost taken an Act of Congress to get her license back last time, not to mention thousands in fees and a good traffic attorney. Once he saw how many tickets she had. . . . Nevertheless, she was stunned when he returned to her side of the car with a pair of handcuffs.

"Get out of the car, please." He stepped back slightly, appraising her with eyes she knew were arctic behind the shades.

She looked at the Start button on her dashboard. She had one of the new ignitions, the kind that started only when the key was in the car. Her foot was on the brake, so she only had to punch that Start button and she could quite literally leave him in the dust.

Be sensible, Mercy Magdalena, she could hear her Irish grandmother pleading from the grave. This was not a good beginning to her first field investigation, and fleeing an officer of the law would not endear her to her federal employers. She looked at him from the corner of her eye. Besides, she might need some help from the local constabulary in looking for Yancy.

He'd stiffened alertly, as if he'd read her mind. His icy politeness softened to a Texas drawl that was somehow more menacing. "Please, do it. Resisting arrest carries a much longer sentence than speeding, and I'd purely love to buy your car at the police auction."

She took her foot off the brake and put the vehicle in Park. "It's not fair that you can drive as fast as you want, but even though I've never had an accident and I've driven on racetracks, I can't go over eighty." She bit her lip when an eyebrow arched above his sunglasses. "Seventy-five, I mean." Slowly, sullenly, she put the car keys in his outstretched hand.

He finished scribbling a ticket and handed her a small board so she could sign. Reluctantly, she did so, stuffing the ticket into her purse without looking at it. "What have I done that's so awful? I was only trying out my new car and no one's even passed us since we've been sitting here." She got out of the car. She didn't like the way he towered over her, so when he moved to put the cuffs on her, she stuck her hands behind her back. "Let me go. Please? I promise not to exceed the limit again." *Until I make it out of this Podunk state . . .*

"Lady, I have a feeling you exceed every limit there is, but that's the judge's problem. You've already made me write my first speeding ticket in at least ten years." He pulled a cigar out of his shirt pocket and stuck it in his mouth, chewing on it as if he badly wanted to light it.

"We all have our temptations," she said pointedly, eyeing the vivid label, which she recognized as a very expensive brand because her Rothschild grandfather, Edgar, smoked the same one. When she tilted her head curiously, eyeing him with bright blue intelligence, he took the unlighted cigar out of his mouth, put it back in his pocket, and continued calmly, "Your hands, please." The next thing she knew, he'd latched cuffs around her hands, put her in the backseat of his SUV, and started up his car.

"You can't just leave it there! Someone might steal it."

"You might be better off if someone did. What kind of idiot gives a speed demon a car like that?"

"My father gave it to me as a graduation present." She thought she heard a scornful, "That figures," but when she glared into his rearview mirror, where she could see his face, his lips were still and set into a very stern scowl.

She hated using this card, but it seemed the last one left. "Didn't you see the name on my driver's license? A Rothschild is many things, but an idiot isn't one of them. I can't believe you're actually arresting me. I don't have so much as an unpaid parking ticket!"

"Ma'am, I don't care what your name is, why you're here, or even that you're going to Amarillo. You're a menace to public safety and your own, and in Texas if I clock you at twenty-five over the legal speed limit, I have the right to arrest you on the spot and confiscate your driver's license. I clocked you at one twenty-five, fifty over the legal limit. Be thankful I've left you your license. For now . . ."

The implication wasn't lost on her. Her temper, always owing more to her Irish mother than her Jewish father, got the best of her. "So sorry I forgot my palm branch and grapes, but if I admit you're the boss, will you let me go?"

The SUV swerved slightly as those shades stared a hole in her. She swallowed the rest of her sarcasm, grudgingly impressed that he got the insult, glad when he finally looked back at the road. Great; no telling how much time and money it would take to get her license back after this escapade. She had to bite her tongue a few times, but she managed to keep quiet after that. Typically she could insult people without their being aware of it, but this cop was obviously well read. She was beginning to suspect he was more than a cop. And she couldn't afford to piss off the chief of police or some other hodunk honcho.

When they finally reached Amarillo, it was bigger and more modern than she'd expected. She looked around eagerly, but their route didn't take them downtown, where she glimpsed a surprising number of tall buildings in the distance. She sank back against the seat, reality hitting home with a vengeance. Her arrival was less than auspicious considering she was cuffed in the back of an unmarked police car. She looked up at the obviously institutional building looming outside the window as he parked in front of it. Typical bureaucratic block construction.

She'd only been to Texas once. When she was a child she'd been dragged by her Catholic grandmother, who had Texas roots, to see the Alamo in San Antonio. She vaguely recalled a very unimpressive cream adobe structure in the middle of a large city. The only hint of its glorious role in Texas independence had been bullet holes in the walls. Lots of them.

Still, when they'd returned to their brownstone flat in Brooklyn, Emm had checked out books on old missions from her school library. As she grew older, her fascination with old buildings increased to a passion. Now here she was, the ink on her PhD diploma in historic preservation barely dry, driving halfway across the country to investigate the misuse of historic resources in Amarillo, Texas, under the auspices of her new employer, the National Parks Service in Washington, DC. They seemed to have a lot of faith in her because the family trust controlling this particular historic block in downtown Amarillo had both money and clout. Sinclair, she'd learned from her research. She was supposed to see the head of the family, the managing member of the trust, someone named Ross Sinclair. The negotiations to stop the demolition of two old office buildings would be tricky at best in a state notorious for its strong property laws.

Especially now that she'd have to hire a driver to get around and hope this indignity didn't get back to her employers.

She realized the officer was holding open her door and got out. He caught her arm and escorted her up the steps. She followed meekly enough because she had no choice and because, deep down, she knew she'd been foolish to go so fast. She noted a prominent Texas Ranger seal on the door, and a bad feeling poked her in the stomach.

It couldn't be . . .

Inside the lobby area, he nodded at a receptionist behind a thick glass wall. She buzzed them in, looking curiously at Emm. Emm was sure she didn't fit the type of the usual culprits paraded through here. Her mug shot should be interesting. She debated sticking out her tongue . . . but she'd already pissed this peace officer off enough.

Please, let him just be a lieutenant or something, she said silently to herself.

When he brought her to another officer's desk—"Corey Cooper," based on the plaque at his desk—and sat her down while he fetched paperwork from a stack in a copy room, she smiled tentatively at the young officer. He looked Latino, so she tried a smile and a polite *"Buenas días."*

He nodded, his dark eyes skimming her legs appreciatively before he shielded his gaze with thick dark lashes. He began filling out the paperwork the other officer had handed him. The tall Texan in the black hat curtly explained the facts of the case and finished with, "We'll take a shared arrest on this one. It may not quite make the record books, but it's close." He unlocked Emm's handcuffs and stuck them in his back pants pocket.

"How fast?" asked the young Latino officer.

"One twenty-five and rising."

Corey whistled, cocking his head as he eyed Emm's expensive but very conservative suit. But he stayed professional and just kept filling out the arrest forms.

Emm read his thoughts, as she was so adept at doing. "I don't look the type, huh?"

The other officer had stepped several feet away and was now thumbing through messages an assistant had handed him.

As Emm eyed him, she remembered his offhand remark, *my first speeding ticket in at least ten years.* He was an upper-ranking officer, obviously. She was in an office with a Texas Ranger seal on the door and a bigger one in the middle of the floor.

She was Irish, or at least one quarter Irish. She kept the shamrock her grandmother had given her in her wallet as a talisman. She couldn't be that unlucky, especially at the start of a new job. No way could he be the Ross Sinclair she'd researched.

Captain Ross Sinclair, Texas Rangers.

Emm looked at Corey but made sure black hat could hear her. "Some people do drugs, others eat too much, some drink to excess. I speed. And while it's something of a compulsion, as vices go, is it really so awful? I'm a very good driver. I've never even had a wreck; check my driving history."

Corey looked like he was about to shrug, but his boss, whom

Emm now realized black hat must be, tossed his messages aside and strode back to tower over her. "If you'd worked as many highway accidents as I have, you'd realize the sheer stupidity of that remark. Sometimes the remains at accidents involving such high speed have to be scooped up. Literally." He swung on his heel and stalked away before she could respond.

Corey eyed her blush with a bit of sympathy. "The captain's brother died in a high-speed accident. He was driving a BMW."

The sharp pang became a knife. Black hat had never showed her a badge, but he'd been so obviously an officer of the law, she hadn't asked to see one. Finally admitting the better part of valor, Emm just shut up and cooperated as best she could to get this over with. While Corey finished the paperwork she looked around, noting all the Texas Ranger certificates on the walls. She eyed Corey's crisp shirt but didn't see a badge. Corey wasn't wearing it, but when she craned her neck, she saw a badge sitting on his desk, where he could grab it. Even she recognized that famous Lone Star.

The knife became the sword of Damocles, hovering over her foolish head. In her background research on her adversary Ross Sinclair, she'd smirked at his occupation, thinking it appropriate enough for a man who liked to boast his authority. Her heart now hammering against her ribs, Emm scrabbled around in her purse for the yellow ticket she hadn't even glanced at when he'd given it to her on the road. She'd signed in the appropriate place but had been too agitated to pay any heed to his name.

She spread the crumpled ticket on her knee. The bold signature leaped out at her.

Captain Ross Sinclair.

Emm stifled a groan, hearing her grandmother's voice more strongly than ever. *Emm, me girl, that temper will get the best of you one of these days.*

Glumly, she eyed the calendar on the wall. This was the day she'd been looking forward to all her life, the day she finally began taking an active role in preserving the old structures she wanted to protect for future generations. Her first case, her first chance to prove herself by persuading a powerful scion of a wealthy family that renovating old buildings was usually better than tearing them down, and she'd blown it before she started. She'd even been taught negotiation tactics in her schooling and had always made As in those courses because she really was good at reading people and being diplomatic—at least where her job was concerned.

And to top it off, her initial research had indicated this Ranger office was also managing the task force to which the Baltimore police had referred Yancy and Jennifer's cases. With the luck she'd had since she'd crossed the state line, Ross Sinclair was probably heading that, too.

Great. Just, great . . .

As they escorted her to her very first mug shot and she stared into the camera unsmilingly, she knew she'd accomplished at least one of her goals: She'd made an indelible impression on Captain Ross Sinclair.

CHAPTER 2

Later that evening, in his vast den with its vaulted, crossbeamed ceiling, Ross Sinclair moodily swirled his brandy as he stared into the crackling fireplace. It was tall enough for him to stand inside, so he seldom used it because of the enormous amount of wood required. It was spring, anyway, chilly at night but warmer during the day. Normally even when he was alone, except for his single employee, a cook/housekeeper/valet/butler, he kept the chill at bay with pashmina blankets and a brandy, but tonight he felt cold and discouraged.

The new eighty-inch LED TV on an adjacent wall was off. His expensive custom sound system, boasting discreet speakers throughout the five thousand square foot ranch house, played soft, mournful Celtic music. His favorite when he was feeling low.

Somehow arresting that Rothschild girl—woman, really, as he'd been surprised to see when he looked at her license—had revived unwelcome memories of the past and incited fresh doubts about his future. The hot little brunette with the blond streaks in her lush mane of hair, driving that ungodly expensive red sports car, had reminded him too much of Elaine. Wealthy, spoiled, and selfish, heiress of a wealthy family, she'd broken his heart, propelling him to drop out of graduate school at Yale on the medical school track and, on a wild hair, move to Texas with a fellow Yalie who had family in Amarillo.

Almost from the moment he'd set foot in West Texas, he'd loved it. Loved the open spaces, the friendly people, the desert climate, the openness to new ideas. While he missed his family, at twenty-three he knew he didn't want to stay in school. He had his bachelor's in political science, which was good enough. If he went back to the sprawling mansion in the Hamptons, his parents would push him to return to Yale, and he was sick of school.

So he stayed. And for a long time, at least, he thrived. It took him a good five years to get settled in the Highway Patrol, another five after that to break into the ranks of the Rangers. Along the way, he'd used an inheritance from his great-aunt, one of the few in the family not scandalized by his desertion from New York, and his own stock market skills, to slowly acquire a hundred-acre parcel and add to it over the years until his ranch was now almost a thousand acres. The recent oil strike had been sheer luck.

He understood the irony. The Sinclairs could trace their New England ancestry back to the *Mayflower* and had birthed a long line of successful tycoons and minor but still respected politicians, and Ross was one of the few of them who didn't give a flip about money. Yet he'd made more on his own than he'd ever inherited. It was his career that truly challenged him and kept him grounded. He'd seen up close and personal the way money, especially inherited money, corrupted. His fortune was purely an accident of birth and geography. Money was little solace for the missing family and passionate love he'd secretly yearned for all his life. Seeing his friend Chad find it in such an unexpected way had proved that it was, after all, possible to combine The Job with the right woman.

But only the right woman. And he wasn't an easy match . . .

As for the future, the job he'd always loved had, of late, been more chore than pleasure. He had almost twenty-eight years under his belt now, enough to retire early on a full pension if he chose. Now that his best friend on the force had become a lieutenant and accepted a desk job in Lubbock so he could spend more time with his infant son and wife, Jasmine, he seldom saw Chad Foster. Even the upcoming annual Sinclair reunion, when Ross's home became a world-class dude ranch, didn't fill him with his usual anticipation.

As he stared into the amber liquid, he finally admitted part of the problem. The fact was, he was getting old. Pushing fifty-two, he could soon retire if he chose, but he still had a long career ahead of him if he wanted it. The question was, did he still want it? He certainly didn't need the pension. Not to mention the second inheritance his grandmother was insisting on bequeathing to him over his protests. He'd already decided which charitable organizations to bless.

Irritated at the circular nature of his thoughts, he tossed back the last of his brandy and fetched the San Antonio paper. The headline blared up at him: "Texas Rangers lead hunt for human trafficking ring ending in El Paso." Tilting the specs he hated onto his nose, Ross read the article. How the hell had Tupperman found out all this proprietary information? He picked up his cell phone and dialed the freelance investigative reporter who'd broken the story. He knew he'd get an answering machine this late, but he had to go on record with his concern. Besides, he golfed sometimes with Curt Tupperman; he even liked the guy.

He minced no words in his message. "Curt, dammit, you know better than to go off half-cocked running a story like that with attribution. One of my assets may be in danger with the cartels, now you blabbed so many details. The cartels have very sophisticated information-gathering techniques, including hackers who can breach your security and get into your files. I want a retraction and a written promise from your publisher not to run anything like this again without clearing it with our office, or so help me, I'll go to Homeland Security and ask them to bring you all up on charges for interfering in our investigation." He hung up, not identifying himself because he knew Curt would recognize his voice.

He wadded up the paper and tossed it into the fireplace for kindling. Being a Ranger captain just wasn't fun anymore. It was bureaucracy, paperwork, soothing the big egos of all the VIPs in various federal departments. Every time he turned around, a new task force was being formed. Turf wars had always been rampant, but just keeping abreast of all the frickin' laws the Texas legislature loved to pass was a challenge.

And technology.

Everywhere, every day, technology was a curse and a blessing. Like all great advancements, it could be used both for good and for evil. Drones, for example. They'd just received their first one, but he wasn't sure he trusted either the guy operating it—he still had pimples and looked like a kid using a very fancy video game—much less the legality of the data collected.

Bottom line: He couldn't keep up even working fourteen-hour days and most weekends.

Glad he'd taken this Saturday off, Ross rubbed his temples, wishing for a cigar, but he'd finally managed to quit smoking totally when Jasmine informed him he couldn't visit the baby very often if he still smoked. Most people didn't dictate to Ross Sinclair, but he adored Jasmine, saw how happy she made Chad, and the baby was so much fun, he'd accepted her decree. He'd been meaning to quit anyway. Still, he was about to get up and see where he'd left that last Gurkha Centurion he sometimes still gnawed on, an elite Honduran tobacco that was one of his few vanities, when the doorbell rang.

He knew José had retired for the evening, and he didn't expect him to come all the way from the top floor just to answer a door twenty feet away from his boss. Still, as a precaution, given all the drug lords he'd pissed off, Ross stuck a Glock in the back of his pants before he opened the door.

He seldom got unannounced visitors, especially this late on a weekend, but when he saw his guest, he was shocked literally speechless.

That Rothschild woman stood there, her hair tangled, her makeup long gone, still dressed in the same, now wrinkled, conservative suit. She was biting her lip nervously and held a small box wrapped in blue paper with a bow. She gave him a tentative smile that stretched her sensual mouth and hit him below the belt. That really pissed him off . . .

"How the hell did you get out of jail so soon?" he finally managed. "Judge Trent wasn't supposed to see you until Monday morning."

"I know how to pull a few strings, and the Texas attorney general is a friend of my grandfather's. I've paid the fine and pleaded no contest, so they let me keep my license. For now. But I told them I'd personally apologize to you for my reckless behavior." Her smile widened hopefully. "So here I am. Sorry to show up so late, but I think we're both people of action."

He swallowed a groan and still glared at her, leaving her standing on the threshold. "How the hell did you figure out where I live? I know the department wouldn't divulge that."

"You told me."

He blinked.

She elaborated. "Remember, you said I almost ran over you when you were coming out of your driveway. My car was towed from just up the road, and the towing company gave me the GPS location."

His ire faded a bit, but she still made him feel . . . funny. He didn't like it; it was a way he hadn't felt in a long time, so he still stood there, blocking her. Texas hospitality be damned. Neither one of them were of Texas birth anyway. A trace of New York came back into his tone as he snapped, "Fine, what the hell do you want?" She tendered the box she held. "I'd have been here sooner, but I had to have these shipped same day FedEx because I couldn't find them anywhere in Amarillo."

He took the wrapped box, and even without removing the paper, he knew instantly what it was from the heft and shape. He stepped aside, waving her in, but he'd get her the hell out as soon as possible without being any ruder than he already had been.

When she stepped inside, he realized she was shivering. The Texas spring was as unpredictable as usual, warm during the day, but now a chilly breeze was howling. "Come inside. I'll warm you a brandy."

He swept a hand before him, and when she entered the great hall, he nodded at one of the leather wing chairs by the fire and tossed the package on the adjacent table. He added a bit more kindling to the dried oak wood fire and went to the wet bar in a corner of the room to pour her brandy into an expensive Waterford snifter. He took time to put the Glock out of sight behind the counter, not wanting to scare her. She was from the Northeast and had probably never even seen a pistol.

When he returned with her drink, she was leaning back against the wing chair, holding her hands to the fire, which was just now beginning to roar, her eyes closed, and for the first time he realized she was very tired. All the more puzzled at why she'd tracked him down so late, he poked the fire up a bit and held her snifter close enough to warm the brandy slightly.

He handed it to her. She accepted it gratefully, warming her hands before taking a sip. She coughed slightly, then took a deeper, more appreciative sip. "Is this Courvoisier Reserve?"

He nodded, not surprised she recognized the expensive taste. Her shivering stopped when he put the pashmina coverlet over her legs. Partly so he didn't have to look at them, but she didn't need to know that.

Her voice slightly husky, probably both with tiredness and the brandy, she asked, "Aren't you going to open your present? It's more than an apology, actually. It's a peace offering."

He obliged, seeing what he'd expected: a wooden box filled with his favorite cigars. This time he didn't bother asking how she knew, because he'd been chewing on one when he arrested her. The fact that she recognized the brand, could afford an entire box shipped the same day, and had gumption enough to approach him to make peace, told him volumes about her character. She had class, she was extremely intelligent, she had her PhD, or so she'd claimed when he arrested her, but she was also courageous and didn't shirk from making tough decisions. All qualities he admired in a woman, but he wanted to keep disliking her. Had to keep disliking her. She wasn't the rural Texas type, to put it mildly.

"Thanks," he said, "but it wasn't necessary."

"I promised the judge I'd apologize in person to you, so it was necessary. I'm very sorry I was so difficult. It had been a long trip, but that's no excuse."

When he only shrugged, she added more forcefully, "Besides, this is West Texas, right? Land of hospitality? Can't we smoke a symbolic peace pipe and bury the hatchet?"

At the image she evoked, he finally had to crack a smile. A small one, but a smile nonetheless. "Are you saying you smoke cigars or that you want to bury a hatchet between my shoulder blades?"

She laughed. "A little of both, maybe, but we can start with the smoke."

She had a sense of humor, too. But since he was refusing to like her, he merely opened the box, took out two cigars, fetched his clip from the bar and a crystal ashtray, and went back to her side. He started to snip the ends of the cigars, but she gently covered his hand. "Let me. I used to do this for my grandfather."

The touch of her soft hand flowed through him, more warming than the brandy, but he told himself it was the fire, which was roaring now. Still, he put the ashtray on the table between the two chairs and handed her the clipper, the lighter, and two cigars.

She went through the ritual, rolling a cigar between her fingers and then smelling it discreetly, a distance from her nostrils. Finally she clipped the end, rose from her chair, and leaned over him to put the flavorful tube between his lips. With an adept, practiced motion, she lit the clipped end. It fired quickly. He took a deep draw, the warm smoke immediately soothing some of his nerves. He made a mental apology to Jasmine, but this woman had brought him an entire box of the cigars he pined for, and he couldn't be rude enough to ignore her peace offering, even if she was a law breaker who put every defense he had on high alert. As a man, and even, for some reason, as a lawman. He sensed a second agenda in her she wasn't admitting to. No matter how she couched it, this extravagant gift was a bit of a ruse.

He caught a whiff of something as she leaned over him. He wasn't sure what it was; it was too pungent for perfume or moisturizer or any of those other female things. When she straightened, her wrinkled jacket coat, already open, fell off her shoulders, and before she shrugged it back on, he saw the slight sweat stains under the armpits on her silk blouse. They were dry now, but had obviously happened when she was bombing along the road in that convertible under the bright sunshine.

Every male instinct in his body went on full alert.

He was smelling a very slight whiff of sweat under her deodorant, but it wasn't disagreeable; in fact, it reminded him of another female part, fresh out of the shower and in his bed. A familiar tingling began in his groin, and he was so discomfited at who'd aroused it that he took a deeper puff, blowing the smoke out forcefully until he couldn't smell her anymore. Pheromones, he told himself, and he was only susceptible because it had been months since he'd visited his local friend with benefits.

Then the woman moved away and lit her own cigar. He didn't miss her slight cough, or the fact that she didn't inhale, but he let it slide. He had a good memory, too, and he recalled her saying speeding was her only vice, so she was going through this ritual to smooth his ruffled feathers and was obviously not a smoker.

The question was—why?

His cigar was half gone when she finally ventured a tentative, "Is there anything else I can do to make amends?"

He bit down on the cigar and the remark he wanted to make— *yeah, follow me upstairs.* Instead, he put the cigar in the ashtray and gently rotated the gleaming bud out so he didn't crinkle the rest of the tobacco. His physical reaction to her was neither welcome nor acceptable, so he decided to fight it the only way he knew. Besides, she owed him an explanation after invading his private space. "Yes. Tell me the reason for this elaborate ruse."

She stiffened slightly. "No ruse. I really am sorry."

"No doubt, especially when you wrote the check for the fine." He slicked back his sleeve to peek at his watch. "Look, it's after midnight and I have to work tomorrow—" A card appeared in front of his nose. He was too embarrassed to put on his specs, so he held it as far away as he could, as if he needed the firelight to read the plain but elegant embossed card. Her name, followed by PhD, above National Preservation Trust Officer and, below that, the address for the National Parks Service in D.C.

Ah, so that was it. He looked from the card to her very still face. Lovely, oval shaped, with a sensual mouth. Waiting, not exactly serene, but as if to say the next move was up to him. She was lovely in the firelight. She had that fair smooth skin, clear cornflower blue eyes, perfect white teeth, and the long, thick, healthy hair of the privileged. Good nutrition, good vitamins, excellent breeding. What else could one expect of a Rothschild?

The top button of her silk blouse had come undone, exposing the slight edge of a lace bra, and he couldn't help it; he fixated on it. She was shaped exactly as he liked, curvaceous instead of the model thinness so the rage in Hollywood.

She looked down. Even in the dim firelight he saw her blush as she quickly buttoned the blouse closed. Well, at least she didn't use her sex appeal like the dangerous weapon so many beautiful women wielded. In fact, she'd tried to downplay her assets, no doubt because of the nature of her job. The fact that she was so sexy and appealing while trying not to be perplexed him, and, strangely, drew him more.

He rose. "I should have realized who you were. The way you were dressed, the East Coast plates. You knew me before you came here, didn't you?"

"I only had to look at your name on the ticket. I knew your name, but you didn't know mine. Shall we start over again?" She rose to face him and offered her hand. "Mercy Magdalena Rothschild. But please, call me Emm. As in Auntie Emm, except my nickname is because of the double Ms in my name."

Reluctantly, he shook her hand. Immediately he released it because he'd felt that unwelcome warmth travel up his arm again, to his gut and below. Great. Just wonderful. He already had enough distractions just now, with the missing girls task force that was proving to be an interjurisdictional challenge and police departments nationwide were sending him new cases. Just today, the press was about to blow their cover. To say nothing of his entire family due to arrive momentarily for the annual gathering he'd barely had time to start planning. And now this.

When he didn't speak, staring over her head moodily, she lifted her chin and said briskly, "Look, I'm sorry we got off on the wrong foot, but I came here with the best of intentions. Preserving old buildings is my calling, just as the law is obviously yours. We're both well-educated professionals. Can't we agree to disagree and not make snap judgments until we have all the facts?"

"I have all the facts, including a soil report and structural analysis—"

"I read them. They weren't conclusive. With so many advances in structural materials, it's quite possible a reasonable renovation could not only meet those tolerances, it could exceed them. I have to see the buildings themselves. Is it possible we could make an appointment for tomorrow?"

"In a hurry to get back to civilization?"

He wanted to call the words back the moment he'd said them, but it was too late.

Those cornflower eyes wilted to grayish blue as they went opaque. She pulled her jacket tighter about her shoulders and turned toward the door. "You have my cell number on the card. I'll check into a hotel and wait for your call, but I cleared my schedule for a number of weeks, so I'll be here until you have time to show me the buildings." She marched toward the front door, where she turned to face him again. "I'm sorry for bothering you so late."

Now he felt guilty. He followed in her wake, feeling both churlish and uneasy, two emotions so unusual for him, he could hardly give them names. He couldn't quite say he was sorry, so he did the next best thing. "I can follow you back to town. It's late and the turns can get confusing—"

"I have a good GPS, thank you." At the door, she turned and offered her hand again.

This time when he reluctantly reached for it, her fingertips barely brushed his. She apparently didn't want to touch him any more than he wanted to touch her. After the way he'd acted, he could scarcely blame her. He wasn't clear on the consequences of a negative report from her, but he knew it would be one more hassle he wasn't capable of handling right now, especially with the family bearing down on him, wanting to know why the development they'd insisted on funding couldn't proceed.

As she reached for the huge front door lever, he said, "Look, I have a full schedule tomorrow, but I usually break for lunch. There's a nice little café called Julienne's half a block from our buildings. I'll meet you there at noon sharp and give you a tour, if we can make it quick. Good enough?"

She gave a brisk nod. "I'll be there. Thanks for the brandy. I hope you enjoy the cigars."

He wanted to tell her no, he couldn't, he was trying to quit, so she might as well have handed him a box of apples. He knew he wouldn't be able to resist the temptation, at least occasionally, but then everything about her was walking temptation, and the fact that she didn't know it only accented her allure. But before he could say another word, the door had closed behind her. Firmly. Not quite a slam, but it was a heavy door.

Grinding his teeth and wondering why this strong attraction to someone totally inappropriate had to hit him at the worst time possible, he stirred down the fire and went up to bed. It was a while before his chaotic thoughts calmed sufficiently for him to get drowsy enough for sleep. The last thought on his mind was Emm. He said her name aloud, his lips stretching in a smile more wolfish than he realized.

No one had ever been named better, and he had to wonder if the nickname came from an old boyfriend. She didn't resemble Auntie Em, or even Dorothy. Her name, when he drew out the taste of it on his lips, was "mmmmm."

Back in town, after a two-hour circuitous route because her Maryland-based brand-new navigation system had trouble with Texas ranch roads, Emm finally opened her hotel room door. She'd chosen an historic boutique hotel downtown, not for convenience but because she'd much rather stay in an old building with character and questionable modern amenities than the steel monolith a few blocks away that no doubt had huge marble baths and steam showers.

She tossed her two small bags on the chenille bedspread covering the brass bed. God, she was exhausted. She'd picked up a San Antonio newspaper in the lobby but was too tired to read it. She took a quick shower in the tiny shower cubicle with a plastic curtain instead of a glass door, dressed in her usual night attire of a teddy, and got into bed. For the first time in a long time she'd looked at herself in the mirror, wondering why she bothered with the sexy black lace teddy when she'd slept alone for a year, but she knew it was her own inner rebellion against propriety, like her speeding. She was a deeply sensual woman and most men hadn't a clue, but her choice of night attire even on a business trip was a tell to anyone with acute observation skills.

Like a Texas Ranger . . .

She expected to fall asleep immediately, but Ross Sinclair's handsome face kept creeping in behind her tightly closed eyelids, as if she could keep him out that way. Without his sunshades, he was every bit as handsome as she'd expected. His thick iron gray hair set off the deep cerulean of his eyes, which were a much darker blue than her own. She smiled a bit herself as she recalled his expression when she finally gave him her card. She was quite sure few people ever put him off balance, but she'd sensed unease in him several times. While she couldn't account for the source, she knew it was probably a good thing as far as her historic investigation went. He couldn't dismiss her easily now because he needed a report from her that stated she agreed the buildings were not appropriate for restoration. Only then could his family legally tear them down because the Texas Resource Commission had filed a stay with the parks department.

She couldn't quite say she had the upper hand as she was still the interloper from the East Coast he obviously disdained, despite the very faint trace of an upper-crust Hamptons' accent she sometimes detected. She knew his background. He knew little of hers, aside from his almost certain recognition of her famous name, though few people realized her father was not from the moneyed side of the family. That was the way she wanted to keep it. The thought occurred to her that if she gave a report recommending the buildings be saved and denied the Sinclairs their development, they could come back and claim she was retaliating for her arrest. But while she hadn't known Ross Sinclair very long, she sensed he was far too honorable for a trick like that.

She fell asleep on the thought, but somehow his perfectly sculpted mouth as he leaned over her with the pashmina followed her into her dreams.

The next morning, when she arose, there was moisture between her thighs, but she only did a quick sponge bath and pretended not to recall her erotic dreams. As Yancy would say in her blunt way, she just needed to get laid.

Nevertheless, she dressed more carefully than she'd planned. She'd met the hodunk honcho now, so she could afford to be a bit more casual. She pulled on skinny pants that molded lovingly to her long legs and added a tunic. The tunic had a slightly military look, with brass buttons and gold braid. She'd paid a fortune for it at a Neiman Marcus Last Call outlet, and with the navy pants and low-heeled boots that came up to her knees, she was good to go even if she had to step over fallen beams and the like.

After a quick breakfast of eggs and toast in the tiny downstairs coffee shop, she walked outside. The changeable Texas weather had fully made the transformation to spring, and it was already in the seventies. She knew the buildings where she was meeting Sinclair were to the right, so she deliberately turned to the left, exploring Polk Street, the most historic area of downtown Amarillo. She consulted the map of structures she held in her hand. She saw some buildings fully restored, even a full-sized Marriott that had taken over what she knew to be an old office building because it was already listed on the National Register of Historic Places, a list compiled and supervised by the federal parks department. After a building met stringent historic criteria, the developer of each historic structure was allocated 20 percent of his construction budget in tax credits. In that way federal tax policy tried to help preserve the nation's historic buildings, and it was one of the few federal programs Emm thought had been slam-dunk successful.

As she walked, she saw other buildings sitting forlorn with boarded-up broken windows. Throughout America, many cities were still struggling with the circular dynamics of reviving their cores. Renovating old buildings took craft, knowledge, commitment, and, most of all, money. Developers wouldn't take on the task without the economic promise of profit. Profit required foot traffic and retail shoppers; foot traffic required fun outlets, restaurants, best of all, private housing. It was a classic demand-and-supply loop Emm figured builders had been facing since the Agora in Athens.

She stopped in front of a vacant building with broken front windows. Windows like that always reminded Emm of the ancient Greek habit of putting pennies on the eyes of the dead. They were empty, lifeless, and it was now both her passion and her calling to bring them back to life.

Her equilibrium restored, she browsed in a cute novelties shop, and then it was time to meet Sinclair. She found the door to Julienne's and entered, the bell tinkling. It was a classic little take on a French café, a delight in a cow town, with checked tablecloths, tiny vases filled with wildflowers, and elegant cut velvet booths. She wondered if he'd selected this location to put her at ease or to accent the fact she didn't belong here. She was a bit early, but he was already seated at a booth near the door. He rose when he saw her and extended his hand.

"Good afternoon. My name is Ross Sinclair, and I'm head of the trust that owns the Draper and Hoover buildings. You must be Ms. Rothschild, historic trust preservation officer. It's nice to meet you."

Relieved he was taking her seriously despite the arrest, she shook his hand, playing along. He wanted a clean slate, and under the circumstances, that was best. "Wonderful to meet you at last, Mr. Sinclair."

"Call me Ross."

"Please call me Emm."

"Emmmm." His lips quirked as he drew out her name, and she flushed as something very male flashed in his eyes when he surveyed her brass button–bedecked chest. But then he handed her a menu with a flourish and told her about the specials.

"You come here often?" she asked as she perused the menu.

"Just about every other day. It's the best food downtown. It reminds me of Paris."

She digested that, ordering the quiche and salad of the day. It didn't escape her he ordered sirloin, rare. They made small talk while they waited, both of them storing up energy for the imminent battle. Despite the truce, Emm was acutely aware of every move he made, from the precise way he folded the linen napkin over his lap to the way he placed his water glass. When the food came, his manners were more a legacy of cotillions than a Texas ranch. Finally she couldn't stand it.

During a lull in the conversation about how Amarillo's booming economy was due, at least in part, to oil and gas, she blurted, "Why have you stayed in Amarillo?"

He blinked, obviously off balance, but only for a moment. He toyed with his napkin, finally admitting, "Because I feel free here."

She paused with her water glass halfway to her mouth. From the way he clamped his mouth shut, she had a feeling he'd been more honest than he'd intended. But she only took a sip, put her glass down just so, and asked the logical question. "Don't you miss your family?"

"Yes, but I see them at least twice a year. I host our annual reunion at the ranch, and they'll all be here for it in a few weeks. And you? Do you live near your family?"

"My parents both live in Baltimore, so I see them weekly. My . . . sister is . . . gone."

His eyes sharpened at her tone and the way she looked away quickly. "Gone? As in traveling?"

She took a deep, steadying breath, wondering if now was the time to explain about Yancy and Jennifer. After all, the cops had told her the Texas Rangers were spearheading the task force, so she figured Ross must be involved. But she had a feeling he'd only clam up and be obstructive to her, what with his obviously overdeveloped sense of duty. Plus, she was the classic outsider. Best to wait until they'd come to some type of compromise, if one were possible, over the buildings.

"Yes. Kinda. I'm trying to reach her, actually." When he opened his mouth for another question, she folded her napkin over her plate and glanced at her watch. "It's almost one and I have some work to catch up on, too. Are you ready to show me your buildings?" She lifted her hand for the check, but he grabbed the bill the waiter brought and tossed down three twenties. Big tipper. She liked that in a man, especially as her first job in high school had been waiting tables.

He stood aside for her to scoot out of the booth, offering his arm with old-fashioned courtliness. Trying to remember the last time any man had offered her his arm, she rested her fingertips on what felt like a camel-hair sleeve. He was dressed as before, in black jeans and starched shirt, though this time he wore a tan jacket. She had a feeling he'd look elegant even in overalls. The walk to his buildings was short, and they made a detour into the hardware store she'd seen earlier. He raised an eyebrow at her sole purchase, a level, but only escorted her back outside.

She stopped outside the Draper and carefully circled the small four-story red brick building. It was constructed in the spare style of pre-World War I, with the plain red brick rectangle accented by arched limestone quoins and an ornate Art Deco–style door that was badly scratched but seemed sound. He followed on her heels, watching the careful way she eyed the foundation. Once she knelt to put the level horizontally against a long flat side of the building. The bubble was very slightly off center. She picked at some crumbling cement near the bottom. The cement had been originally constructed in such a way, built up with a trowel, that it resembled stone. All the way around the building, the stone effect was crumbling.

"See the problem? This entire foundation is crumbling."

She straightened. "That's not part of the foundation. It's a curtain wall, purely decorative, and repairable." She tested with the level again on the opposite side of the building, where the curtain wall was intact. "See? Almost perfect after nearly a century. If the foundation was bad, the wall would be leaning slightly on each side. It isn't."

He scowled.

"Shall we go inside?"

Once inside, she eyed the long sweeping staircase and iron railing and banisters that led to the second floor. "Nice." She tested everywhere: support walls, a decorative pilaster accenting a half wall, door frames. On the third floor there was a slight crumpling in the old linoleum where she pushed the level flat against the wall, perpendicular to the floor. At this point, the level's bubble teetered far to the side.

He jumped on the opportunity. "How can you expect us to conserve something that isn't structurally sound?" he demanded.

Her only response was to take a Swiss Army knife with every imaginable attachment from her purse. She carefully levered up the cracking linoleum near the wall to reveal wood flooring beneath. The wood flooring was warped.

"That's what I thought." She stood and looked up. Near the wall joist was an ugly brown stain in the ceiling. "You have a leak. Must be a pretty bad one to come down two floors. We'll have to get confirmation from a structural engineer, but I don't think this is structural. The wood flooring has bowed beneath from the moisture. Fix the leak and the floor and you should be fine."

He glared at her. She smiled, sweeping her hand in front of her. "After you. Let's see the roof. We'll have to move carefully if there's a leak, but I know what to look for."

She was noncommittal for the rest of the tour. The survey of the Hoover building, which had a larger floor plan but was only three stories, went equally quickly. When she was finished, she dusted off her pants, only leaving more marks from her dirty hands. She shoved her loosened hair, which she'd swept back with an elegant clip, away from her cheek as once again they met on the sidewalk. She was totally unaware she'd left a streak of dirt on her cheek. She wondered why he kept looking at her face that way, eyeing her cheek, then her mouth.

This time he glanced at his watch. "I have to go. I have a two thirty meeting."

"That's fine. I need to see the 'as builts,' which I believe you told me you have at home. In the meantime, I suggest you let me bring in an historic resources expert to confirm my findings before I write an official report. It will probably cost around ten thousand dollars, but if I'm wrong, it may get you your development. But I don't think I'm wrong. Both buildings were very well constructed for their time, and I saw no evidence of foundation damage. Everything you noted to me in your e-mail is easily fixed and would be addressed in any complete renovation."

"I bet you're never wrong."

She lifted her chin at his sarcasm. "All the time. But seldom in my work. As far as men go . . ." She shrugged.

He put those mirrored shades over his darkening eyes, but not quickly enough. She saw something flash that reminded her of a shark circling deep blue seas. *Back at ya, lady.* While she was debating whether she'd just been insulted, he finished curtly, "I'll have the 'as builts' for you later this evening at my house. Eight?"

She nodded and watched him walk away. March, really. He obviously wasn't happy with her review, but she couldn't help that. She'd given him her honest opinion, but, like she'd said, she could be wrong.

Back at the hotel, she was appalled when she saw the dirty streak on her face. No wonder he'd stared at her so strangely. She changed her clothes and took a quick shower. Then, more depressed than exhausted, she reclined on the bed and opened the paper she'd picked up yesterday but hadn't read. She stiffened at the blaring headline: "Texas Rangers lead hunt for human trafficking ring ending in El Paso." She read the rest of the article so quickly, she didn't blink. It described how the authorities were one step behind the notorious Los Lobos cartel thought to be behind the nationwide kidnapping of many missing persons, mostly young women. The article further identified the FBI Agent in Charge, Rosemary Reed, and Captain Ross Sinclair, Company C of the Texas Rangers, West Texas division, as heading the investigation. The reporter didn't come out and say it, but the implication was that both Ross and the FBI agent were incompetent because there were no strong leads even after months of investigation. The article went on to name a couple of operatives who had recently been wounded in a border skirmish with the cartel.

A warehouse filled with feminine goods, apparently hastily abandoned, had been discovered in Amarillo, the reason the authorities believed the city must be a stop on the pipeline. The article gave a partial list of items. She read it carefully, stiffening at one line: "A green dragon-shaped marijuana pipe, along with other drug paraphernalia."

Yancy had a pipe just like that, and she always kept it in her purse. An old boyfriend had it custom made for her, and she said her weed never tasted the same without it.

When she finished the article, Emm went to toss the paper aside. As she did so, her eyes finally focused on the reporter's name: Curt Tupperman. She froze. Curt? She knew him, not just slightly but well, because he was one of Yancy's old boyfriends. She'd introduced them after she met him at school, and at first Yancy had liked him, but after a few months, as usual, she'd lost interest. He'd been working for the Baltimore paper, but when he went freelance about a year ago he'd moved home to San Antonio, though he roamed nationwide pursuing stories. She'd have to call him, press him for details.

She rubbed her forehead as she debated how best to open her own unofficial investigation. She'd only be here a few weeks, so she didn't have a lot of time. Logically, she needed to see that pipe; it was her first concrete link to Yancy. If she just told Ross who she was, that she'd filed the missing persons reports on both Jennifer and her mother, would he let her see the evidence? She was sure there must be rules against that sort of thing, and he was none too happy with her at the moment.

So how? Legal or illegal, there had to be a way . . . and heck, he was already pissed at her, so what did she have to lose?

CHAPTER 3

Seven thirty rolled around all too quickly for Ross. After another long, tedious day of paperwork and phone calls coordinating resources between the six different agencies he was managing in the human trafficking task force, Ross was in no mood for company. He'd only been home for a few minutes, and he had to drag his carcass up the stairs to his bedroom to freshen up. He brushed his unruly hair, trying to quell its tendency to curl a lock into his eyes, then his teeth, checked his deodorant, and put on a fresh shirt, resolving to get the damn woman out of there as quickly as possible. He cursed himself for not taking time to have the plans copied so he could give her a set and solve the problem, but it was too late now.

He was barely at the top of the stairs when the doorbell rang. He glanced at his watch. Eight exactly. She was punctual, at least. He liked that in a woman. Especially in a beautiful woman. He waved José away. "I'll get it. See you in the morning, amigo."

José gave the bottom of the stairs a curious glance, then looked back expectantly at his boss.

Ross hadn't said a word to him about his late-night guest, but José had the hearing of a bat and the olfactory capability of a blood hound. Plus Ross knew he wanted his boss to have a señora to help run the ranch. Ross needed to work less and socialize more, or as José, who was as much a friend as a retainer, put it with a sly wink, "Dancing with señoritas *bonitas* is better for hombre looking *por una esposa* than—" and José mimed pushing papers around and stapling a pile, making up in acting ability what he lacked in English vocabulary.

Ross had always given José a lot of latitude, but he wasn't in the mood for another one of their fruitless debates on the subject. José recognized his narrow-eyed glare and wisely closed the door to his small suite of rooms as Ross started down the stairs. *Yes, maybe I need a woman, but this isn't the right señora,* he said to himself as he opened the door. But when he saw her, his critical thoughts scattered, and he froze at his own entrance.

Emm had obviously dressed and showered away the dust of the building tour. This time she wore a buttercup yellow sundress. Over her shoulders she'd draped a yellow Mexican shawl embroidered with enormous silk flowers and ending in a multicolored fringe. Again, he was nonplussed, trying to read her, for at first she'd looked more like a Vera Wang devotee than an earthy hippie type who loved huge flowers and fringe.

She extended her arms, showing off the shawl. "You like it? I found it downtown at a souvenir shop. They told me it was *hecho en Mexico.*"

Her unexpectedly perfect pronunciation of the Spanish broke the spell. Wasn't there anything the damned woman couldn't do? And must she always look luscious while doing it? When she tilted her head, looking at him curiously, he gathered his wits and swung the door open. "*Mi casa es su casa,* señorita."

She playfully bobbed a curtsy and entered. He had the plans spread on a long console table behind the sofa, but he hadn't had time to lay a fire, and now that the sun was down, the air was growing chilly. His mouth was literally watering at the sight of her, so he walked to the bar. "Can I get you something to cut the chill in the air?"

She put her fingertip to her chin, tilting her head. "Let me see . . . how about a Lemon Drop martini?"

He glared at her over the bar. "I might be able to scrounge up an extra dirty one because I have olives, vodka, and vermouth, but that fancy stuff you can order in town."

She had to grab the shawl as it slipped off her arm, so her response was somewhat hurried. "I just thought you must have already juiced some lemons. Because of the look around your mouth."

Sourpuss. She was calling him a sourpuss. He wanted to stay remote and rocky as Gibraltar, but a laugh slipped out. "I deserved that one. But it's not you. It's . . . the day I had." He nodded at the chair by the fireplace. "Please, sit. Tell me what you saw in town today."

While she described the retail stores she'd visited and what she could see doing with some of the old buildings still vacant, he expertly mixed up two martinis in the shaker. He poured one for her, one for him, and added two premium garlic-stuffed olives to both.

She'd been using her hands to describe a building she particularly liked and seemed not to have noticed the slipping shawl. He noticed. The sundress wasn't low cut, but it had a lace-up ribbon bodice that emphasized her curves. This time, when he leaned over her, she smelled of roses. Not Chanel, or any of those other, even fancier names that ended in vowels. Just roses. Again, it was unexpected that this complicated, wealthy, well-educated woman would scent herself with smells of the earth instead of an expensive perfume.

When she accepted the glass, their fingertips brushed. Fire tingled up his hand. He jerked away so fast, the liquid sloshed in the martini glass, dribbling on her dress. He flushed. "I'm so sorry. Let me get a towel."

She brushed at the dribbles. "No problem; the garlic will cover the scent of the vodka and the hotel has laundry service." She took the olive out of the glass and ate it with gusto in two bites. "Do you have some more olives?"

Glad for the escape from the scent and sight of her, he went behind the bar and dumped half the contents of the olive jar into a small glass dish. When he took it back, she was nursing the martini and staring into the cold fireplace. She opened her mouth, closed it, and used the toothpick he'd given her to spear another martini olive, but he caught her slight shiver.

Sighing, he did the right if not the expedient thing and took the time to stack firewood in the grate, enough for a good-sized fire. She put her glass down to help, but he waved her back.

He had a gas log, so the kindling was already catching by the time he dusted off his hands and sat in the second chair to sip his own martini. He caught the sideways looks she kept sending him and finally asked, "Have I grown two heads, or do you just like keeping people off balance?"

She took another sip for courage and rushed out, "I was just wondering why you made the fire. It's late, and I know you have to work tomorrow. This really isn't a social visit, so I'm fine if we just get on with the plans—"

"I could see you wanted one."

That really tilted her head sideways as she stared at him. "I'm in a tiny apartment in Baltimore and I miss having a fireplace, but you couldn't know that."

He shrugged. "It was in your face, and you shivered." It was his turn to eye her speculatively. "I'd have thought you owned your own fancy townhome with lots of windows and an itty-bitty lawn."

"So you've been to Baltimore?"

He nodded. He'd been to more than one fancy, power-elite party thrown by various family members.

She opened her mouth to say something obviously vehement, thought better of it, finished her martini in a gulp, and put her glass down with a snap. "No, I don't live in a townhome. Anyway, thanks for the drink and the olives, but it's getting late, so we need to get to the plans."

Now what had he said to make her go evasive like that? Ross wondered. He could usually read people early and well, probably the main reason he'd risen in the Ranger ranks as quickly as he had, but she was an enigma. When she got up to open the old, yellowing plans he'd spread out on the sofa table, her face and form limned beautifully by the firelight, he thought she must fit Fibonacci's famous golden ratio in the balance of her form and face: 1.618. The ideal of true beauty and symmetry . . . what would she look like naked?

She'd already flipped through the entire set of plans while he was drooling over her. "See this structural schematic?" She pointed at a structural blowup drawing of the area where they'd stood beneath the brown ceiling.

He had to physically grip the edge of the table to master his restive urges and force himself to listen. Dammit, why must she smell so good?

"See this structural red iron beam that supports all the floor joists? We can get a good read from a structural engineer and the soils analysis to discover whether it still meets these tolerances. Then we'll know for sure if I'm right that the leak is cosmetic." She let the plans roll back up again. "We'll need to have these copied so we can give him a complete set. I have someone in mind who I've worked with before, but if you have your own firm, that's fine. . . ." She trailed off to stare at him.

Only then did he realize that he was standing all too close but not looking at the plans where she pointed. Instead, he was staring fixedly at the hollow of her throat, at the pulsing beat of her heart. He felt like a vampire, so badly did he want to taste that vibrant rush of blood and life and test it with his tongue. He reddened at her expression and stumbled back a step, his own flush so bright it heated his face even in the warmth of the fire. What the hell was wrong with him? His booted foot brushed against one of the wing chairs and he stumbled slightly.

Automatically, she reached out to catch him, but by then he was a good six paces away. "Mr. Sinclair, is something wrong?"

Everything, he wanted to retort, but with this much distance he was able to master his out-of-control libido. "No, I'm just tired, stumbled a bit. You go ahead, contact whoever you think is best for the job. The structural inspection we had done was several years ago and was only a walk-through, so I can see we need something more thorough. Just have him send his scope of work and estimate to my home e-mail before he starts." He scribbled his home e-mail on the back of one of his work cards and handed it to her, careful not to touch her fingers. "Would you like another drink before you go?"

She got the message. Shaking her head, she grabbed up her shawl and wrapped it close around her shoulders. Not quite a protective cocoon, but he also got the message: hands off. "Would you like me to have the plans copied, or do you want to do that?"

Her voice was very cool, and because he was all but rushing her to the door, he couldn't blame her. Wordlessly, he wrapped the rolled plans back in their brown tube and handed them to her. She accepted them in one arm and slung her purse over her shawl on the other, turning for the door.

He drew a sigh of relief but followed her to courteously open it. She moved to cross the threshold but stopped and looked up at him. "Do you have . . . a public information officer on the task force for human trafficking?"

He blinked. What the hell? How did that have any bearing on the debate over his buildings?

She must have seen his confusion because she said primly, "I'm looking into the disappearance of . . . a friend. I was told in Baltimore that she was probably brought through Texas to Mexico, and that the Texas Rangers are heading the task force. I saw your name listed yesterday in the San Antonio paper—"

Ross pulled her back inside and slammed the door. "Is that what this has all been about?" Dammit, he knew she'd had some kind of hidden agenda beyond her job. "Even if I wanted to, which I don't, I couldn't give you details of an ongoing investigation." He read the words trembling on her tongue and said bluntly, "And even if you could help in some way, which you can't, I wouldn't be the one to question you—"

She took the ire out of his words with one simple sentence. "I know." She walked back to the bar to set the plans and her purse down. Then she turned to him and said simply, "But I may have information about a key piece of evidence." Quickly, she explained about the dragon-head pipe. "Couldn't you, like, test for fingerprints to see if it's really Yancy's?"

"Yes, of course, but that won't help us find her, at least not yet."

"But at least I'd know."

The silence was broken when a log fell with a crackle and burst of fire. Ross saw his budget for the quarter in his mind's eye, already in the red. He was about to tell her no, it was a futile exercise, but the dark desperation in her normally cloudless blue eyes troubled him. "What is this Yancy to you?"

She took a deep breath and then admitted, "My half sister. They took her daughter, my niece, too. That's how Yancy went missing, looking for her. Her name is Jennifer. They're both . . . natural blondes and beautiful. Yancy has green eyes and Jennifer's are blue."

Few knew what that meant better than Ross. Women like that were highly prized in various rough corners of the globe. He felt a bit sick to his stomach as he visualized which corners, and what two such women were doing right now. Despite his distaste at her now obvious attempts to grease the flow of information with a box of cigars, Ross understood exactly how she felt. He escorted her back to the armchair and, without her asking, mixed them both another martini. He knew this time he'd have to let her have a guest room rather than drive, or stay up with her for at least another few hours, but he sensed the anguish behind her quiet, waiting expression.

She was getting to him in a way he didn't like, and he knew he should keep any meetings between them impersonal, but a missing sister and niece were anything but. Gratefully, she accepted the drink, as before, concentrating on eating olives with each sip.

"Have you had dinner?" he asked.

Again, she seemed surprised that he'd read her hunger. "Is my stomach growling?"

"No, but you just ate through half a bottle of olives."

She looked down at the empty little dish and gave an embarrassed shrug that pushed the shawl off her shoulders.

His gaze fell to the hollow of her throat, and to disguise his own hunger, he stood abruptly. "Follow me. Bring your drink."

And so it was that Captain Ross Sinclair, forced by circumstance and the common courtesy drilled into him since he could walk, played host yet again to a woman who represented all he'd rejected when he'd left Elaine. While he hastily threw together a couple of sandwiches with glasses of milk and homemade cookies for dessert, he asked questions.

Fifteen minutes later, he knew the what, where, when, and how of the case, but as to why . . . ?

She bit into her sandwich, took a few appreciative chews, swallowed, and said, "Well, in Jennifer's case, she was hanging out with the wrong crowd. Some of them were doing drugs, even heroin, brought in from Mexico. It's only a theory, but I think one of the cartel's suppliers saw her at a party or something and staked her out. At least she disappeared two days later . . ."

Sitting across from her at the large granite-topped island in the gourmet kitchen that was his favorite room in the house, Ross nodded and wiped his mouth. "Most of the drug cartels have also started human trafficking. Oftentimes they use the same transportation pipeline or tunnels under the border to move victims out of the US."

She leaned forward eagerly, her sandwich dropping to her plate, forgotten for the moment. "But if you know that, why can't you track them?"

"As soon as we find one tunnel, they dig another. Remember, we're fighting not just a lone kidnapper but an organization with increasingly international ties and almost unlimited funding. We think there may even be some connections between one of the most vicious gangs known here in the US as the Los Lobos cartel and some of the Chechnya extremists."

Frowning, she nibbled at the edge of a potato chip. "That's the cartel Curt mentioned in his story. He admitted he didn't have proof yet, but he said there were indications their web of allies stretches nation-wide."

He smiled bitterly. "Yes, well, his little theories make it that much harder for us to collect concrete evidence, especially when he broadcasts the names of some of our contacts."

She was nodding, and he realized she must have done her research. He shoved his half-eaten sandwich away. "This dragon pipe . . . if I get you in to view the evidence we're still collating from that warehouse, do you think you could ID more of their belongings?"

She nodded enthusiastically. "Yes. Jennifer and Yancy and I went shopping together. A lot."

Of course they did. Everything about this woman said she had money to burn. But he didn't let her see his thoughts as he rose and dumped the rest of his food into the trash. When she finished, he took her plate, ignoring her protest that she'd do it herself, and scraped the remnants of her bread crust and chips into the trash, too.

He'd been thinking furiously, and he turned to her with a new suggestion but stopped with it half formed on his lips when he saw her sitting there patiently, hands clasped together on top of the granite. His reluctant respect for her grew. She knew when to push and when not to. He also noted she'd barely touched the martini. While he still felt a bit used, he couldn't really blame her for being manipulative in hopes of getting information about her sister and niece. And he knew if he turned her over to the system and she tried to go through appropriate channels, she'd get stonewalled. He had visions of her breaking into the evidence warehouse. While he was still getting to know her, it was patently obvious the two of them shared one trait: sheer bull-headedness.

"Do either your sister or your niece have any distinctive habits or needs that might set them apart and give us a paper trail? An ailment, a special food they have to eat, or a custom shoe, that kind of thing."

She frowned, concentrating, then she said, "Yancy has a mild case of hemophilia A. She usually controls it with oral meds, but if she goes off them for long she has to have intravenous shots. She's allergic to the other protocols."

"You know the name of this drug?"

She stared into space. "I've seen her take it often enough . . . Effluenatasis. It hasn't been available long and it's made in the US. It's got to be hard to get in Mexico."

"That at least gives us somewhere to start." He scribbled down the name of the drug.

She worried her shawl fringe again. "Do you . . . think they'd quit treating her and just let her bleed out? If she's been off her meds most of this time . . ."

He wanted to tell her no, her sister was valuable, and they'd try to keep her healthy, but he couldn't lie to her. All the cartels were notorious for cutting their liabilities ruthlessly, and Yancy was much older than their usual targets. He stayed silent.

Her mouth trembled, but she managed, "Thanks for not lying to me. I guess there's really no way you can give me an answer to that."

He almost reached out to take her hand but stuck his hand in his pocket instead. It was dangerous to touch this woman, even in comfort. He cleared his throat. "Her picture is on all the missing persons sites?"

She nodded. "And the police in Baltimore distributed it, but the only hit we had didn't lead anywhere except . . . maybe here."

"What is your sister's last name?"

"Russell. Yancy and Jennifer Russell."

The names didn't ring any bells, but Ross seldom saw the case files themselves because he was managing the investigation. He rarely got involved in fieldwork. "You have pictures of them?"

She pulled her cell phone from her dress pocket and flipped it open. The picture of two gorgeous blondes who looked more like sisters than mother and daughter had a background of the Bellagio hotel in Vegas. Ross recognized it instantly. "So your sister likes to gamble?"

She nodded.

Ross handed the phone back. "Thanks. Well, I don't know how much good it will do, but it always helps to associate a name with a face. I'll do what I can to get you into the evidence room, but I'll have to clear it with our attorneys." Privately, as she wiped the granite while he washed the few dishes they'd generated, Ross suspected her sister and niece would never be seen again. Women that beautiful were just too valuable. . . . And Yancy resembled her younger sister, at least in the perfect bone structure and sparkling intelligence in her eyes, and no doubt, in determination. One sister had gotten herself taken by conducting her own investigation, and it was his duty to see that Emm didn't suffer the same fate.

For about the sixth time since he'd met her, Ross wished this woman had never come to Amarillo. It was hard enough remaining impartial about human trafficking so he could dispassionately conduct his job, but now he would be haunted by those two gorgeous blondes, not just how they'd looked on their fun vacation spree but how they probably looked now . . . if they were even still alive.

The next day, Emm rose late after a night of tossing and turning. Because she'd barely touched the second martini, she'd been fine to drive last night and had insisted on returning to her hotel even when Sinclair halfheartedly offered her a guest room. She sensed he didn't want her embroiled in his private life, and given the circumstances, she could hardly blame him. But to herself, at least, she could admit she was strongly attracted to the iron-haired and iron-willed Ranger captain of Company C. "Horrid timing, you idiot," she said under her breath as she dressed. "He's only the key to successfully resolving my first case and to finding my sister and niece. Hands off."

With that resolve in mind, Emm quit looking at her cell phone, hoping to see it ring with his name, called the structural engineer she knew from Fort Worth, and explained the issue, plus that this was something of a rush as she was staying in Amarillo until the results came in. Then, after a quick light lunch, because she still hadn't gotten the approval from Sinclair to go to the evidence warehouse, she decided to visit the downtown Amarillo library.

The Web was fabulous for research, but only to a point. Older research materials, such as newspaper articles from several years back or old case files from prior kidnapping cases, were seldom online. She'd already performed some cursory research before she'd come here and had stumbled across mention of a cold kidnapping case from three years earlier that had been reopened after a body had been found in a shallow grave in the scrub outside Lubbock. The dental records had matched a missing girl from Baltimore, and the little she'd read about the case had eerie similarities to Yancy's circumstances. Black truck, two men, girl missing from a downtown Baltimore bar. The case had been referred to the Baltimore police and then handed back to the Texas Highway patrol, who had jurisdiction over the area of the grave site.

But Emm knew local papers often carried stories the big dailies wouldn't. If she searched the database the library subscribed to, she was hoping the Amarillo paper had been digitized at least three years back and would carry more detailed information. After she registered and was given a swipeable ID card, she sat down before a vacant bank of computers. She entered the girl's name and was surprised when five hits came up. All but one of them were highlighted in blue, which meant she could click on the full article. She clicked on the oldest article first, her pad beside her so she could make notes. She could print the articles and read them later, but Emm loved libraries and was grieved they were struggling. Just like seeing a movie in person, researching next to other seekers of knowledge held its own charm.

Two hours later, she'd filled three pages with various tidbits of information, and as she read what she'd compiled, she felt a frisson run up her spine. She sensed she'd stumbled onto the victim profile of the human trafficking conduit that had swept away Yancy and Jennifer. The girl was the same age as Jennifer, the same wild, party girl type, and from the picture in the article, she even looked like Jennifer. Now she had the name of the bar where the girl had been taken, Emm was pretty sure it was even in the same seedy Baltimore area as the bar Yancy had been searching when she was grabbed.

Why had none of the authorities picked up on this link? Or had they, and dismissed it as circumstantial? She knew the Baltimore cops she'd worked with had never mentioned this missing girl. Surely they'd made the connection? Emm debated calling them and demanding they follow up on their end now that the missing persons case had become a murder, given the discovery of the body. But she knew the Baltimore cops would have sent all their findings to the Texas Department of Public Safety, especially after the case was reopened as a murder investigation. Sinclair would probably have information in his files. She closed out the menus she had open and logged off, debating whether she should raise the issue with him or contact the TxDPS office in Lubbock, which now had jurisdiction.

She was so deep in thought that as she slipped down off the stool, her elbow caught the bag of the woman sitting next to her and knocked it to the ground. The contents spilled out. "I'm so sorry," Emm began, but she froze in reaching out to help pick everything up when she saw a small revolver gleaming on the linoleum.

A large, capable hand nonchalantly put the gun back. Still kneeling, Emm looked into the sharpest gray eyes she'd ever seen. The woman waved a dismissive hand as she stood to her full, imposing height. "No problem; I should have shoved it to the other side." She offered a hand. "Hermione Abigail Doyle, just arrived in Amarillo a few days ago."

"Mercy Magdalena Rothschild. I just got here, too." Emm was much shorter than this Amazon, and she tried not to feel intimidated as she shook the woman's hand, which swallowed her own.

"And on a similar mission, I perceive."

Emm was puzzled. "Uh . . ."

"Investigating human and drug trafficking. I believe we may be interested in the same case, for different reasons. You're from Balti-more?"

Now Emm was floored. "How could you possibly know that?"

The woman nodded at the key fob attached to Emm's purse. "There's only one BMW in the parking lot and it has a Baltimore dealership above the Maryland plate number." That laserlike gray gaze zeroed in on the articles showing beneath Emm's notes. "'Human Traf-ficking Texas Task Force Offers Rewards,'" she read off the title.

Impressed in a way she seldom was upon first meeting someone, Emm shoved her notes and articles back into her briefcase. "Great deductions." She looked the tall woman up and down, noting the con-servative gray suit and plain white cotton blouse that boasted no adornment. Even the buttons were hidden. "Your parents were from England, because there's a trace of it in your voice. And you have to hide how smart and capable you are because you're a woman in a man's field."

Those gray eyes flickered in surprise, and it was obvious few peo-ple ever used Ms. Doyle's own deductive reasoning against her.

Emm smiled warmly. "In that way we're kindred spirits; men dominate my field, also." She reached into her pocket and pulled out a card, which she offered.

After reading the card, Abigail smiled and reciprocated with her own card. Emm read, "Dr. Hermione Abigail Doyle, Consultant." Below that, in smaller print, was the title, "Forensics, Texas Rangers." The address was in Austin.

Emm carefully stuck the card in the zipper pocket of her purse. "It might be helpful if we compared notes. Would you be available for lunch?"

Ms. Doyle hesitated. Somehow Emm knew this imposing woman

was not married, not only because she didn't wear a ring but because she probably intimidated the heck out of most men.

"I can't share much with you."

"I know. But I can share with you. I have a feeling you catch things other investigators might miss. Most importantly, we both very badly want to see this human trafficking ring broken into bits, do we not?"

Ms. Doyle didn't bother to deny either assertion. She motioned a hand before her. "Lead on, Ms. Rothschild."

Emm led the way to the parking lot.

CHAPTER 4

It was almost five when Ross finally took time to eat his take out sub sandwich, now stale, but he hardly noticed. He was growing increasingly frustrated at the progress—or, more accurately, lack thereof—of the human trafficking investigation, no matter how much money they threw at it. Public awareness of the problem had finally brought in billions in federal dollars and more than six hundred million from State of Texas funds to purchase gunboats, drones, listening devices, weapons, surveillance cameras, and even seismic equipment to help them locate tunnels at the porous 1,241-mile border between Texas and Mexico. Hundreds of new Border Patrol agents had been hired, and the governor had once even called in the National Guard to battle the flow of illegal immigrants.

However, though the unaccompanied minors fleeing Central American violence were trying to get into the US, as opposed to the young women being smuggled out, the modes of transport were very similar and often involved the same coyotes and gangs. And both were highly lucrative for the myriad criminals and Mexican nationals involved in the trade, with money greasing palms all the way down the line from cartel boss to *paisano*. It was literally impossible to keep up with all the potential links because they were so fluid. By the time they had proof enough to arrest a source, like the independent big-rig driver who'd been stopped at the border with drugged women hidden in the false bottom of his cargo bay, the conduit moved to another location and another trafficker.

As he scarfed down the last of his sandwich, Ross glared at the towering pile of files leaning against his office wall. On the rare occasion when he got to send one to the dead files after it was marked, "Case Closed," it seemed three sprang up to take its place.

In 2009, the TxDPS had established a special Ranger division known as the Ranger Reconnaissance Team. They had authority throughout Texas to conduct in-depth, military-style covert investigations designed to infiltrate and stop the drug cartels. Rumor had it they even had access to high surveillance aircraft. Most of their operations were on the Texas–Mexico border, and it was their intelligence gathering that offered the best hope of rescue for the kidnapped women. Not even Ross was privy to their detailed tactics or information unless he went straight to the head of their unit, a privilege because of his status as a Ranger captain, but one he seldom utilized, knowing from his own cases that the fewer eyes and ears on sensitive data, the better the chance of keeping it under wraps.

However, with the murder of the kidnapped girl in Lubbock, and now, just today, another case from another bar in downtown Baltimore, as well as the abductions of Emm's family, it was time he used that privilege. He needed to see if they could collaborate to trace this part of the trafficking ring back to the East Coast source. So many cases in a year from the same area had to mean it was a conduit; somewhere at the top and the bottom of the route, someone, probably an upper echelon crime boss for the East Coast, had all the information to bust the entire chain. . . . Ross pulled two new files from the teetering stack on his desk and opened them to read as he nibbled on apple slices. He'd requested copies of all the files linked to Baltimore after Emm's pleas last night, and he was still trying to absorb everything.

As he'd noted when Emm showed him their photos on her phone, Yancy and Jennifer looked more like sisters than mother and daughter. The vast majority of the kidnapped girls were in their teens, as the sleazebag johns tended to prefer younger women. But it wasn't unheard of for one of the cartel members to take a shine to an older woman, especially if she came with a daughter who looked like her. Ross flipped through Yancy's thick file. The Baltimore cops had been thorough: They had everything, including her application to the city of Baltimore, where she'd clerked in what appeared to be one of many odd jobs. Sure enough, she was listed as fluent in Spanish. He thumbed through Jennifer's much smaller file, but there was nothing on her language proficiency. He made a mental note to ask Emm.

His apple slices forgotten, Ross stared into space. He'd worked human trafficking cases for years, though only in the last few had they become so pervasive and difficult to crack. These days, the cartels hired their own hackers and were increasingly creative in their money laundering. Usually, no matter the crime, if you tracked the money, it would eventually lead to the perps. But girls forced into prostitution barely left a trace, and they were usually shuffled around frequently under assumed names, making them even harder to track.

But if Yancy had been lucky enough—or unlucky enough—to catch the eye of a cartel honcho, there was a slim possibility she was still in cartel custody along with her daughter. That, allied with the expensive drug she was on, might trip their databases with a lead, but what he had in mind would require very sophisticated analysis. All his men were swamped, as was he, so Ross turned to his computer. He was looking for the introductory e-mail he recalled from a division meeting. A new consultant had been hired, a former MI6 operative who'd moved to the US, become a citizen, and opened her own consulting firm. She was said to be the best the department had ever worked with in data collection and forensic analysis.

Facts she'd doggedly traced had already led to the arrest of a new cartel boss and the seizure of a thousand pounds of marijuana and cocaine. Hiring her would put a big dent in his already battered budget, but his gut told him he was right and this was their best chance to trace the head of the cartel's trafficking operations. Natural blondes were rare, especially in Mexico. . . . He had an opportunity to help Emm, as well as use her family's cases and unusual profiles to crack the pipeline wide open.

Ross dialed the number on his screen.

Sitting across from Ms. Doyle at a cute diner several miles from downtown Amarillo, Emm swallowed the last of her sweet tea, wiped her mouth, and pushed her half-empty salad plate away. She'd spent most of the luncheon talking about Yancy and Jennifer; not just the facts of the case but who they were and why she was so worried about them. She knew Yancy, and possibly Jennifer, too, would resist captivity even if it meant extreme peril. "I . . . have a feeling if they're not found soon, it will be too late," she said, signaling for the check as Ms. Doyle's phone rang.

Ms. Doyle rummaged in her briefcase and removed her cell phone. She glanced at the caller ID, then put the phone back in her briefcase without comment. "You do realize it may already be too late," she said gently.

Emm nodded, a knot in her throat. Her fingers trembled a bit as she opened her wallet, but a large, gentle hand took the tab away from her.

Ms. Doyle nodded at the waitress, brandishing a credit card. "Allow me," she said over Emm's protests. "Your story has been most elucidating and this is a deductible expense for me."

Emm couldn't argue with that.

After she signed the bill, tipped and thanked the waitress, and pocketed her card, Ms. Doyle rose, sweeping a hand before her toward the exit. Their cars were parked next to each other. "You have my card," Ms. Doyle said. "Call me if you think of anything else pertinent." She gave what was, Emm suspected, a warm smile for her severe countenance. "Call even if you don't. I don't know anyone here either. I'm about to go to the DPS offices. They've hired my services to assist them with drug interdiction, but drug and human trafficking are most often committed by the same cartels, so there is much crossover data."

Emm nodded, waved, and got into her own car. That night, after another light restaurant meal that didn't appeal to her, she scowled at her silent cell phone. She'd hoped all day it would ring with Ross's number. She was expecting him to call with the evidence warehouse address so she could view the pipe. She hoped he hadn't gotten cold feet. . . .

She tried to concentrate on the historic study she was writing on a building she'd surveyed in Baltimore before she left. The investigation with Ross hadn't taken much of her time so far, so she was scrupulous enough to put in her hours in other ways, and she had plenty of work. This particular building had been purchased recently by an experienced developer of historic properties. His intent was to do an apartment loft conversion, but his initial application for historic tax credits had been denied. He'd appealed that decision, bumping it up to Emm.

She already knew the building, so reviewing the pictures, plans, and current zoning information should have been easy for her. Instead, she was having a hard time concentrating. She started when a firm knock came at the door. She was in her teddy, sipping a glass of wine, so she called out, "Give me a minute," while she dug through her suitcase for her robe. She finally found it and wrapped it tightly around herself. There was a view hole in the door, but she wasn't surprised to find it opaque. Lots of little things tended not to work in old buildings. Besides, she felt entirely safe, so she flung the door open.

"Oh, hello . . . Ross. Mr. Sinclair."

Ross smiled. "I like the first one better."

She flushed as a thorough blue gaze ran over her from her mussed hair to her makeup-less face and down the old chenille robe, fraying at the sleeves, to her slippered feet. Wishing she'd taken time to buy that new robe she'd kept promising herself, she opened the door wide and stepped back. "Would you like to come in?"

"For just a moment." He entered as she closed the door. With that all-seeing, all-encompassing gaze she'd noticed the first time she'd met him, when he wrote her the ticket, he took in her worktable, laptop, files, and messy, half-open suitcase. His smile had disappeared as he reached for something in his pocket. "I had this brought up from evidence today. Is this your sister's custom pipe?"

Emm's stomach fell in disappointment. She'd wanted to see more of the evidence than just the pipe, and he knew that, damn him. Still, she carefully turned the plastic bag over. It had a series of numbers written on it, along with Yancy's last name, but even through the bag she recognized it instantly.

"Yes, that's it. I've seen her smoke it often enough . . . but I thought you said you wanted me to view more of the evidence, clothes and the like?"

"This is enough authentication because the lab already confirmed it was custom, one of a kind." When she still stared at him, his gaze fell. "I decided this was quicker and easier than taking you to the warehouse."

For me or for you? The words almost escaped before she swallowed them. She knew he was trying to keep distance between them, and she knew why, because she felt the same electrical current every time he was near. It was raising the hairs on the nape of her neck now.

Her voice was cooler than she intended, but she had to know. . . .

"What happens now? Now that you have confirmation from a family member that Yancy and probably Jennifer are in this group of women taken by the Los Lobos cartel, what else can I do to help?"

He shrugged. "It's not your job, it's mine, but this was helpful.

These men are extremely dangerous, as should be evident given the way your sister was snatched when she was looking for her daughter. I promise to keep you apprised of any progress . . . an easier task, of course, when you're here. . . . You heard from the structural engineer?"

"Yes, he's working up a proposal. If it's okay, I asked him to copy me on it as well."

"Of course."

"He's swamped, so he said it might be a week or so before he can get here to do the survey."

"As long as we get it done before my family comes to Amarillo, that's fine. They're going to start arriving toward the end of the month."

"We should be able to make that." She sat down on the bed, waving him into the one chair, crossing her legs and bouncing the fluffy slipper on her heel. She could tell herself she was just fidgety, but in reality she knew she was transferring sexual energy to kinetic energy. The motion also caused the bottom of her robe to gap open, but she was feminine enough to want him to look, to provoke at least some of the same vulnerability she felt in his presence. His gaze raked her legs compulsively, but he quickly looked back at her face.

"I never figured you for chenille."

The words took a moment to click. "Why don't you say what you really mean?" At his guarded look, she added softly, "You'd rather not have to figure me at all." Her foot perversely bounced faster and her slipper flew off, brushing him in the shin.

She expected him to kick it aside, but instead he picked up the slipper and knelt at her feet. When she stayed frozen in shock, he calmly lifted her foot onto his bent leg and put the slipper back on. Then he held her foot on top of his knee, appraising her legs closely and thoroughly, so thoroughly that she blushed. She snatched her foot away, the fleeting contact making all her feminine parts excruciatingly sensitive.

His lips curving as if he saw right through her downcast eyes, he stood. When she was brave enough to lift her gaze, she noted his blue eyes had softened somewhat. Instead of the corny Cinderella reference she expected, he said, "You have lovely feet and legs. Why do you hide them in sensible footwear and those frumpy suits you wear?"

"I want people to pay attention to my acumen, not my looks." Her flush fading, she looked down, mortified to see that her favorite robe was not only frayed, it was ripped at the last two button closures, so that her legs were bare almost to her hips. She moved to pull the robe closed, but she was sitting on the fabric. Finally, she just rose, twitched the robe closed, and, with her other hand, gave the pipe back to him. "You don't really know me, nor do you, from what I can tell, feel inclined to a closer acquaintance. Which is fine by me. Just business."

"Just business," he echoed. He stuck the pipe back in his pants pocket, stretching the black jeans in a way she noticed and wished she hadn't. He loomed so large in every way in the small room that she had to back away. Not because she was scared, but from the sheer impact of his presence. And deep inside, in a place she kept curtained away even from her own eyes, she knew they both lied. This man had the potential to be much more to her than just business. She was several steps away, but she could still smell his scent. His aftershave was faint and spicy, not too sweet, just like him. Direct, alluring because it didn't bother to entice with hidden ingredients. It was what it was, take it or leave it.

Emm badly wanted to put his hands-off attitude to the test, but she knew she might as well play with dynamite. Safely, she backed away another step. Her hip brushed the small round table, knocking a folder and a card to the floor. He bent to pick them up for her before she could, a lock of hair flopping across his forehead.

This time, the temptation was too great. Before she could stop herself, she tenderly brushed his hair back into place. His eyes widened, delving deeply into hers. She jerked her hand back, or tried to, but it was too late. Catching her wrist to pull her close, he dropped the folder and card, papers flying, and jerked her into his arms. Then that finely shaped, stern mouth lowered over hers. Right before contact, the lines softened to the same rampant sensuality he incited in her.

All protest died at the first brush of his lips. The feel of his mouth was soft in a way she hadn't expected, but the kiss itself was not. It was hard, needful and arrogant. It dared her to keep things businesslike, but subterfuge was beyond her. Instead of pulling away, she wrapped her arms around his neck and pulled him closer to slant her mouth over his. To give to the nth degree as he demanded, but also to incite him to give back even more. This tempest had been building between them since he'd cuffed her on a desolate stretch of Texas road, and whether it buffeted her into a lonely place or not, she had to yield to the storm. She not only brushed her lips from side to side over his, she also took tiny nibbles from the corners of his mouth on each slide, caving in at last to all the forbidden emotions he made her feel.

She was rewarded with a tortured male groan and a tongue pushing past her teeth to learn her taste and texture. Normally, she didn't like French kissing early on, but her reaction to this man had been anything but normal. She opened her mouth to his invasion, sighing her pleasure against his lips. He took the sweet sound like the gift it was, the kiss gentling to a deep, thorough caress. The very tip of his tongue explored the inside shape of her lips, the caress so gentle but so arousing that her heart literally skipped a beat. When he opened the robe that had loosened in their embrace, she was too far gone to care.

His own breathing ragged, he drew back to look at her. His eyes were closed at half mast, and they were so blue they looked incandescent as he traced a hand down across her silk teddy from the deep vee of her bosom to the beginning of the vee on her lower stomach. She did something else she'd never done with a man on the first kiss: She lay back against his other arm and let him look. No, she reveled in the passion flaring his nostrils, his quickened breathing, and the hard lump in his black jeans. If he'd lowered her to the bed, she wouldn't have resisted him.

He took a deep, raggedy breath. For an instant, as if by sheer strength of will, he forced his hand to drop away before he touched her where she most needed it, but then he froze, his hand on the curve of her hip, staring down between her legs. And then he brushed between her thighs, spread to help support her weight as she leaned against him. One finger touched between her legs, high up. She went rigid, firecrackers where her nerve endings used to be; only when she saw a drip of pearly moisture on his fingertip did she realize how wet she really was. Holding her gaze, he brought the pearl to his nose, his nostrils flaring as he absorbed her scent. Then he licked it away, as if it were a delicacy to sustain him, body and soul.

The shocking intimacy of this moment with a man totally inappropriate for her finally galvanized her into motion. With a strangled gasp, she fled into the bathroom and slammed the door shut. She looked at the sensual woman in the mirror, knowing that even after five lovers, she'd never seen this person before. Lips swollen, pupils so dilated her irises looked black, nipples erect against the torture of the silk she longed to rip away so she could know that skillful mouth there, too. *Am I easy or do I just need to get laid?* she silently asked. There was no answer.

Shamed, she turned the faucet on cold and splashed water over her heated face, using a washrag to roughly bathe between her legs. Then, her senses still incredibly alive, she listened, hoping to hear the hotel room door open and close. Instead, she heard outside his heavy breathing, gradually slowing, but his presence was still so vital she could feel it even through the door.

Dear Lord, she could barely face herself, how could she face him? And why was he the only man she'd ever met who incited this degree of physical chemistry so quickly? There could be no future for them . . . After they concluded their business, she'd move back to the Northeast, and he was a confirmed Texan. He didn't even like her, not really. He thought she was a spoiled heiress out to prove herself in her first case by denying his family the property rights to develop their land as they deemed suitable.

She had to clear her throat, her voice was so husky. Finally, she managed through the door, "Is there anything else? I . . . need some sleep and it's getting late."

"That's not all you need. For that matter, I need it, too." The words were guttural, as if he ground them out against his will. She didn't answer because any denial would be a bald-faced lie and they both knew it. She was still afraid to open the door.

Then a note of laughter softened his tone. "Are you ever coming out?"

"Actually, I'm thinking of staying awhile. If I stare into this mirror long enough, eventually I'll see someone I recognize."

Silence on the other side of the door, and then it opened. She'd dropped the robe onto the floor to wash, so she stood before him bare in body and soul, or at least that's the way she felt. "Hey," she protested, "maybe we shared a kiss, but that doesn't give you the right to invade my privacy."

"You're right. I just want to be sure you're okay and then I'll leave." This time, he studiously kept his dark blue gaze on her face. "If you want me to . . ."

Stay—the word leaped to her lips, but she didn't give it freedom.

She was still too shaken by their passionate embrace. If she followed her instincts, yet more complications would result. "I can't."

The incandescent blue died down to a simmer. "I understand." And then, like the gentleman he was, he picked up the robe, wrapped it around her shoulders, holding it while she stuck her arms in each side, and belted it tightly. "You need a new robe and slippers," he said lightly, backing out of the door to give her room to exit.

"I know; this one is just so comfortable. And . . . Yancy gave it to me for my birthday a long time ago."

"A very long time ago . . ." he teased. He bent to pick up the scattered papers. He stuck them back in the file, then flicked the business card against his thumb. "Where did you get Doyle's card? She's a consultant for the Rangers."

"I met her at the library today. We were both researching trafficking, though I think she said she'd been hired to look into the drug trade more than kidnappings."

"The two are intertwined."

"That's what she said."

"Did she say who hired her?"

Emm shook her head.

He frowned, his eyes narrowing. The last of the lambent flames had died away and the stern Ranger captain was back as he growled, "This is not an association I approve of. She knows what she's doing, but you don't, and if you spend much time with her, I could see you trying to trail after her like a puppy—"

"At least give me the dignity of a bloodhound analogy instead of a puppy—"

"And as it happens, I received the okay just today to hire her to help look for your sister . . . and the other missing women, too, of course."

Arguments died on her lips. "Thank you."

"So you found her competent?"

"Beyond competent, though I shared more details with her than she did with me."

He nodded approval at that. "By the way, do you recall if your niece speaks fluent Spanish?"

Emm tilted her head as she did when confused. "Yes, and so does Yancy. They both spent a summer and several holidays in Spain."

"I see." With a last look between her and the bed, a look that made her blush again, he went to the door. "Okay, well, let me know when the structural engineer will be in town. I want to be present for at least part of the survey."

She nodded, holding her robe closed, and walked him the short distance to the door. "Thanks for stopping by." The banality should have been comforting, but it wasn't. She stuck her hands deep into her frayed pockets to avoid the urge to catch him around the neck and pull his head down. And then . . .

They both studiously avoided looking at the bed.

His wide shoulders blocking the hallway light, he turned back to look at her in that thorough, head-to-toe way again. "No—thank *you*." He waited, and only when her flush deepened did he give that lazy smile. "It's only a matter of time, you know."

She pretended to misunderstand. "I know, I should be out of your hair in a month or so—"

"Until *you* sweep *me* off to bed. You're a very passionate woman. You need it almost as much as I do. Why not save us both a lot of time and frustration and admit it?"

"Oooh!" She slammed the door on the kiss he blew her.

But as his footsteps retreated, she stared into space. He was right, damn him, as he'd been right about almost everything else. "Just business," she repeated to herself as she flung off her robe and slippers and climbed into bed.

But as sleep claimed her, the mantra had changed to, *Just once, what can it hurt? Just once . . .*

CHAPTER 5

Two days later, Ross tossed the last file into a large box and taped it shut himself. He'd spent most of his working hours compiling every piece of evidence they had on the Los Lobos cartel, including both drug and human trafficking leads. The day after Emm had told him Doyle had already been retained by the West Texas district of the DEA, Ross had called the head of the division and suggested they split the cost and share the information. He'd readily agreed.

A knock on the door interrupted his thoughts. "Come in."

Dr. Hermione Abigail Doyle was as imposing in person as she was on paper. She stood almost six feet tall, and her conservative black pant suit didn't disguise a lithe, fit form. Ross glanced at his watch. Plus, she was punctual, almost to the second. He stood and offered his hand. "Thanks for coming."

"My pleasure, Captain Sinclair." She sat down in the chair in front of his desk.

"Call me Ross. I have a feeling we'll be working together closely. You executed all the agreements and waivers I e-mailed you?"

"Indeed. I appreciate your confidence in my services." She pulled a thick envelope out of her briefcase. "I've attached a card with my address while I'm in town so you can mail the countersigned documents to me."

"Excellent." He put the envelope on his desk and nodded at the large cardboard file boxes stacked next to her feet. "I've spent the last two days compiling all the information we have to date on the Los Lobos cartel, including both drug and human trafficking intel. You have a few burned CDs as well. Our servers are, of course, encrypted, but I thought it best if you received the most sensitive information the old-fashioned way."

"It will take me a few days to come up to speed. I know time is of the essence."

"Always, but thoroughness rules the day here, so follow whatever protocol you find most effective. I compiled an evidence list, and it's at the top of the box, with a very tentative ranking of the information that seems most promising, at least to me. You might start with tracing the drug one of the victims uses to control her hemophilia. It's fairly new, and rare in Mexico. We began tracing it using the accounts we subpoenaed from the US manufacturer, but we lost it across the border. Hopefully you'll have better luck."

A glimmer of humor softened the severe lines of her face. "As they say in Texas, this isn't your first rodeo."

He laughed. "Somehow that cliché sounds better with a British accent." His smile faded, and he gave her the same square, dead-on look he gave his Rangers. "Your reputation precedes you, but know this: I expect results."

She nodded coolly and rose. He shook her proffered hand. "I'll have someone follow you to your car with the boxes."

She'd turned toward the door when he added reluctantly, "Ms. Doyle?"

She turned with an inquiring look.

"I heard you met a certain Emm Rothschild a couple of days ago?"

She nodded.

"I'm sure you're aware of this, but sharing information with private citizens, especially those with an agenda, is frowned upon. Everything in the boxes is need to know."

That erect back grew ramrod straight. "I read in full the nondisclosure clause, and it is no more limiting than the others I've signed."

His cheeks flushed a dull red because he knew she was right. "I'm sorry, it's not you I doubt; it's my knowledge of Ms. Rothschild's proclivities that concerns me. To be blunt, don't let her near the files."

The straight back relaxed a bit. "You fear she's like Pandora?"

"No, I fear she'll stick her nose where it doesn't belong and become victim number ninety-two."

She nodded, this time thoughtfully. "A valid concern, based on my short acquaintance with the lady." She turned in the doorway after she opened the door. "You have my word she shan't see a thing. And Captain Sinclair . . ."

"Yes?"

"I won't tell her you're so concerned for her welfare." A smile flickered at the corners of her long mouth before she mastered it. "Unless you wish me to."

All he could come up with was, "Good. Don't." Then he rested his head in his palms, elbows on the desk, and groused, "Why do things have to be so damn complicated? Why can't we just be two lonely people who find something they need in someone of the opposite gender? Isn't that the way it's supposed to work?"

"Perhaps, but it's seldom that easy. I promise to keep your secret." A soft laugh trailed her as her heels tapped across the linoleum, her footsteps as precise and measured as her character. Ross went to the door and called an office assistant to take the boxes out. Then he closed the door, staring into space, a bit unsettled now he'd met the legendary Ms. Doyle. He found her even more imposing and astute than he'd expected, which was good as far as the case went. Not so good as she obviously used the same eagle eye on her clients as she did her perps. She'd seen through his concern for Emm in an instant. He could only hope she kept quiet, as she'd promised, because Emm didn't need any more weapons to wield over him . . . They'd both agreed on the parameters of their relationship: "just business."

Righto . . . Disgruntled, he powered on his computer again and sorted through his umpteen e-mails.

Outside in the parking lot, Emm saw Abigail getting into her car after a young man had put several bulky file boxes in her trunk. She could just make out the word "Evidence" in big block letters. She hurried over, releasing the arm of the man who had escorted her out of her own vehicle. "Dr. Doyle!"

Abigail powered down her window. "Abby, remember?"

"Abby, I'm glad you're here; I was just going to call you. Would you care to have dinner with me and Curt Tupperman? He's a freelance investigative reporter based in San Antonio, but he's writing a book on human trafficking in Texas. He has information he wants to share with us."

Abby opened her door and got out, offering her hand to the tall, fair-haired man who towered over her own considerable height. "Good afternoon."

He nodded, pumping her hand, his blue eyes twinkling. "Is this Abigail Doyle? Dr. Hermione Abigail Doyle?"

Abby nodded. She pulled away from his tight clasp.

"I've been following your exploits since your days at MI6. I'm thrilled to meet you."

Emm looked sharply at Abby. "MI6?"

"Long ago. Before I emigrated to the US. And I was never a field agent, just an analyst."

"An analyst so well respected she was assigned to a joint CIA/MI6 task force investigating terrorism after 9/11," Curt clarified. Abby looked away from his sharp gaze.

Emm clasped his arm lightly before he could say anything else as the subject obviously made Abby uncomfortable. "Anyhoo, will you join us for dinner tonight at my hotel? My treat."

Abby looked at her hand, comfortable on Curt's arm.

It was Emm's turn to be flustered. "I'm sorry, I should have mentioned I met Curt several years ago in Baltimore, while I was working on my doctorate. We ran into one another downtown near my hotel and have a mutual interest in the human trafficking case."

"MA, Criminal Justice," Curt offered. "So see? I'm harmless and something of a professional, too. And anything you share will be strictly off the record."

"I cannot promise the same, Mr. Tupperman."

He nodded quickly. "I understand. Please, join us. And call me Curt."

"Very well." After they arranged a time and location to meet, Abby waved briskly, got back in her car, and drove off.

Comically, Curt shuddered. "Wow, that's one fearsomely intelligent woman."

"Is there such a thing as being too intelligent?" Emm walked up the steps and reached out to open the door, but he bolted up and beat her to it. At her jaundiced look, he shrugged sheepishly.

"Guess not." When they entered the foyer of the Ranger offices, he took a deep breath.

She sensed his unease. "What's wrong?"

"I'm bracing myself. Sinclair and I are acquaintances. We've even played golf together. But my last message from him was, well, rather . . . curt."

Emm was still digesting that when Sinclair exited his office. She recognized that starched spine and cool gaze, but she wasn't sure whether his disapproval was aimed at her or Curt. After she explained her connection with Curt, she added, "We thought we might shanghai you for an early glass of wine. Curt has information to share about some evidence he's collected from South Texas."

"Not exactly collected," Curt said hastily when that cool gaze turned on him. "I was included in a press briefing on the Valley papers, but it's all public knowledge."

"Then I'll be informed as well," Sinclair pointed out.

"Eventually. It might help to have the information now, especially if Dr. Doyle is collating all the data."

Sinclair frowned. "How do you know that? I literally just retained her."

"You can blame that on me," Emm inserted. "We ran across one another outside, and when we saw the boxes, well, they were marked evidence. . . ."

Now that glare turned back on her. "Which you are to stay away from, correct?"

Emm intended to count to ten, but she only made it to five. She lowered her voice to be sure only Sinclair and Curt could hear her, but her tone was no less severe. "Look, Mr. Sinclair, we'll get much further if we work together. Surely you've figured out by now I'm not the type to stand around and do nothing when someone I love has been kidnapped and probably forced into a despicable trade. I am excellent at research." She rummaged in her capacious bag and pulled out a thick sheaf of papers, holding it up for Sinclair to see. "This is the Texas Human Trafficking Prevention Task Force report from December 2012. The final recommendations are summed up in the words of Attorney General Eric Holder."

Clearing her throat, Emm read from the first page of the report's conclusion: "'Human Trafficking is not just a global problem. It's a national crisis—one that every parent, every teacher, every policymaker, and every law enforcement official must work to understand—and must help to address.'"

She crammed the report back into her purse and stabbed a thumb into her chest. "Policy maker, that's me. While protecting historic resources is not strictly speaking being a first responder, we have had cases where we've dealt with immigrant and human trafficking victims in abandoned buildings and had to coordinate with other federal agencies." When she saw the disagreement trembling on Sinclair's tongue, she took an aggressive step forward and raised her voice.

"And the attorney general of the United States, while not my direct superviser, is certainly somewhere in my chain of command . . . and yours."

Sinclair looked at Curt as if pleading for support, but he seemed to have a strong interest in the plaques on the wall.

With a rueful laugh, Sinclair held up both hands in surrender. "Shall we agree to a mutual information sharing? With the understanding that whatever intel we exchange not leave our little trio."

Emm frowned. "I have to let the Baltimore detectives know what's going on. I promised them I would."

"Can you at least trust me with that much?" Sinclair groused. "It's part of my job to keep other agencies in the loop . . . My God, what a control freak."

This last was muttered, but Emm heard it. She had to bite back her response that he was the one who'd taken total control of her in her own hotel room last night, but the memory colored her cheeks. When his eyes narrowed a bit, she turned toward the door. "Very well, then, shall we find a quiet spot for a glass of wine?"

"Let me get my hat," Sinclair muttered, marching back to his office.

Curt eyed that starched spine, then lifted an interested eyebrow at Emm.

"None of your business," she preempted the very reporterlike question she saw him about to utter about the sparks flying between her and Sinclair. "I'll see you at the bar."

On the short drive back downtown, Emm gripped the wheel tightly, hoping that among the three of them they could stumble across something, anything, that would lead to Yancy and Jennifer. For the umpteenth time, she uttered a silent prayer for the safety of her sister and niece.

On the outskirts of Mexico City, Yancy Russell patted the heads of the three Rottweilers she'd long ago befriended, tossing them the dog biscuits she'd filched from the kitchen. This secluded estate, on the hills outside Mexico City, was such a fortress that it had taken her months to learn how to circumvent its defenses. The corner of the vast gardens was the only place invisible to the electronic eyes surveying the entire compound. She only knew this because she'd saved her pocket change, doled out to her every week by her "benefactor,"

Arturo, to bribe one of the security techs who periodically came in to maintain and tweak the equipment. One of them, an aging expat American hippie with a guitar tattooed on his forearm, had been susceptible to her smiles and wiles. When she could duck her own constant companion, aka jailer, several times she'd joined him in the kitchen for fajitas and mojitos.

The kitchen staff had long ago turned a blind eye to her little rebellions against Arturo, for in that way she was no different from the innumerable beauty queens, models, and barrio girls who became the mistresses of various cartel leaders. Their careers were short, dictated by their youth and beauty, and to a woman they utilized every female guile at their disposal to milk jewels, designer clothes, cars, apartments, and even trust funds from their benefactors.

Yancy, the servants of the vast mansion agreed, was older and smarter, though still very lovely. If she wanted to share a drink with the other help, it was a small transgression in a kingdom where food tasters and armies with advanced tactical training were the favored vassals of the patron. She was just a Yanqui cast out from her own wealthy family who was lucky the patron had been at the merchandise drop when she came in and had taken a fancy to her. It was said he'd noted her resemblance to the pretty blonde his son had snatched for himself months earlier, and he'd been titillated to think of the fun he and Tomas could have with a gorgeous American mother-daughter combo.

And, since in the last five months or so Yancy had never tried to escape or, from all the eyes and ears on alert wherever she went, even tried to use a phone other than the restricted one they allowed her, her jailers had relaxed enough to leave her alone occasionally. Besides, as she herself had told Arturo on more than one occasion, she'd never leave Jennifer behind. Because Jennifer had tried to escape several times, and slit her wrists once, she was kept under constant armed guard. Yancy was allowed to see her on supervised visits once a week.

And that visit was tomorrow, and was the reason for her risky maneuver. Yancy patted the dogs again, hitched her tight red silk dress above her thighs, kicked off her heels, and climbed up the brick wall. She'd always loved rock climbing, and from a distance this wall looked too smooth to scale, but there were breaks where the mortar was loose, and with the stakes so high, she had no choice but to chance it.

She slipped once, scraping a knuckle as she scrabbled to hold on, but using the upper-body strength she maintained by calisthenics in her room when she was alone, she topped the wall, dangled her legs down the first six feet, and dropped the remaining four feet to the asphalt road. She knelt down, staying in the shadow for a moment to get her bearings between the cameras watching the road and the wall. She ignored the slight wound on her hand, aware that it was still bleeding—Arturo had been slow to get her very expensive meds for her in the last month or so, and she hadn't been able to take them consistently. The little money she'd saved would have to go toward the pills for Jennifer, which were also expensive and hard to get in Mexico.

She confirmed there were no cars in sight and then darted across the road. She rounded the corner and went through a small copse of trees to a tiny clearing, expecting the little red Fiat to be there, where it always was. Her heart sank when she saw the empty clearing. What now?

While she stood there debating, she heard a very smooth, powerful engine approaching the bend. Crap; she recognized that sound. Only an armored Rolls-Royce Corniche could sound that quiet and powerful all at once, which meant Arturo had returned early from his meeting.

Her heart pounding, she ducked behind a tree until she heard the electric gates open, and then she tore back across the road, using a stump to vault herself as high as she could toward the top of the wall. She scrambled down the other side and high tailed it toward the back door that led to the kitchen, plucking a few roses from the lush grounds on the way. She stuck her dirty feet into her red stilettos, glad she'd selected pumps so her soles were covered, and entered the kitchen, calling for a vase.

She wrapped a paper towel around her hand to staunch the blood, but it was still welling up. As she arranged the flowers, she heard her name being called in that mellow basso voice that in other circumstances she might have yearned to hear. "In the kitchen!" she called back in Spanish. His English was broken at best, another reason, she was sure, he'd selected someone proficient in Spanish as his latest mistress.

Arturo entered, smiling indulgently when he saw her trimming rose stems, but his smile faded when he saw the bloody paper towel on her hand. He took her hand and removed the towel to look at the small wound. "I've told you before to have the maids cut the flowers for you, precisely for this reason," he scolded. He gently wrapped a fresh paper towel around her hand, pressing on her cut to try to staunch the blood. His dark brown gaze, which could go brandy hot with lust and the next instant take on the cold glare of a snake, traveled down her form, pausing on a couple of snags on the tight silk.

She ducked her head over her task, muttering, "They never get the right ones. I snagged my dress on the bushes. I was going to change before you came, but you're early." She put the last rose in the vase with her free hand and stepped back, eyeing her handiwork as she pulled gently away from his touch. She'd learned early on that resistance only made him more brutal.

He slipped the towel off her hand. The blood had slowed to a dot. "Good. I will send María into town for more of your medicine. You're out?"

She nodded, cupping his cheek with a faux tenderness and gratitude he seemed to take as genuine. At least so far.

Mollified, he embraced her, muttering, *"Pobrecita, idiota,"* and kissed her ruthlessly on the mouth. She did what captive women have been doing since time immemorial: She stifled an urge to kick him in the balls and kissed him back, running her hands through thick hair graying at the temples.

She had one imperative: to survive one more day and to protect her daughter until they could escape . . . And with her second breath she gave a plea to the only other person on the planet who really loved her and Jennifer. "Emm, I hope you haven't given up on us. . . ."

In downtown Amarillo, Emm, Curt, and Ross sat near the back of the dark little bar, each nursing a glass of wine. The exchange of information had begun slowly, with Emm sharing what she'd learned in the library. "Girls had been disappearing in Maryland long before Jennifer, and I found at least one victim who was originally from the Baltimore area but was found in the Texas Panhandle . . . Baltimore could be a hub for this particular group."

Sinclair shared what the lab had deduced so far from the warehouse of confiscated items. "We traced clothes, purses, shoes, even some of the makeup, but other than your sister's custom weed pipe, most of the things were cheap knockoffs sold in any city in the nation. We're trying to trace them but haven't found anything of interest yet."

"So that's why you hired Dr. Doyle?" Emm asked.

"Partly. It's a massive amount of evidence and I just don't have manpower enough to thoroughly vet everything. She'd also already been retained by the DEA to assist with the Los Lobos cartel on the drug-smuggling end of the spectrum, so it just made sense to share her fee."

Curt's eyes narrowed. "You think this Los Lobos gang is the one behind the human trafficking in Baltimore?"

Sinclair shrugged. "I can't make that connection yet, but we have confirmed they've broadened their focus in the last few years to include trafficking."

"How do you know that?" Curt asked.

Sinclair hesitated, his eyes taking on an icy sheen in the dim glow of the shaded lamps. "Off the record?"

"I told you I wouldn't print any of this," Curt protested.

"Yeah, well, you said that before I found my name and one of my operative's names broadcast all over Texas in your glad rag."

Curt sipped the last of his wine and placed it just so on his napkin, his bright head bent but a flush coloring his cheekbones.

Looking between the two men, Emm intervened. "My niece and sister won't care who gets credit for what . . . if they're even still alive. Our only chance of finding them is to work together . . . Please . . . Can you tell us how you know the Los Lobos cartel is in the human trafficking trade?" She focused on Sinclair.

He shoved his half-finished wineglass back and said shortly, "Surveillance picked up a semi crossing back into the US from Mexico. ICE agents found a false bottom in it that was empty, but there were traces of human hair and no drug residue whatever. The driver was a known accomplice of the Los Lobos gang. We arrested him, but he's refused to talk even under threats of life imprisonment, which, frankly, we probably can't make stick without more evidence. We can't deport him because he's a US citizen." He saw the words trembling on Emm's tongue and held up his hand. "Of course we took samples, but in most cases these girls are young, with no record, so we don't have DNA on them to cross-reference anyway."

"Yancy has a record. Disorderly conduct, possession, even a

shoplifting charge when she was younger," Emm pointed out. "It's possible they took samples on her last arrest."

Sinclair nodded. "I know, it's in her file. If we get any matches, we'll know at least where she went across, but this semi was searched just a month ago, long after she and your niece disappeared."

"And were you able to trace ethnicity on any of the ... hair fibers?" Emm hated the word *merchandise*, and *victim* was equally stark. "I know DNA tracing has advanced hugely in the last five to ten years."

Sinclair nodded. "We found seven fibers, two of one vic, the other five across the spectrum in ethnicity: Irish, English, Scandinavian, American Indian, Hispanic, Jewish."

"In other words, the hairs could belong to just about anyone in the US," Emm said.

Sinclair nodded grimly.

Curt asked, "Were you able to trace when and where the driver came across the first time?"

"Of course. He checked out with a full load of manufacturing equipment for a new factory in Sinaloa. The agents who cleared him vaguely recalled the vehicle and driver. Both said they heard zip from the cargo bay, smelled nothing, and the dogs didn't alert anyone." Sinclair fiddled with his napkin in a nervous way uncharacteristic of him, which Emm realized spoke volumes about his state of mind. "Tests indicated the occupants of that cavity were so drugged they were undoubtedly comatose, so they couldn't make a sound. And any scent the dogs might have picked up on was disguised by cans of paint and chemicals, part of the shipment. It was also the type of truck with built-in vent fans that are on continuously."

Emm pictured a stifling cargo hold, pitch black, with barely enough air to breathe, and women—no, girls—bouncing against one another, the hell of where they were still better than the hell of where they were headed. She looked down to disguise her tears as she thought of what Yancy and Jennifer must have done in the last year to survive. If they survived ...

Sinclair's hand on top of hers was comforting in a way she couldn't think about right now, but she knew she needed a clear head, so she equally gently withdrew her hand from his. Again, Curt looked curiously between them.

"All right, I suggest we all take a week to work the case and then see where we are," Emm proposed.

Sinclair just looked at her, but she knew him well enough by now to read disapproval behind that opaque stare.

"I'm not doing anything but research. Heck, it's no different from what I do in my job, or what I had to do to get my PhD." When he still looked at her, she snapped, "If you want to stop me, there's only one way." She crossed her wrists over the table in front of him.

"Don't tempt me. A few weeks in lockup would do you good." He stood so quickly the table leg scraped on the floor, but he only picked up his hat and pinned her with a gaze that was very clear now, and pure threat. "There's a reckoning coming between the two of us, whether either of us likes it or not. Watch your step, because Rangers are pretty touchy about people interfering in their investigations." Smashing his black hat on his head, Sinclair stalked out of the bar.

This time, Curt ignored her don't-ask signal. "Why don't the two of you get a room and get that part of this equation settled?"

Emm glared at him, tossing down enough cash to cover the tab. In another measure of Sinclair's unusual behavior, she realized he'd forgotten to pay for his drink. "Don't be crude."

"Hey, babe, I'm a reporter. I see what I see. And I've never seen Ross Sinclair so off balance because of a woman."

Emm stood and grabbed her car keys. "It's not me, it's the case." She stalked out, trying to ignore the scornful sound he made in her wake.

Still, on the short drive back to her hotel, she had to ask herself: Was it possible she confused Ross Sinclair as much as he intimidated her?

Ross had intended to go back to the office, but he was so flustered when he walked out that he decided to go home instead. He had plenty of files to read there. On the drive to his ranch, he kept remembering the tremor in Emm's full mouth, the shaking of her small, warm hand as he covered it. He couldn't question her terror for her sister and niece, but on the rare occasion when she let her guard slip, she showed a feminine vulnerability that reached deep inside him. And, instinctively, he'd tried to comfort her . . . He pulled into his driveway, still deep in thought, but a big grin stretched his face when he saw the new SUV parked in front of his house.

He leaped out of his own unmarked SUV and ran inside, bellowing, "Where's my boy?" as he went.

Chad Foster poked his head out of the den. "So he's yours now, huh? Okay, I'll have you come give him his two a.m. feeding tonight."

Ross held his arms out for the curious and alert blue bundle. Chad tilted his hat back to proudly watch two of his favorite people in the world eye each other. Trey junior had his brother Trey's blue eyes and at least some of Trey's sense of mischief: He blew a raspberry that spattered Ross right in the face. Ross just used a piece of blanket to wipe his cheek and grinned like an idiot down at the infant. "He gets bigger every time I see him."

"That's common with such exotics as pronghorn antelope and newborn boys," Jasmine teased, stepping up to kiss Ross's other cheek. She eyed the practiced way he supported the baby's head on one arm, folding the blanket tighter with the other hand. "You're very good at that. You really need your own."

Ross's smile dimmed. With a last gentle kiss on the rosy cheek, he offered the boy back. "I'm getting too old for that. So what brings y'all into town from Lubbock?"

Jasmine gladly accepted her son, even if she looked skeptical at his remark.

Chad only shrugged. "Took a few days off to handle some business."

"Great; you're both welcome to stay here, you know that. I even have a bassinet somewhere that I keep for the reunions." When they hesitated, Ross insisted, "Believe me, I'm glad for the company."

"I like to stay at the homestead when I'm here, check up on things," Chad replied. He waited, then added, "Besides, you may have other things to do. I hear there's a new arrival in town. Someone from back East?"

Jasmine and Chad exchanged a look. Ross noticed. He scowled. "Can't a man keep one little thing private around here?"

CHAPTER 6

Chad had grinned tauntingly. "I never could. To your great delight, I might add. I remember a certain ribbing I took, complete with a leather-holstered sex kitten above my desk."

Jasmine laughed, cradling her son closer to her impressive bosom. She'd rounded out since she'd given birth to the Foster heir. She was still trying to lose the last fifteen pounds, but based on the pride and adoration oozing from Chad's every pore, he loved her just as she was. He put an arm around her and murmured something in her ear that made her blush.

Ross squelched a sigh, feeling like a lovesick idiot, but he couldn't help it: Jasmine's pale green eyes suddenly became blue, her rioting auburn curls a straighter, deeper brown that begged for a man to bury his hands in those thick tresses, and . . .

"Ross? You okay?" Chad's head tilted slightly to the side in that way he had when he was confused.

Emm did the same thing . . . Ross turned to the bar to hide his flush. "I'm sorry, woolgathering; it's been a tough week. How are y'all liking Lubbock?" He mixed them each their favorite, a margarita with fresh lime juice and Añejo premium tequila.

Accepting their drinks, they sat down on the couch, very close together. When their son began to doze, Jasmine set the boy down next to her and piled pillows on the edge of the plush couch to keep him away from the edge. Ross noted that, just in case, she also kept her hand pressed on the edge of the couch in front of the pillows to stop them from sliding to the floor. Chad handed Jasmine her drink from the table beside him periodically as they discussed the little things in life, like her new coursework at Texas Tech, Chad's new boss, and how they both liked Lubbock but missed the ranch. Ross noted Chad always seemed to sense when she was ready for another sip and gave her the glass without her saying a word.

He'd observed that strange empathy between the two of them almost from the beginning, the unspoken ability to read each other's thoughts and wishes. He was convinced it was the sixth sense only couples shared that was the real glue holding marriages together. Superficial things like status and looks waxed and waned over time, but this warm bond grew stronger with the years. If it was there to begin with . . .

Again, Ross had to collect his scattered thoughts when Chad asked, "So, what's happening with the family's buildings? I hear the conservator who came into town is quite a looker."

Succumbing to their curiosity, Ross admitted, "Yes, and a royal pain in the ass. We're waiting for a structural survey, and then she can make her finding and boogie back East, where she belongs."

Jasmine eyed his averted face. When he still concentrated fiercely on the dregs of his own margarita, she smiled slightly. "She sounds interesting. We're at the ranch for a couple of days . . . would y'all like to come out for lunch this weekend?"

When Chad grasped his throat and made a choking sound, she whacked him lightly on the thigh. "I'm trying to be a better cook, but since Trey junior came—"

Chad's hands fell, but he scooted slightly away from Jasmine as he needled, "Poor kid, it's good he's still on milk because your cooking might stunt his growth." He had to dodge a halfhearted whack.

Jasmine's mock glare became real. "We're not paying all this money for law school so I can be Suzy homemaker. If I don't make law review, my dad will have a conniption, especially as he's funding me now so I can spend my savings on the ranch . . . You can take over cooking once in a while, Mr. Hotshot Lieutenant—"

Ross picked out the pertinent information from her complaint. "Lieutenant? When did that happen and why didn't you tell me, you SOB?"

"That's one reason we made this trip. Took a few days off to celebrate, and see to some repairs at the homestead." Chad accepted Ross's warm handshake. "I really have you to thank for it. I took your approach into the Lubbock office with me and our conviction rate has climbed twenty percent in a year because our evidence methods are so much more ironclad. They noticed and promoted me accordingly."

Ross sat back down, unable to resist his own jibe. "No more Texas-style justice?"

"Yessir, it just works better if it's slow and maybe." Chad and Ross shared a laugh, and then Chad pulled his scowling wife under his arm and kissed her cheek. "'Course it doesn't hurt to have two attorneys in the family. Keeps me on the straight and narrow." He bent his head to kiss her caustic comment away.

That envious pang gripped Ross's midsection again as Jasmine resisted for a nanosecond, then kissed her husband back so passionately that she didn't notice when a cushion fell to the floor. Little Trey still slept peacefully, even when Ross rose to set the cushion back in place.

Jasmine seemed to sense his presence, and she pulled away from Chad, thoroughly kissed and thoroughly embarrassed. "I'm sorry, he likes to tease me."

"Hmm, I can see that. Tell me, when I come to the old place, will I find a leather harness hanging from the beams?"

Chad burst into laughter as Jasmine turned her glare from him to Ross. "Am I never going to live that down?" she complained.

Both men said, "Nope," simultaneously.

She joined in their laughter, and Ross felt the shadows that had been lengthening of late in his home retreat to darker corners, where they belonged.

Emm stared across the table at Dr. Doyle. They'd shared a nice meal, discussing the generalities of the case and the troubling statistics of human trafficking. Emm said, "The latest statistics I saw estimated seventy-seven percent of the women forced into trafficking are put into the sex trade and the remainder go into some type of menial labor."

Dr. Doyle nodded. "Yes, thereabouts. And, of course, you probably know that of the people kidnapped or coerced, at least seventy percent are female."

Emm nodded grimly. "So we should all be on the lookout?"

"Well, certainly those of us in law enforcement."

Emm scowled. "Look, Dr. Doyle, I've had this lecture from Ross

Sinclair. While I'm awaiting the structural engineer's report on the Sinclair buildings, I have some time to look for my sister. And as you've already admitted, I'm excellent at research." When Dr. Doyle neatly set her fork and knife over the edge of her plate and pushed it away instead of replying, Emm's voice grew more insistent. "If you'll just share some of the evidence with me, I'm sure I'd recognize anything owned by Yancy or Jennifer. . . ."

"I've already sorted through the clothing and such left at that warehouse. Cheap overseas goods that can be bought at any discount store in the U.S, very difficult to trace. . . ."

"Oh yeah? How come I had to tell Mr. Sinclair about Yancy's custom pipe? And I only learned about it because of Curt's article."

"Ms. Rothschild, I admire your tenacity, truly, but these cartels are very dangerous, and there are indications they have accomplices throughout Texas, likely even Amarillo. Accomplices that don't fit the profile; probably upstanding professionals who assist with the money laundering and currying political favors. A few Border Patrol agents and customs officials have even been paid off to look the other way."

Emm wadded up her napkin and tossed it on the table. "So bug out and sit down and shut up. Just on the off chance I might be taken, too?"

Dr. Doyle sighed. "I'm not saying that. But as bright as you are, you're not a law enforcement or intelligence professional, and these alliances are so wide ranging and difficult to track that just accumulating enough evidence to convict some of these people is very difficult. You could impact that information gathering without even knowing it."

Emm gnawed at her lip. "I don't care what the reasons are. Jennifer has been missing over a year, and Yancy over six months. Time is running out for them, if it hasn't already, and traditional law enforcement moves far too slowly to save them. They're more than an evidence file number to me . . . Who else will advocate for them?"

A long moment passed, and finally Dr. Doyle glanced at her watch and took out her phone. "Do you mind if I record the rest of this conversation?"

Emm shook her head. "I'm not sure I can be of much help. Everything I know is in the file—"

"There are always more details. For example, were there any embittered ex-boyfriends with drug connections?"

"Jennifer was dating someone her mother and I didn't like, a rocker, but the Baltimore police didn't find any connection between him and Los Lobos."

"And you spoke yourself to their friends?"

"Yes, more than once. Yancy hadn't dated in a while, but Jennifer was into Internet dating because she liked older men, said guys her age were too immature."

"And did you meet any of her other dates?"

"A couple. They seemed harmless enough. The police said neither of them had a record."

"In this type of crime, that's not always a tip-off. It's their very respectability that makes them valuable to the cartel. There is a link somewhere between Baltimore and Texas. Too many of the victims were from the same area, and I suspect that someone, likely someone of influence who travels the two areas with equal ease, is assisting the cartel with advance intelligence of police and agency movements, which is why we can't find a trace of their conduit."

Emm tried to picture anyone she knew contributing to this heinous crime, but she failed. Not a single person came to mind. "So it would have to be someone privy to law enforcement information and tactics. Someone who traveled frequently between Baltimore and Texas. Someone respected and possibly influential in the community . . ."

Dr. Doyle nodded. "Exactly."

Emm stared into space. She could only think of one person who fit that profile, and no way could he be involved. He'd even dated Yancy for a while. . . .

Dr. Doyle must have seen something in her face because she leaned forward. "Any idea, no matter how far-fetched, needs to be considered."

Emm opened her capacious purse and rummaged around. She'd kept the article, intending to send it to her father, but hadn't gotten around to mailing it. She pulled it out and offered it to Dr. Doyle.

She read the byline and her gaze narrowed, then shifted to Emm's face. "Are you offering Mr. Tupperman as a suspect?" She seemed genuinely shocked.

"He fits the criteria. When he's in town, he frequents some of the same bars as the women who were taken. He knows both Yancy and

Jennifer. And he had a bad breakup with Yancy a few months before she disappeared. He certainly has tons of connections in both politics and banking. And he has very expensive tastes. He recently bought a nice condo and an elite sports car. On a reporter's salary."

"Hmm . . ." Ms. Doyle ruminated, and then nodded. "I'll check his financial records. If he's involved in the procurement or laundering, there will be signs."

"Quietly," Emm suggested. "No subpoenas."

Dr. Doyle sighed heavily. "As discreetly as possible, but there's only so much I can deduce from the public record."

Feeling a bit better now they had a tentative plan, Emm signaled for the check. Dr. Doyle accepted with a gracious nod. As they waited, Emm said quietly, "And there's one other piece of evidence that I think should be given priority." Emm told her about Yancy's hemophilia and the new drug she'd found to be most efficacious.

Dr. Doyle nodded. "Yes, Captain Sinclair had already flagged that as a high-priority item on the evidence list. I've started searching databases of drug shipments, but this formulation is so new it's not showing up very much even domestically. Things get a bit more complicated when I try to cross-check specific drugs and who's prescribing them with Mexican pharmacies. But I'll keep trying. I do have a few contacts in Mexico's larger cities."

Both women stood. Impulsively, Emm hugged her. "Thank you so much. I finally feel the tiniest smidgen of hope. At least I'm doing something productive."

Dr. Doyle smiled, her severe face taking on a mischievous look. "I suspect you'd be doing 'something productive' with or without my help."

Emm smiled but said nothing.

Shaking her head slightly at Emm's expression, Dr. Doyle led the way out.

Ross sat at his desk in his home study, reviewing the structural engineer's proposal. It sounded much more involved than he'd anticipated. The engineer was bringing along a soils guy, who had to take borings at strategic points on the lots based on the survey they'd had updated and a preliminary look at the "as builts," which Emm had already scanned and sent to them. The final report would take a while even after the survey was complete. The engineer was asking for approval, so Ross gave it by e-mail and copied Emm. He was a bit surprised when she responded almost immediately. She must be back in her hotel room.

An image of how she'd looked in that silken teddy sent a tingle through him. Then he remembered her wetness on his fingertip. His nostrils flared at the memory of the feel and smell. All woman, sheer ambrosia that made him hunger for more. The tingle grew more tangible, and he was so aroused that he reached for his cup of coffee to distract himself. He fumbled it, and it fell into his lap, scalding him. He jumped to his feet, letting the mug fall to the floor, cursing and using the napkin to wipe at his pants.

He was in this predicament when José knocked perfunctorily and came in to fetch the dinner tray. He saw Ross hopping around with a napkin to the front of his pants and the broken cup on the wood floor. A twinkle appeared in his eyes as he bent and calmly picked up the shattered crockery and sopped up the coffee. "Señor is usually not . . . how you say? Clumsy?"

Ross slammed his napkin down on the desk, only to curse and move it quickly as it dampened some of his papers. He swung it around one finger, eyeing his trusted manservant as if contemplating flinging it at his head.

But when José stood back up and faced him, that twinkle deepening in his mellow brown eyes, Ross blew a bitter sigh and plopped back in his chair. He handed the napkin to José. José neatly folded it and stacked it on top of the dirty dishes and broken crockery.

"My family wants to meet with the historic preservation officer," Ross said abruptly.

José nodded. "*Es bueno*, yes? So you can get her out of your . . . hairs?"

"*No es bueno*," Ross disagreed grimly. "My aunt and mom will pick up on the . . . tension between me and . . . Ms. Rothschild immediately. Not to mention they won't be happy at her likely refusal to let us proceed with the development, if she's right that the building is structurally sound."

José shrugged. "You don't need money."

"It's not the money, it's the principle. I came out here partly to get away from interference in my affairs. We have the right to develop the property as we see fit." Ross scowled as José made a murmuring sound that Ross knew usually meant his disagreement—and an imminent lecture. Ross braced himself. But no one he knew, including the other Sinclairs, including even Chad Foster, cared for him as deeply as this old retainer.

"In my village in Chiapas, we had an old church," José said mildly. "It was, how you say, broken?"

"Dilapidated."

"But the old women of the village, they still prayed at the altar, and lit candles for loved ones even when the alcalde lectured them that it was not safe. And he began asking for funds from the governor of Chiapas to tear it down. But the women said it still lived with the spirits of their dead. When the men came to tear it down, they joined hands in front to stop them. The *federales* came, and two of the old women were hurt." José picked up the tray and headed for the door.

Ross knew his chain was being yanked, but he still had to know. "Dammit, what happened?"

José stopped at the door and turned to face his boss. "They tore the church down, and one of the old women died. A year later, a gas leak in the new church reached the candles as the alcalde was praying. They only found pieces of his body." José steadied the tray again. "With no church as its center, the village died with the old women. Only a few paisanos live there now, and they say they hear the whispers of the dead every night where the old church stood."

"Is this when you crossed the border into the United States?"

"Sí, a few months later."

Ross waited, but José was silent, obviously reflecting. The sparkle had faded from his eyes, leaving them somber.

Ross demanded, "Okay, you old buzzard, spit it out. Your little stories always have a moral. You should have been named Aesop."

"Even in Mexico City, one of the largest cities in the world, it is the old buildings that are the heart of the city," José said simply. "It is so easy in this country to tear things down . . . but do we give up a little of our spirit with every broken brick?" He exited.

For the dozenth time, Ross reflected that José was a wise old soul for a man in his early sixties. What Jose said could be extrapolated to include the Sinclair buildings, but they were hardly the center of Amarillo, and they certainly weren't holy. Besides, the decision wasn't just his. . . . He turned to the catering quote he had for the reunion, wishing he could turn away from his sexual urges as easily. He really had to give that widow he sometimes "dated" a call. . . .

When she got back to her hotel room and checked her e-mail, Emm was glad to see the message from Burt, the structural engineer. She reviewed his proposal, noted he'd copied Sinclair, and e-mailed both of them back that two days from now would be fine to do the examination, provided Ross Sinclair approved the time and materials listed on the proposal. Emm was surprised to see that confirmation had come almost immediately from Ross.

Because she was pretty sure he didn't do personal e-mails at work, she figured he must be at his ranch computer. She tried to envision him, lord of his domain in that big, lonely house, feeling a pang of longing to fill it with their mutual laughter. She squelched the impulse, logging off her computer and shutting it down. *Just business,* she told herself. Two days to the actual survey, probably about a week to get the results, perhaps another day to write her own findings and present them to the family. By then, she'd heard, much of the Sinclair family would be in Amarillo at their annual reunion. She made a mental note to request an actual time slot from Ross, as he'd already suggested she speak to all of them.

As she slipped into her teddy, yawning, she reflected that she'd be back in Baltimore within a couple of weeks. She waited for a sense of relief, but it didn't come. West Texas had grown on her. The hot spring days yielding to soft nights in the sixties, the flat prairies offset by red outcroppings. The glorious sunsets, colors deeper and more intense than any she was accustomed to because of the residual dust in the air. Ross had recommended she take a guided tour of Palo Duro Canyon before she left, and she just might do that. Usually after a full day like this one, she'd fall asleep quickly, but this time she tossed and turned, finally snapping on the TV, but she barely listened to the late-night talk show.

The true source of her restlessness stood a bit over six feet in custom cowboy boots and an expensive Stetson. Once she left here she'd likely never see Ross Sinclair again, and the knowledge haunted her.

Idiot! she scorned herself. *You just landed the job you've been dreaming about since you were a child and you go and get yourself enamored of a Texas lawman, one who's never been married to boot.* She had to smile at her own accidental choice of words, but the smile faded quickly as another, far less pleasurable image, came to mind.

Yancy . . . Jennifer. She couldn't get the thought out of her head that both of them were either dead or wished they were. . . . If she left here, where the trail was most likely to lead across the border, she'd probably never see them again either. Two victims lost in one of the most heinous and yet hardest to solve crimes in the entire world. The cartels were, despite their brutality, business enterprises. They operated on a risk-reward basis, like every other business, and sex trafficking was high reward and low risk. Not only were the victims hard to trace but the revenue stream the women produced lasted for years.

Knowing how Yancy would struggle against such debasement, Emm closed her eyes and whispered yet another fervent prayer that the information sharing she was doing with Dr. Doyle and Ross would yield a hot lead. And Curt? Emm frowned and beat her pillow. Surely her suspicions were wrong. She'd been his friend for over five years and knew him for a gifted writer with an instinctive nose for news. Yet she couldn't forget that he drove a Porsche 911 Carrera and lived in a penthouse in one of the nicest parts of San Antonio. And she knew for a fact that, like most dailies, the San Antonio paper for which he wrote most often struggled with declining circulation and dwindling ad revenue, and had been forced to lay off staff and even cut salaries and perks.

While she couldn't trace his bank accounts, she might be able to trace his movements. His car was very distinctive, and the last time she'd seen him in Baltimore he'd driven it up from Texas. She could call the Baltimore cops and ask them to run his plate through all the surveillance databases to see if there were any hits near downtown Baltimore at the time Jennifer and, later, Yancy, disappeared, or the other two girls from Baltimore, for that matter.

Feeling better now she finally had a plan, Emm dozed off after snapping off the TV. Dreams came to her, as they usually did, and they were troubled ones, vividly depicting Yancy and Jennifer chained to beds with faceless men laboring over them, and more standing in line. In her nightmare, a scream pierced their cries of despair, and her viewpoint shifted to another bed, where another woman was held down by a heavy Latino man. At first she couldn't tell who it was, but he finally moved aside and she saw the victim's face . . . The scream reverberated in her dream, and only when she knocked her head against the headboard did she hear her own scream as she started awake.

Shaking, she got out of bed and went into the bathroom to bathe her flushed face, telling herself over and over that it was just a nightmare. Must be that late cup of coffee she'd had.

But the water didn't help much. Nightmare or not, the victim's face was all too familiar: her own. Trying to shake the visceral fear, telling herself she didn't believe in omens, Emm snapped the lights off and got back into bed. It was a long time before she slept.

At about the same time, Yancy gave her sexiest smile to the men outside Jennifer's door, but they were unmoved. They were among the cartel's oldest and most loyal soldiers and stared at her blankly when she lifted a bag filled with toiletries, letting them look inside. "I'm just bringing her some cosmetics she asked for. Just a minute?" It wasn't time for her usual visit, but Arturo was gone again on appointments, and she'd managed to filch a few pills from the woman who supplied the drugs to the brothels. Jennifer needed them, and she needed them now. Arturo's son Tomás had just returned from a long business trip to the States and they'd not seen much of him in the last few days as he stayed in his room with Jennifer, but he'd finally surfaced to go into the city.

The guards fingered through the female pots and tubes. She'd slipped the three pills into one of the compacts and hid a sign of relief when they didn't open it. "We will give them to her."

"Uh, yes, but I need to ask her about something. She wanted a new pair of shoes for the fiesta, but I need to see her dress to match it properly."

The two men shared a look, eyeing her up and down. The upcoming fiesta was a very big deal to the entire household, with many of the far-flung cartel members in attendance, and Arturo had told his staff to be sure the two Yanqui women were dressed for the occasion.

One guard spun his finger in a circle, and she obediently did a 360-degree turn. The other patted her down, lingering a little too long near her breasts, but she pretended indifference as she'd become so adept at doing, when she really wanted to kick his balls up so high he'd have a most unsightly new Adam's apple.

The older man, obviously the shift leader, gave her a last warning look and took a set of keys from his pocket to unlock not one, not two, but three locks. Yancy's heart sank as she realized they'd added a new dead bolt since her last visit five days ago. That meant only one thing—Jennifer had tried to escape again. Dammit, didn't she realize she only made them watch her more closely?

"Cinco minutos," the leader said, opening the door and shoving her inside with the bag.

The room was so dark Yancy had to stand there and blink before her eyes adjusted. "Jenn?" she said softly.

She heard a stirring of the covers, and then even in the dark room she caught the shine of her daughter's beautiful golden hair. She crossed quickly to the bed and snapped on the bedside lamp.

Jennifer's mascara had run and she rubbed her eyes, smearing it further. "What time is it? How'd you get in?"

"I told them I needed to see your dress for the fiesta so I could figure out the best shoes to buy you next time I go into town. Always use as much truth as possible. . . ." Yancy quickly dumped the cosmetics out and opened the compact, showing the three small pills. "Here, let me get you some water—" She hurried to the bathroom, but by the time she returned a few seconds later, Jennifer had downed not one but two of the pills, so desperate that she'd swallowed them dry. "Jennifer, you shouldn't overdose on these damn things. You might spot, and Tomás would know what you're doing."

"I don't care, I hope he kills me," she said dully, lying back on the pillows. "All I want to do is sleep."

Yancy saw that Jennifer's dinner tray was untouched. She sat down on the side of the bed and took her daughter's hands, squeezing them tightly. "Jenn, you have to hold on. I think we might both be able to slip out during the fiesta. There's no way they can watch us as closely with so many guests. We just have to be smart about it. We can hide in someone's trunk as they're leaving. I'm working on it now."

"Then where do we go? With no money and no friends?"

Yancy bit her lip. "Once we make it to the city, we can go to the US Embassy. I have a couple of jewels I can barter, and so do you."

"And you don't think Arturo and Tomás will have every single vehicle stopped and searched when we disappear? You know half of the Mexican authorities are on his payroll. Once they get us back . . ." Jennifer began crying again, burying her face in her pillow. "I'm so tired . . ." she murmured, and then she was asleep again.

Yancy realized she'd taken Xanax from the pill bottle beside the bed. Tomás, the bastard, gave her the meds to keep her quiet when he was gone, and she feared her gifted, honor student daughter had become addicted. It was better than cocaine, she tried to tell herself, but her eyes welled up despite her best intentions.

Yancy stroked her daughter's bright head, tears falling hotly. She was having a hard enough time controlling her own fear and hatred; how could she keep Jennifer strong enough to escape when she herself was only holding on by a single emotional thread? Then the door opened. Yancy wiped her eyes on her sleeve and turned with a blank smile. "I'm coming."

The older man eyed the pill bottle beside the bed, the sleeping girl, and Yancy's tearstained face. Something that might have been sympathy flashed in his eyes. Yancy saw it, realizing he must have a daughter of his own, but she also knew he'd never betray his *jefe*. He merely jerked his head at the door. Yancy scuttled, only then realizing she'd forgotten to look at Jennifer's fiesta dress.

As she went downstairs, she saw Arturo enter the hallway and look up at her.

She faltered, recognizing that expression, but merely went down the stairs with that hip-swaying gait he liked. She kissed his cheek, asking him about his meetings, as a good mistress should.

He shrugged. "You saw your daughter without permission? Your meeting with her is not for several days." Arturo smiled slightly, as if it was no big deal, but she knew that smile shielded a keen, active mind that was always assessing, looking for betrayal or advantage.

Yancy's fallback with him was the same one that had saved her from many a beating or being auctioned off to the highest bidder: guarded honesty. "I'm sorry, but you know how worried I am about her . . . Do you think maybe we could cut back on her meds?"

His smile became rueful. He shrugged elegant shoulders. "My son insists, and she is his. . . ." He trailed off.

Yancy said bitterly, before she could stop herself, *"Puta."*

His smile dropped away clean, as if she'd sliced it off his face. "I've been too lenient with you, *mujer.* You want to see how a *puta* is really treated?" Grabbing her by the hair, he pulled her into the living room and slammed the door. He ripped her dress down to her waist and shoved her scant bra up to suckle harshly at her nipples, bumping his erection into her as he shoved her back on the couch. He fumbled at his pants.

Usually, she suffered his attentions with feigned enjoyment, but this time worry for Jennifer and fear that her delicate dance was about to come to a violent end combined to make her temper flare. Teeth bared, she leaped back up as he unzipped and kicked him in the shin with her stiletto. She would have preferred hitting him higher, but even in her anger she knew better than that.

His high cheekbones flushed with either rage or lust—she didn't know or care—and he caught her foot in his hand and used it for leverage, shoving her off balance over the plush arm of the couch. He tilted her hips up, moved her scrap of underwear aside, and took her there, more brutally than she could remember, calling her *puta* all the while. And to her horror, she heard him chuckling as he did so, and realized her defiance had only inflamed him.

She hated him then, as never before. She tried to shove him off, but he was far larger and stronger, harder than he had been in some time, and finally she subsided.

But this time she made no pretense of response.

This time, with every brutal stroke, she counted the ways she would kill him when she had Jennifer safe.

CHAPTER 7

Emm was still asleep the next morning when her cell phone rang. Yawning, snapping awake from yet another bad dream, she grabbed it. "Hello . . ." She cleared her husky voice and tried again. "Hello."

A brief silence on the other end was broken by the rich male chuckle she recognized. "I always knew you were a dilettante." Ross waited. As usual, he was goading her.

She bolted upright. "What do you want?"

"Cranky before we have our coffee, are we?"

How did he know that? She looked at the clock beside the bed and was shocked when she saw it was almost eleven. "I didn't realize it was so late. I couldn't fall asleep last night."

"I can call back later." Now he sounded genuinely contrite.

She put her feet on the floor. "No, I need to get up anyway and finish some docs for my boss. What can I do for you?"

"Tomorrow's Saturday and I've decided to take the day off. I was . . . wondering if you'd like to go with me to meet a couple of my friends. I think you'd like Jasmine . . ." He sounded almost hesitant, unusual for the arrogant Ranger captain.

She was touched and wary at the same time, but she was so eager to see him again that she agreed before she realized it, "Sure. When and where?"

"I'll pick you up at eleven in the morning. My friends, the Fosters, have a ranch outside town and they've invited me—that is, us—for lunch. They have a new baby boy I thought you might enjoy meeting. See you soon." He hung up.

Emm slid the bar across her phone, disconnecting the call. She stared into her sleep-puffy face in the mirror, her heartbeat accelerating at the knowledge she'd soon be seeing him again, and this time in an entirely social setting. What happened to his maxim, "Just business?"

Idiot, why didn't you tell him no? And why the heck was he even asking her to such an intimate luncheon with what were obviously some of his best friends?

That entire day crawled for Ross, but in between administrative tasks such as disciplining one of his men, assigning two others to new cases, and adding new DEA-sourced evidence to the human trafficking case file, he couldn't stop thinking about Emm. He'd invited her to join him for lunch on impulse, partly because he knew Jasmine and Chad would finagle a meeting if he didn't, but also partly for a far more basic reason: He had to see how she was around little Trey.

Despite what he'd told Jasmine, Ross badly wanted kids. His father was still sharp as a tack well into his seventies, but Ross knew he needed to start a family soon if he wanted one at all. And he still did . . .

Most women were instinctively nurturing, but Elaine had been sadly lacking in that area, even going so far as to inform him she wasn't sure she wanted kids. That had accelerated the knock-down, drag-out fight that led to their breakup, but as devastating as it had been at the time, now he was glad he'd not been caught in a doomed relationship; plus his unhappiness had partly led to his first trip to Texas.

Now, over twenty years later, another pampered rich girl had quite literally roared into his life in a 100k sports car driving 125 miles an hour. Since she'd revealed her sensual side in her hotel room, he'd started wondering—could she be the only woman since Elaine he could contemplate spending his life with? The thought scared him, but something drove him to find out anyway. She came from an even richer, more influential family, but her sincere concern for her niece indicated she must have a close relationship to the girl. Yet bearing and raising an infant and being an aunt to a teenager were two different things, so he'd decided to go through with this little test.

She'd be livid if she found out why he'd invited her, but he certainly wouldn't tell her. He only hoped Jasmine didn't figure it out and let it slip. . . .

He was packing up his desk a number of hours later when his assistant buzzed and told him Abigail Doyle had arrived and asked for a brief meeting.

"Send her in." He rose and offered a warm hand as she entered. As usual, she was dressed conservatively, this time in a brown pant suit with a white blouse. Her thick brown hair was pulled back from her severe face, but he wondered if she realized the hairstyle only emphasized her penetrating gray eyes and aquiline nose.

After they shook, she moved forward to the edge of her chair, hovering there, and his curiosity increased. Hesitation was unlike her, but whatever she had to say obviously wasn't easy for her. He smiled slightly as encouragement. "I've been getting your updates in my secure in-box. I can see you're being very systematic and thorough, but if there's a smoking gun to lead us to the end of the pipeline, I haven't seen it."

"That's why I asked for this meeting." Abby took a deep breath. "There is no way to sugarcoat this, and I didn't want to put it in an e-mail. How long have you known Curt Tupperman?"

What an odd way to open the conversation, but he played along. "Over ten years. With his national connections as an investigative reporter on various dailies, he's one of our best sources when we need to leak news, though he can be a bit overzealous at times. . . ." He trailed off as the implication of her question hit home. "Are you telling me you think he's somehow involved in the cartel's human trafficking?"

She nodded. "He lives a very rich lifestyle for a reporter. Ms. Rothschild actually is the one who flagged him and asked me to investigate."

"I thought they were friends. That they'd even dated."

"Apparently, he dated her older sister Yancy for over a year, and their breakup was . . . difficult."

Ross's mouth dropped open. "Are you telling me you think he was instrumental in Yancy being kidnapped?"

She pulled a red file from her capacious bag and shoved it across the desk. It was stamped "Private and Confidential." "I had to call a federal judge I know to subpoena his bank account and phone records because they cross international lines. I didn't scan this. You're holding the only copy. I found no calls to Mexico—he's far too smart for that—but there are very large sums being transferred to his US account from one in Belize about every two months. All the records are here. I want another set of eyes on this before I dig deeper, as I understand he's very well connected, and this could cause problems for your office if we move forward without substantial proof."

Ross was still struggling with disbelief, but he pulled the folder forward and reviewed the bank account record. He saw that as much as one hundred thousand dollars was indeed being deposited into Curt's San Antonio bank about every two months. Unless Curt had won the lottery and didn't tell anyone, Ross had no idea where he'd be getting those kinds of funds. Book royalties, which were supposedly quite substantial on his latest expose of the finance industry, would come from New York City, not Belize. "And we can't access the Belize account?"

She shook her head. "Despite an IRS crackdown on offshore accounts, some banks still evade reporting and keep most of their digital transfers interbank. Even the original deposit slip shows only a transfer by wire paid from 'cash,' with no depositor listed. But look at his phone record on the day before Yancy disappeared." She flipped through the pages and showed him a highlighted telephone log of an outgoing call made from Curt's phone to what Ross knew was Yancy's cell phone number. They'd spoken—he counted—three times on the day before she disappeared.

Grimly, he stuck the phone log back and snapped the file shut, putting it in his own secure file drawer and locking it while he contemplated this new evidence. It was hard to believe Curt could be involved in anything so disgusting, but Ross had seen far too many otherwise upstanding citizens fall prey to greed to discount the evidence as coincidence. Like most law enforcement professionals, Texas Rangers didn't believe in coincidence, anyway. "How far back did you go in your search?"

"The prior twelve months. Six deposits from Belize, totaling over a half million."

"I authorize you to go back thirty-six months, because that's about when we think this particular conduit started operating from Baltimore. I'll call the judge and make the request myself for the rest of the records. If we can find when the deposits started, maybe we'll be closer to the head of the snake. Did you access his credit card bills?"

"No, I wanted to start with banking and phone records, but it's a good idea. Please include that in your request of the judge." She smiled ruefully. "I try to keep a low profile, but females high in law enforcement seem to be particularly rare in West Texas. Much less forensic experts with decidedly marked British accents."

"Shucks, ma'am, why do you think I worked on losing my Eastern nasal twang?"

They both laughed at that. But Abby's smile faded soon enough. "This is not my place, but I'm worried about Emm Rothschild."

Ross's smile was wiped clean, too. "How so?"

"She's the one who made the connection with Curt Tupperman, and if we don't give her, ah, something productive to do in the investigation, I fear she may take matters into her own hands. With both the chain of evidence and her own safety at risk."

"What the hell do you expect me to do about that? Arrest her?" He was irritated that she'd picked up on his own very strong and very reluctant attraction to Emm. Was he really so transparent?

Abby's rueful smile returned. "By all accounts, you already tried that." When Ross wouldn't meet her eyes, she only added mildly, "I'd suggest you find another way to keep her occupied."

"We're having the survey of the Sinclair family buildings in a couple of days, and that should keep her busy for a week or so. After that . . . she may be going back East." Ross couldn't disguise his own desolation at that thought, at least not from those uncommonly perceptive gray eyes.

But Abby only nodded and stood, allowing him his privacy. "I'll be off, then."

"And the hemophilia drug? Have you had any luck tracking that?"

"I have several sources in Mexico searching for me but nothing conclusive as yet. You do realize all the women in this particular pipeline may have been funneled overseas by now . . ."

Ross sighed heavily. "Of course. The alliances between the cartels and other crime syndicates worldwide are always in flux, but the latest intel suggests the Los Lobos cartel is working closely with Italian Mafia and Chechen rebels. There's even some talk they may be putting out feelers to ISIS. Any woman who disappears into that network is unlikely ever to be seen again, especially as human trafficking violations aren't high on the list of priority cases with the intelligence agencies overseas. But they're making millions every day, and anywhere there's money like that, Los Lobos will be attracted."

Abby looked revolted. "Surely even Mr. Tupperman wouldn't do business with ISIS?"

"Unlikely he'd even know. Arturo Cervantes is by all accounts extremely tight-fisted both with his money and his authority. We think only he and his son, Tomás, know all the particulars of everyone they conspire with, which is one reason why they've been so hard to track."

Abby nodded, understanding completely. "I'll be back in a few days, after I've had time to examine the new evidence."

Ross nodded and walked her the short distance to his door. "I'll find a way to keep Emm occupied." His smile suddenly grew sensual. "Who knows, it could be fun."

Outside, Abigail Doyle carried the recollection of his sensual smile with her to her car. She'd immediately seen the strong attraction between the two Easterners and thought it would be a shame if Emm returned to Baltimore without admitting her own feelings. For a second, as she drove back to her lonely hotel room, she toyed with the idea of playing matchmaker, but she dismissed the notion equally quickly. She'd done that once before and ended up not only losing a friendship she cherished but spoiling the nascent relationship she'd been forging with the only man she'd ever met who appealed to her on every level.

She unlocked her hotel room door and looked around at the neat, tidy little room that was such a perfect metaphor for her neat, tidy little life. Disarray upset her, and even when she traveled, she unpacked immediately, folding her clothes neatly into bureau drawers and hanging her suits with colors complementing the appropriate adjacent blouse, the sensible shoes matching each outfit centered exactly beneath on the closet floor.

For a moment, she lay back on the neatly made bed and closed her eyes, but seeing Sinclair's Cheshire cat grin had hit her like a gut punch. She couldn't squelch a dart of envy. Emm had no idea what she'd started; Abby had picked up immediately on the fact that her new friend was more of an egghead than a socialite. No doubt she'd had a number of boyfriends, but she would have few defenses against a man of the world, and a Ranger captain to boot, like Ross Sinclair. Abby had a feeling Emm's life in Baltimore was about to take a big detour west.

Abby had moved to Texas from even farther away, and had few regrets despite the curiosity and sometimes outright prejudice she faced as an outsider. Even in England, her parents had been from Cornwall, the most southerly county in England and the most fiercely independent. When they passed about a year ago, she had been coming off a bad breakup with an Oxford don she'd met at a social event in London. He was the heir to a lower earldom but had long since lost his country house to taxes and the rising cost of upkeep. All that remained of his family's wealth was a London townhome that needed a good polish, and his prickly pride, which made him extremely difficult to please. Had he not been absolutely brilliant, with a dozen best-selling tomes of British history under his belt, he'd have been let go from Oxford, too. He'd been twice divorced when she met him, and he'd had to court her to get a first date. Only when she quit MI6 to care for her parents in their last months had she really accepted his attentions.

Mentally, he was one of the only men she'd ever met with whom she was compatible, though even his analytical ability paled compared to hers. Physically, they were more than compatible; his creativity extended between the sheets. Even thinking about some of their role playing heated her in body parts she seldom thought about anymore. But emotionally? When she quit laughing at his sophisticated jokes and tried to open up a bit with the man she'd grown to love, he turned back to his books and froze her out. Even when her parents both passed within a week of each other, he didn't come to the funerals. He was off to a new conquest, and only then, too late, had she realized he was a serial womanizer who got his self-worth as a man from the women he wooed and deserted.

In her quiet hotel room, Abby buried her face in her pillow and gave a frustrated grunt, which was as close as she came to an emotional outburst. Seeing Sinclair restless with a sensual need he could scarcely control made her realize it had been well over a year since her last partner. So what? Grimly, she moved the pillow away, tucked it back under the spread, and smoothed the fabric. Then she went to the mirror, combed back her disarranged hair, and tightened it even higher on her head, quelling her impulses with the same ruthless sense of order. Then she went to her evidence stash and opened a new box, sitting down with her checklist.

* * *

Saturday morning, Emm was more careful with her makeup than usual. She even penciled in a bit of eyeliner, wanting to look her best. *For this couple she'd never met or for Ross?* she asked her own flushed face in the mirror. "For myself," she said firmly, turning away.

She'd dressed in the yellow sundress again as her wardrobe was too spare to allow for a new outfit every day, but she'd seen the appreciation in Ross's eyes that night at his place when she last wore it. She slipped on low-heeled sandals and gold jewelry, spraying on a dab of her favorite rose-scented spritzer.

Lastly, just as the knock came at her hotel door promptly at eleven, she slipped the flowered shawl over her shoulders. Her smile stretched wider when she saw Ross. Usually he wore starched white shirts and black jeans. Today he was dressed in short sleeves that displayed his muscled, tanned arms and worn blue denim that clung to his thighs and other places she tried very hard not to notice but did.

"You look lovely," he said, kissing her cheek. "I like that dress."

"Ditto," she said shyly.

He grinned. "You like my dress or I look lovely?"

He always looked lovely to her, and she suspected he was one of those men who would age so gracefully that he'd still be stunning at ninety. But she only shook her head at him and followed him out. "So tell me a bit about this couple."

He helped her up into his big SUV. As he drove off, he said reflectively, "They met in a very strange way, almost as strange as the way you and I met. She was a suspect in Chad's brother's disappearance, and he went all the way to LA from Amarillo to grill her. Chad's not much of a womanizer—he's from a Ranger family turned ranchers from way back—and she led him quite a little dance, appropriately enough, as she was an exotic dancer. An exotic dancer working on her law degree at USC." He smiled at obviously fond memories, but his smile faded as he said gravely, "She risked her life to help him catch the real perp, her onetime boss, but unfortunately they were too late to save Trey."

"So Jasmine knew all along that they were a good fit?"

He shrugged. "Chad sure didn't. He has brass cojones and an even harder skull, plus there was another redhead who confused the picture. But women are always better at that emotional stuff." He sent her a sideways glance that made her so warm she had to slip the shawl off her shoulders. "Right?"

"So how does she like Texas?"

"Turned out she was from Houston until she ran away from home when she was eighteen. Chad contacted her father and helped reunite them, and that was all it took. They were married a few months later and within a year had little Trey. She's almost finished with her law degree now. Her father is a judge."

"How long have you and Chad been friends?"

"Oh hell, I've known him ten years at least, but now he's stationed in Lubbock with a different company, we've become close because I'm not his supervisor anymore."

"Interesting." Emm was still a bit puzzled as to why he'd included her in an intimate luncheon with his best friends, but she was happy to be with him in the bright day, for once not worrying about Yancy and Jennifer.

When they arrived a few minutes later, the old clapboard house had a fresh coat of paint and new shutters, along with a big rocking chair on the wraparound porch. Ross helped her from the car. As she got out, her shawl slipped again. He caught it with automatic male courtesy, wrapping it back around her shoulders. His knuckles brushed her exposed flesh in the vee of the dress.

They both froze. The bright Texas sun seemed to melt and pour into her veins, and when she looked up at him, she saw only his head limned in the light. But he could obviously look into her eyes, brilliant blue in the sunshine, and she was wondering what she'd revealed when his head lowered and his mouth covered hers. His movements were jerky, and she realized he was as compelled as she.

And then she couldn't think . . . she could only feel.

Though it was only the second time they'd kissed, their bodies melded together as easily as old home day. As if they'd done this hundreds of times before, as if they belonged this way. Emm tilted her head back, pulling his head down to slant her mouth even closer against his. His knee moved between her legs, winnowing her feet apart. She felt the hardness in his worn jeans, and a deep, irrepressible need made her move one foot between his spread legs and tilt her hips upward, answering that need, even as she slid the tip of her tongue into his mouth.

A strangled gasp rewarded her, and again, most unlike her, she took advantage, exploring his delicious mouth more deeply. He tasted of spearmint and passion. Their tongues dueled as their hands began to wander.

One of his hands had cupped her breast and she was unbuttoning his shirt when a discreet cough penetrated her sensual haze.

"Uh, welcome," said an amused masculine voice.

Emm's eyes blinked open, filled with sunlight and embarrassment. She jolted away, teetering unsteadily. Ross finally came out of his own sensual haze with a jerk. He still had presence of mind enough to steady her with a hand on her waist.

"Howdy, Chad."

"Howdy, Ross."

His own cheeks brick red, Ross led her forward to the bottom of the steps. "Sorry; we were a bit distracted."

"I noticed." Chad's mouth was suspiciously straight.

Ross scowled, daring him to go on, but Chad only offered his hand to Emm. "You must be Ms. Rothschild. Pleasure. Welcome to my ranch."

Emm had to clear her voice twice before she could calm herself enough to answer, and even then she sounded squeaky because she could not recall ever being so mortified. "Thanks for inviting me. Ah, may I borrow your restroom?"

He showed her where it was, down the hall. She splashed water on her face, not surprised to see she was as scarlet as the flowers on her shawl. What had possessed her to act like that in a stranger's yard? She glared at her own dilated, deeply blue eyes in the mirror.

She took a deep breath and touched up her makeup. One thing was certain: She couldn't leave here without giving herself the gift of Ross Sinclair. Afterward, she'd miss him even more, but it would be worse to wonder for the rest of her life what it would have been like. And based on the incendiary way he responded to her, he wanted her almost as badly, so she doubted she'd have to seduce him. Still, she'd never made such blatant overtures to a man before, so she was in uncharted territory.

When she came back out, her cheeks were still pink. Ross was sitting on the couch, both arms stretched along the back. He had a fixed smile on his face. Chad was grinning. Emm glanced between them, but a beautiful, voluptuous redhead exited a room down the hall, carrying a blue-wrapped bundle.

She smiled warmly at Emm. "I'm so glad you were able to come. I'm Jasmine. And this is Trey."

Emm looked at the sleeping face. Her throat closed up even more. All she could do was smile like an idiot.

"You can touch him. He won't break. Babies are much tougher than people realize."

Emm gently stroked the soft head with one finger. Trey didn't even stir.

She felt an intense focus on her and looked up. Ross was frozen in place, staring at her.

She tilted her head slightly, wondering at his expression.

Jasmine handed the baby to her husband. "Have to get back to the kitchen. Do you want to come with me?"

Emm was relieved to be able to escape the living room and its strange undercurrents. "Sure. What can I do to help?"

A few minutes later, after she'd dusted the last of the chicken in a paper bag full of flour, Jasmine had a streak of flour on her chin and her cheeks were heat flushed in the old kitchen where she'd obviously been cooking for hours. The cabinets looked recently painted and there was an old, scarred oak table in the middle. The stove was ancient but obviously cooked well as several dishes sat covered and ready to be dispensed. A huge cast-iron skillet held sizzling fried chicken that filled the air with a mouthwatering aroma.

"Do you mind setting the table?" Jasmine asked as she turned back to the skillet. "Use the good dishes in the hutch."

Emm carefully pulled out gold-rimmed bone china. It looked old. "Are you sure you want to use this?"

"Yes. It makes me think of Chad's mama. I wish I'd known her, but she passed before Chad and I met. But the two of us wouldn't be together without her."

Emm paused in setting out the plates. "How so? If you don't mind me asking . . ."

"Not at all." Jasmine pulled the last piece of fried chicken from the skillet, critically eyeing a few dark spots. "Texas Rangers are a different breed, and women tend to gravitate to them. Chad's not conventionally handsome, like Ross, and the first time I met him I thought he was an asshole. But after I got to know him . . . he has a tender side he lets few people see, and that all came from his mom. Family means even more to him than his job, and I know if I ever need him, he'll be there through tornado, pestilence, or famine." She looked at the piled-high golden brown chicken. "Of course the latter isn't likely to happen around here."

Emm laughed with her. "So you met him while you were in law school?"

"Sorta in spite of it." Jasmine smiled, her pale green eyes dancing with mischief. "He wanted to arrest me first thing because I was a no-'count stripper who tempted his brother Trey to LA after suckering him out of his land. Dancing was the only way I could afford law school, but Chad softened toward me when I helped him gather evidence against my old boss that proved he was behind Trey's kidnapping."

Emm vacillated between shock and laughter. "Must be a Texas Ranger motto; instead of 'one riot, one ranger,' 'see a woman you like, arrest her.'"

The men came back into the kitchen to gales of female laughter. Ross looked suspiciously between them and then at Chad. "Why do I get the feeling they're laughing at our expense?"

Chad only grinned. He dabbed a paper towel in water and wiped the flour off his wife's face, kissing the same spot. "We'll get our own back, but after we eat. She finally used my mama's fried chicken recipe I've been offering her for over a year and I'm afraid if we don't eat now it may disappear like a phoenix."

"Keep it up and I'll brown your share extra well," Jasmine threatened.

Chad poked at a leg suspiciously. "Looks like you already did that."

"Hey, I never made any promises. You should have known I can't cook when the best meal I ever made you at my place was a grilled cheese." Jasmine sat down in the chair he pulled out for her.

Ross did the same for Emm. He was smiling indulgently as he listened to their banter. He caught her eye and winked, his hand caressing the top of her head before he sat down next to her. She wondered what he'd said to Chad about their embrace. It was obvious Chad had been teasing him.

Blushing, she unfolded her napkin into her lap. She had to squelch a sharp pang of envy along with an even more powerful wave of curiosity as to why Ross had invited her into this scene of domestic bliss. If only such scenes were part of her own life. Ducking her head, she wiped her mouth to hide the sudden tremor, but then Jasmine and Chad's ribbing about prior cooking disasters made her laugh. She bit into a juicy piece of chicken. Delicious; a bit crispy, true, but tasting of home and the many generations of women who had used this exact recipe. Tradition on a plate.

After dinner, Chad and Ross insisted on washing up. Emm offered to help, but other than letting her clear the table, they wouldn't allow it, so she went back into the living room to find Jasmine feeding little Trey. Earlier, Emm had been afraid to hold the boy, but this time, when Jasmine burped him, she offered him up to Emm. Sitting next to her on the couch, Emm carefully held Trey as his mother indicated. Jasmine put her breast back into her bra and had just buttoned her shirt when Chad and Ross came back from the kitchen, laughing at some male joke the women were not privy to.

Chad sat down in the battered recliner, but Ross had stopped so abruptly the swinging kitchen door hit him in the rear. He watched Emm and the baby exchange a long look.

Chad and Jasmine both looked between Emm and Ross, but for once he seemed oblivious. On the edge of her consciousness, Emm knew they were all watching, but she was so enchanted she didn't care. She whispered to the baby, "You're going to wow the girls someday with those big blue eyes." She moved the blanket back from his face and he latched onto her finger, bringing it to his mouth and sucking it. She froze, thinking of nothing to say but an inane, "My hands are clean."

Jasmine chuckled. "He likes you. Usually he only sucks my finger, and Chad's occasionally. I'm not sure he likes where it's been."

Chad's eyes fired up as he looked at her partially unbuttoned shirt.

Jasmine fastened the last button. "Don't say it."

Emm scarcely heard them. Tired of suckling her finger, Trey reached a chubby hand to her necklace, wrapping it around his fingers. He gurgled up at her, liking the shiny gold, and laughed.

Emm was so entranced tears came to her eyes. "Precious," she said, and kissed his cheek. Then she offered him back to Jasmine, rose, and ran for the bathroom to collect herself. Lord, they'd think she had female problems, but she was dealing with emotions she'd never known before and they felt so private she wasn't sure how to handle them.

* * *

Inside the living room, a pregnant silence ensued. Ross sat down on the edge of the furniture arrangement in the only hard chair in the room and tried to calm himself. Emm had exquisite manners, but the tears in her eyes were too genuine to have been inspired by politesse. He stuck his hands in his pockets to hide their slight tremor, but Chad wasn't fooled.

"That doesn't help. Trust me, I tried it. Maybe you should grab what you want instead. Would have saved me and Jasmine a ton of trouble if I'd done that. You know that as well as anyone."

Ross couldn't evade his friend's gray eyes any longer. "So what do you think of her?"

"I think she belongs here; she just doesn't know it yet. And I think you want her for more than a night or two. I've never known you to be swept away with passion like that on someone else's doorstep."

Jasmine looked between the two, unsure about that last part, but she only said, "She's delightful, Ross. Are things . . . serious between the two of you?" Jasmine patted Trey's back as he rested against her shoulder, his eyes fluttering drowsily.

"I . . . don't know. Maybe." Ross couldn't lie to his two best friends. He'd wanted their opinion of Emm and he had to rush, knowing she'd be back any moment. "She's a Rothschild, you know."

"So?" Chad shrugged. "You're a Sinclair. Seems like a good match to me."

"She reminded me instantly of Elaine."

"That's your baggage, amigo, not hers."

As usual, Chad cut to the chase, but Ross realized he was exactly right. He could hardly complain about being alone if he wasn't willing to take a chance on the only woman to truly draw him in more years than he cared to recall. By the time Emm came back into the room, her face free of makeup, her cheeks pink, Ross realized she'd been so moved by little Trey that she'd had to scrub her face. Probably for the second time in an hour.

His mouth spread into a smile more sensual than he realized. Chad cradled Jasmine beneath his arm while he looked at his old friend with a what-are-you-waiting-for? challenge.

Ross watched Emm play with her shawl and realized she was having a hard time dealing with the feelings this visit had aroused in her.

He took pity on her, rose, and expressed his profuse thanks to Jasmine for the delicious meal, then said they'd have to be going as he had a ton of things to catch up on at his ranch.

Emm expressed her own warm thanks. Jasmine and Chad walked them to the door, Ross carrying the paper bag of goodies she'd packed for them from the leftovers.

"We'll be back in a few weeks," Chad said as they approached the SUV. "We'd love to do this again. Maybe we could pull out some cards or dominoes."

Emm looked at Ross. "That sounds lovely, but I may be . . . gone by then."

Chad looked at his old boss. "We'll see," he only said, ushering his wife back inside.

Ross helped Emm into the car, wishing he felt as confident as Chad. He had his answers. . . . She'd make a wonderful mom. And Jasmine and Chad both really liked her.

Now what?

CHAPTER 8

That Sunday, in Mexico City, Yancy argued with the cook in voluble Spanish about the menu for the fiesta. Arturo had slowly given her more authority in the household over the past few months, especially when he saw her talent with flower arranging and managing the kitchen. After his attack in the living room, Yancy had bitten her tongue more than once, and whatever suspicions he might have of her seemed to have abated. He was in the middle of finalizing some big deal, she knew, because she'd seen Euro-type trash in expensive suits, covered in tattoos, coming and going at all hours, arriving and leaving in armored limousines. They spoke Spanish with heavy Eastern European accents, she guessed from Bosnia or Chechnya.

If she'd been less worried about Jennifer, she might have tried to eavesdrop to get details for her eventual escape, but she knew if she was caught it wouldn't just be she who was punished. So she played the submissive mistress, planning the fiesta with the servants. As a reward, that morning in his bed Arturo offered her the hemophilia meds with a flourish. "Hard to get, so make them last." Yancy kissed his cheek in thanks, watching him dress.

"I will be busy all day today. You have all the supplies you need to decorate for the fiesta?"

Yancy pulled the silk sheet around her naked torso and tucked it under her armpits. "I still need more lanterns to light the walkways, and shoes to finish my dress and Jennifer's."

He tossed a huge pile of pesos on the nightstand. "Take the car for half the day and get everything else you need. I'll tell Gustav."

Gustav was the head chauffeur.

Yancy nodded, yawning, for he'd kept her up late. She sometimes wondered if he took Viagra, or if he was naturally so virile. The more she submitted, the more gentleness he offered, even occasionally calling her *querida* at the height of passion. But she still hated him, hated him for making her into his personal sex slave, hated him even more for letting his son turn her lovely honor student daughter into an addict.

After tying his Hermès tie, he hauled her up in the bed, jerking the sheet away and running a possessive hand down the pleasing arc of her body. He lingered at the base of her spine, as he usually did, tracing the howling wolf tattoo she'd had imprinted at her tailbone. It had been this tattoo that had so intrigued him the first time he saw her naked, with the other victims in the sterile fluorescents of the warehouse where they'd been unloaded after making the trek over the border, drugged and quiescent, in the false bottom of a big rig.

With her blonde hair and green eyes, she was unique among the other girls, even though she was obviously older. She so resembled her daughter that he knew immediately she was related to Jennifer. But when he saw the tattoo, his eyes fired with an unquenchable lust that still, many months later, showed no signs of abating. She knew in his twisted logic that because he was the alpha male of the Los Lobos cartel, the tattoo marked her as his property. This rebellious symbol of her youth had saved her, along with her fluency in Spanish, from being shipped overseas and separated, probably forever, from her daughter.

He slapped her rear hard enough to leave an imprint. "Until tonight, *mujer*." And with a drug lord's version of tenderness lingering in the room, filling Yancy's nose with his expensive cologne, he left, whistling a popular Mexican pop tune.

All was right with his world, the bastard.

The minute he was gone, Yancy took the pillow he'd slept on and used it for a punching bag. She beat it repeatedly, wishing it were his face. Then, exhausted, she resolved to use this trip into the city to set up a route for their escape. She'd have to be very careful because Gustav was a suspicious man, and the armed guards always sent to escort her were very difficult to ditch. But she didn't have much choice; the fiesta was in five days.

The house would be full of guests and everyone would be occupied. It was their best, perhaps their only, chance to escape. As she drifted off to sleep, she remembered Jesús was supposed to come by later today to drop off the money from his last shipment. Arturo had asked her to meet him, apparently trusting her to take the huge green-back bag. He knew she wouldn't dare take any of the money because he also knew the exact amount he was due.

Still, as her eyes fluttered closed, a small smile stretched her lovely mouth. Arturo didn't know everything. Or that of late, Jesús's loyalty was suspect and centered more on Arturo's mistress than Los Lobos . . .

Then, exhausted from lack of sleep and her spent emotions, she slept.

While Yancy was plotting an escape, Emm was trying to figure out how she could sneak into Abigail's hotel room. The survey was scheduled for tomorrow morning, a Monday, and she figured within a week or so she'd be finished and on her way back to Baltimore. If she was going to find out anything that might help break open the case, she didn't have much time left. She knew what she was con-templating was potentially a felony, but Sinclair clammed up any time she brought up Yancy and Jennifer, and Abigail had also grown evasive when she met her for drinks or for lunch.

She also intended to invite Curt to dinner tomorrow after the survey. He was staying around Amarillo for now, ostensibly to research his next book, coincidentally or not on modern human slavery in Texas. Abigail had been evasive when she'd asked point-blank if she'd pursued an in-vestigation of his finances, and Emm was resolved to pump him for information herself. She'd always trusted her instincts and they were clamoring an alarm right now. Curt Tupperman was somehow involved in all of this. He was the only clear Baltimore/Amarillo connection, and even for a reporter, he knew a lot about what was going on.

She left a message on Curt's cell phone voice mail and then, her ex-pression grim, powered on her laptop and went to YouTube, Googling "how to pick locks." Abigail had told her she was spending all day today in the library, so time was a'wastin', as they said here.

In his home office, Ross Sinclair was also having trouble concen-trating. All the logistical details of the reunion had come together, and the bills were even more astronomical than usual. He eyed the three-page RSVP list, wondering who some of these people were, but he'd never complained when various family members brought guests. He'd had sprawling guesthouses built just down the hill behind his home for this very purpose, and normally, he was glad of the company. Still, the list grew every year, and Ross wasn't sure he even enjoyed the events anymore. But he eyed the schedule he'd compiled in an Excel spread sheet and typed "historic analysis of our buildings by Emm" in one of the only blank slots lined up for next weekend, shortly after everyone arrived. He'd run the time past Emm to be sure, but he was confident she'd want to state her case and save the buildings.

A perfunctory knock came at the door, and José entered with his dinner tray. Ross sighed and pushed back from his desk. "I need a break—why don't you join me in the kitchen?"

Nodding, José carried the tray back out.

He arranged the dishes in the middle of the granite island with bar stools, Ross's preferred place to eat. His movements were quick, efficient, for they shared meals together often. In the right time and place, Ross had little use for social restrictions.

He ate a couple of bites of the huge sub sandwich José had made, but his stomach was tied in knots. He shoved the plate back, despite its appetizing array of fresh veggies and homemade ranch dip along with a pasta salad. José had spent years learning to cook *yanqui*, as he called it, and everything he turned out was delicious. Ross just wasn't hungry. Feeling antsy, he stood to pace.

José systematically demolished his own food. Very little ever put him off his feed, and he had the rotund form to prove it. With his lugubrious countenance, which incongruously stretched often into humor, he was also a walking contradiction of many parts that Ross cherished, jumbled as they were.

Uneducated but wise.

Sharp sense of humor but tinged by melancholy.

Missing his home in Mexico, but staying in Texas with the man he trusted most.

He felt José's dark eyes following him, but when he whirled to face that somber gaze, José merely took a bigger bite of his pasta salad. He chewed slowly and carefully, but Ross knew he was stewing over something when he went so quiet.

"Spit it out. Call me an idiot, why don't you? Chad pretty much has already."

José shrugged. "If you know this, I do not need to state the, how you say . . ."

"Obvious? Why is it so freaking clear to everyone I'm closest to that I should go on bended knee before a woman I scarcely know who has proved to be a royal pain in the ass?"

"Because you wish me to state this obvious . . ." José wiped his mouth and pushed away his empty plate. "I have been your servant for almost twenty years now—"

"*Mi* amigo—"

José was more aware of the conventions than his boss and said steadily, "Your family retainer, I think they say on such shows as *Downton Abbey*. But señor, in all that time, after you have had many women companions, I have never seen you unable to sit still at the thought of never seeing a woman again." Having said his piece, José stood and collected his plate to take it to the sink and rinse it, then put it in the two-drawer dishwasher.

Damn the man, how did he know that's what was really bothering me? Ross asked himself. Ross took his plate and dumped the contents into the trash, then offered it to his "family retainer." He hesitated, even with José, but the words came of their own accord. "I don't know what to do to get her to stay. She just got this job, and with a new PhD in historic preservation, how could I ask her to come to provincial Amarillo even if she wanted to?" He saw the question hovering on José's tongue and explained, "Provincial means small and countrylike."

"She loves old buildings, no? You own two of them." José smiled into Ross's blue eyes. "Besides, it is the *mujer's* choice, *sí*?" Placidly, José cleaned Ross's plate, too.

With his usual ease, José had cut to the heart of the matter. Ross played with that solution, but like everything with Emm, it was complicated. For one, he didn't own the buildings, only his share as managing member. It would be quite costly to acquire them. For another . . .

While he debated the pros and cons of that idea, José dried his hands on a towel and turned to face him, his mournful countenance lightened by the devilment in his eyes. "Mees Jasmine came by to give me some of her first batch of fried cheeken, and she told me about your . . . deesplay, she said, in their front yard."

Ross's cheeks colored a bit. "So?"

"So, if Mees Emm kissed you back, so . . . *bueno,* then you can show her another reason to stay." José folded the clean towel over the towel bar by the sink. "All things between *mujer y hombre* lead to that, señor, and not just in Mexico. Be the *jefe*." Jose gave his boss a last macho smile and exited, leaving Ross alone in his very expensive, sparkling kitchen that, God help him, he wanted more than anything in the world to be graced by Emm Rothschild, barefoot and pregnant. Mmm.

While Ross was envisioning her in his bed and his life, Emm was breaking into his forensic expert's hotel room. Emm had earlier taped off the corner surveillance camera with black electrical tape, being careful to keep her face out of the camera angle, using the chair near the elevator to reach it, but she knew she didn't have long before someone from security came to investigate why the camera had gone dark.

The tutorial she'd watched on YouTube didn't seem to work very well with this old lock. She kept an ear out for anyone passing in the corridor, but this late on a Sunday she had the hallway to herself. She moved the pick she'd bought very gently from side to side, then up and down, but didn't hear the click she was supposed to. She knelt on the carpet, looking through the keyhole, but she couldn't see any light behind it. Like most hotels, even older refurbished ones like this, the door was opened by key card rather than key, but Emm figured it still had to have a tumbler release.

She was digging into her purse for a different pick when she heard the elevator stop at this floor. She looked up and down the hallway, but it was long, with nowhere to hide, so she could only stand up and pretend to be walking toward Abby's room when the elevator opened and someone walked out. With her back turned, Emm didn't know who it was, but she stopped at Abby's door and knocked.

"I'm here, Emm." Abigail Doyle stopped behind her. "As I informed you earlier, I was at the library, but somehow I knew my presence was urgently required."

Emm turned with a big smile. "Why, Abby . . . I was just in the area and thought I'd stop by to see if you wanted to have a late cocktail."

Abby eyed Emm's big bag and too bright smile, her gaze now fastening on her black pants. "Indeed? You must have fallen on the carpet because there are fibers on the knees of those lovely black pants. What a shame." She sent a look down the hall toward the taped-over camera. When she looked at Emm again with a stern expression, Emm had the grace to flush and look away.

Abigail sighed and took a tiny remote from her purse and clicked it. The light on the key card slot flickered but stayed red. Two loud clicks sounded in sequence, and only then did Abby take her card from her purse and insert it in the lock. After a third click, the key card light turned green and the door opened to Abby's gentle push.

Inside, stacked neatly against the wall, Emm caught a tantalizing glimpse of the same evidence file boxes she'd seen that day in Abby's trunk. Still, she kept her smile bright, but it took an effort. Of course Hermione Abigail Doyle, former MI6 and CIA, had had special electronic locks installed, given the sensitivity of the evidence within. Damn the woman, she was one of the few people Emm had ever met who made her feel inadequate. "Oh well, it's late and I can see you're tired. . . ."

Abby's noncommittal gaze went cold. "Not yet." She waved Emm inside. Emm entered, this time reluctantly, her gaze fixed on the boxes of evidence, but Abby was angrier than she'd ever seen her.

"Don't you think it's time we dispensed with this roundaboutation? If you persist in this imprudent behavior, I will be forced to inform Mr. Sinclair, and he will be forced to arrest you. Is that what you want?"

Emm's smile fell like the façade it was under Abigail's full frontal assault. "No, but I don't have many options. I've tried to get you both to tell me more and you won't."

"We are bound by law and sworn duty to keep our evidence secure. Surely you understand that there is a chain of evidence procedure here we must follow if we want to eventually bring these perpetrators to justice?"

"How much meaning will that far-in-the-future result have if both Yancy and Jennifer are dead?"

Abby waved Emm into the only chair. "Very well; if we are at an impasse, I must contact Captain Sinclair." She picked up her cell phone, but Emm leaped to her feet and covered her hand.

"Please don't. Can't we do this on the QT without telling anyone? I swear on my sister's life I won't tell a soul if you let me look at the evidence." When Abby stayed very still, glaring at her, Emm's voice grew passionate. "Ross is a Texas Ranger captain, and he has to do things by the book. I'm a concerned private citizen who has tried the legal route by filing the appropriate police reports, handing out flyers, and so on. I got diddly. Once I return to Baltimore, obviously I'll be at the wrong end of the trafficking pipeline. Call me reckless if you want, but I seem to be the only person on the face of the earth— including my mother—who is really trying to find Yancy and Jennifer. If I have to bend the law a bit to do that, I do so with full awareness of the possible consequences."

Abby's stern mouth relaxed a bit. "So you are willing to go to prison for a first-degree felony?"

Emm sat back down more heavily than usual, but she was suddenly very tired. "If it secures their release and return to the States, yes."

Abby sighed. She put the phone back in her purse. "Tell me why you think you might see something we have not."

"I know who and how often Jennifer and Yancy dated, I know the foods they like, the music they listen to, and the places they've traveled. Any one of those things could have influenced their movements and how they were captured. A concert, a restaurant, a trip."

Abby hesitated, but then she went to a box of evidence, opened it, and removed a file folder marked "Jennifer Russell Internet Communications." She set the file on the table before Emm, but when she shakily reached for it, Abby held up a cautioning hand.

"The only way to make this legal is for me to interview you as a family member. As such, you would be privy to some of these communications. In fact, I've seen your name more than once, so here you make a viable witness." Abigail removed a small recorder from her purse and turned it on. "Ms. Rothschild, you've approached me with a request to review Jennifer's e-mails, Facebook pages, and Tweets three months before she was taken. I'm allowing this unusual exchange, given you are the person closest to both victims. The MO of the Los Lobos cartel shows fast action in their pick of merchandise, and they gravitate to beautiful young women who have little family and are imprudent in their behavior. We suspect they would have taken Jennifer Russell shortly after they became aware of her vulnerability and beauty. If there is a link you can see in these communiqués, it could facilitate our ability to find whoever took her." Abby shut off the recorder. "Proceed."

Emm fell on the file like a rabid dog.

* * *

Ross glanced yet again at the clock on his bedside table. He'd resorted to brandy and cigars to calm his nerves, but they were not as effective as usual. He'd resolved to go to bed early—he had a full day tomorrow. It was almost ten, but he remembered Emm also had problems sleeping. Every urge in his body bade him to go to her now, to stake his claim, but if he did that, he'd be creating a clear conflict of interest. Maybe no one else would know, but he would.

He pounded his pillow and tried the other side of the bed, but thirty minutes ticked away. He was rising to warm himself some milk when his cell phone vibrated. He looked at the text. It was from Abigail Doyle and only said, "Sorry for the hour, but we have a possible new evidence vector. Can you come straightaway to my hotel room to meet with me and Ms. Rothschild?"

Ross was reaching for his clothes before he finished reading.

Thirty minutes later, Emm and Abby were sitting in an uncomfortable silence. After she'd highlighted several of Jennifer's e-mails as possible clues, Emm had asked to also look at Yancy's file and been denied. Abigail said only Ross Sinclair would determine how to proceed from this point, but first he had to hear why Emm thought these e-mails could lead to a key piece of evidence on how the women were snatched.

A firm rap came at the door.

Abigail got up and unlocked the door. "Thank you for coming so late."

Ross was scowling when he entered, and Emm noted that he hadn't taken time to comb his hair, which was mussed. His shirt was even buttoned crooked. This evidence of his haste and concern might have touched her at a less tense moment, but at the look in his eyes, she had to force herself to sit very still rather than defend herself. She let Abby do the talking and was touched when, to some degree at least, the woman covered for her.

Abby said, "Ms. Rothschild came by late to see if I'd care for a cocktail, and when I invited her in, she asked about Jennifer Russell's Internet communications. Given I've seen Ms. Rothschild's name many times in both victims' e-mail accounts, I thought it might be of use to interview her. Forgive me if I overstepped my bounds and should have brought her to your office tomorrow, but . . ."

Ross waved an impatient hand. "I trust you to do what's right,

Abigail, and I'm also sure you know how to conduct an interview. You recorded it?" When Abby nodded, some of his sternness was piqued to eagerness. "What did the two of you find out?"

Abby spread out three different pages of the printed Internet communication file. "There are three e-mails from an account we previously dismissed as junk mail from one of the many bars Ms. Russell frequented in downtown Baltimore. A flyer announcing live music, another inviting Ms. Russell to karaoke, and a third advertising a St. Patrick's Day party." Abby looked at Emm. "Please tell him what you told me."

"I was at that St. Patrick's Day party a bit over a year ago," Emm said. "The bar owner has his own publicity firm—they did the flyer and e-mail blast—but that was the night Jennifer met him. His name is Brett Umarov, a former rock star whose stage name was, I think, Reefer Marty and the Stoners."

Ross's eyes narrowed. He looked at Abby. "That's a Chechen surname. You cross-reference it?"

Abby nodded, showing him the master list of the users of each IP address. "There is no e-mail account under either of those names."

"I'm not surprised if Jennifer kept her contacts with him mostly quiet," Emm inserted. "The night she met him, she was swept away by his guitar playing and stayed out all night, the first time ever, upsetting Yancy. I'd forgotten about this until I saw the flyer. Jennifer was an honor student, and Yancy tried to get her away from this guy, a former rock star who opened his own bar and introduced her to the wrong crowd, but Jennifer was at the rebellious age and wouldn't listen to her mom."

Emm tapped the next e-mail listing Abby had highlighted. "This was the karaoke event Yancy invited me to, but I was preparing for my orals and didn't go. I don't know precisely what happened, except that she and Brett had some type of confrontation and Jennifer moved out of Yancy's apartment and into his." She looked at the date. "This was only a month or so before she was grabbed. The last event I missed, too, for the same reason, but I know it was a big rock music concert, and Jennifer dressed entirely inappropriately." Emm showed Ross her cell phone. "I e-mailed these pictures to the Baltimore police, but they seemed clueless. They told me they interviewed the employees at this bar but didn't find anything that led to a person of interest, even though Jennifer disappeared a few days later. I believed them and didn't realize how key the dates were until I saw these e-mails."

Ross looked down at the photo of Jennifer in skintight jeans with holes and a tank top that revealed her slim waistline and impressive cleavage. "E-mail me these pictures, please."

Emm nodded. "Anyway, Yancy told me after Jennifer disappeared that she thought Brett had introduced her to cocaine at that concert. She said the powder was everywhere like snow, and that she suspected he might be a dealer as his band had never sold a bunch of CDs, yet they seemed to have very expensive equipment and played gigs nationwide that she was pretty sure they had to pay for. She'd enlisted me to go with her to Brett's place to try to talk Jennifer away, but by the time I could schedule it, Jennifer was gone." Emm's eyes filled with tears. If only she'd put that meeting first, before her own ambitions . . . Emm started when Abby put a gentle hand on her shoulder and squeezed.

"It's not your fault," Abby said. "This is indeed a very viable lead, and we should have questioned you earlier."

Ross skimmed through the rest of the e-mails. Emm saw his strong throat flexing from some emotion, but she wasn't sure what. She got control of herself, blew her nose fiercely on the Kleenex Abby offered, and then asked, "Now what?"

Tossing the e-mail list back, Ross said, "Now you come into the office tomorrow for an official finding. Abigail, would you please bring Yancy's Internet communications also, so we can get Emm to take a look at those? And I'll put my best people on, making follow-up phone calls tomorrow, do some more digging on the activities at this bar, see if we can come up with some witnesses at these events. And I'll ask the Baltimore police to interview this Brett character again in more depth."

Emm frowned. "Don't you have someone besides the Baltimore police who can interview him? They already did and said they got nothing. I don't fully trust them."

"That's obviously out of my jurisdiction, but I can make a couple of phone calls. You think they're incompetent or . . . ?" Ross trailed off, obviously not liking what he was hearing, but drug and trafficking money turned a lot of formerly good cops into crooks.

"I don't know, but the older cop—Ruiz, I think his name is— makes me uneasy. He was very . . . dismissive and cursory in his analysis, so far as I could see," Emm replied. "I asked about Brett specifically at one point, and he said they'd interviewed him, but he seemed clean and genuinely upset at Jennifer's disappearance."

"I see. One of my colleagues is high up in the DEA on the East Coast, and I know he's also trying to track the Los Lobos cocaine pipeline. If this Brett character is involved in distributing, as it sounds like he might be, there's plenty of probable cause here to collar him for a more in-depth interview."

Emm took a deep breath, feeling for the first time in over a year that there might actually be a breakthrough imminent. "Thank you. Both of you." She stood and kissed Abby's cheek.

Abby reddened, and Emm realized the brilliant forensics expert was far better at tearing cases apart than accepting physical affection. Emm offered Ross a tentative smile and got one in return that brought red to her own cheeks.

"Don't I get a kiss, too?" His drawl this time was pure Texas, with no hint of a New York accent.

Emm said before she could correct herself, "I think you've had enough of that for one weekend."

Abby's eyebrows shot to her hairline as Ross laughed.

Emm scurried for the door. "I'm available for an interview the day after the survey. Thanks for listening."

Ross's taunting laugh and its promise of more to come followed her through the door, into the corridor, into her car on the short drive to her hotel room, straight into her dreams.

CHAPTER 9

The next morning, Emm dressed very conservatively for the survey, as if that could make up for the eroticism of her dreams. Ross Sinclair spent most of the night making love to her in front of his roaring fire, then doing unspeakably sensual things to her in his bed, then . . .

Emm shied away from her own flushed face in the mirror. "Traitor!" she muttered to herself, grabbing up her stuff and slamming out.

On the way to the buildings to meet Ross and the engineer, she tried the bromide, *Just business*, but it was no more palliative than sleep had been. No matter how she lectured herself on the facts—that she'd be gone soon, that she didn't belong in Texas and Ross would never leave, that she'd just landed her dream job and couldn't quit— she felt inevitability hovering over her like the thunder brewing in the distance.

In the end, as with most complicated things when they were distilled to their essence, reality was both stark and simple: She wanted Ross Sinclair. And he wanted her, too. Regrets aplenty she'd have afterward, but she'd always been a very poor practitioner of what might have been. At least she'd have a few happy memories to sustain her, for she had a feeling she was unlikely to ever again meet a man similar to Ross Sinclair.

Feeling at peace with herself for the first time since her arrival in Amarillo, Emm didn't have to pretend a big smile when she saw Ross waiting in the lobby of the unlocked old building. He did a double take when he caught her expression, as if he'd never seen it before. His own eyes darkened, and his pupils dilated. He'd just opened his mouth to say something when the structural engineer arrived.

The next few hours were very professional. If the engineer, Burt, caught the strange undercurrents between Emm and Ross, he didn't let on. He measured and took borings of the foundation and curtain wall, while the soils engineer took borings in the parking lot to confirm the soil was still supporting the old structure as designed after almost a hundred years. The soils analysis would also be the determining factor in whether more square footage and height could potentially be added to the building.

Explaining he was conducting something called a Rapid Visual Screening, Burt squinted at the "as builts" Emm had copied for him and walked every corridor, looking for signs of weakness or failure. He made notes on his iPad, and when Emm looked over his shoulder she saw a complicated Excel matrix he was feeding into as they investigated. He even took stud samples at a few places that showed a bit of sagging. He walked the basement and, with Ross's permission, exposed a beam he was concerned about by using a small saw to cut a neat long hole in the wall. He took tiny scrapings of the old iron beam and shined a flashlight in both directions as far as he could see, testing its vertical stability with a laser-held device. Then he did the same on the higher floors and finally reached the roof. He walked it, staying away from the crumbling, darker area but agreeing with Emm that it was probably the source of the leak she'd found below. He took more measurements with the laser, making notes on his iPad until he was satisfied.

Then, shortly after noon, he bade the two of them good-bye and promised a detailed report in a week, about the same time the soils analysis was due.

"Twelve thousand dollars later . . ." Ross grumbled as he watched Burt saunter away.

"The bulk of his time is the analysis he'll spend a week compiling, not the survey itself," Emm pointed out.

Ross glanced at his watch and then back at her. "Do you have time for a late lunch?"

"Don't you have appointments for the rest of the day?"

"I cleared my schedule until four or so."

"In that case, I'd love to."

He opened the door and escorted her out. "Where would you like to go?"

Emm hesitated so long he gave her that curious look behind half-mast eyes that was becoming both familiar and beloved to her. He raked his hand through his hair, leaving it more mussed than usual, and she realized he was nervous, too.

That knowledge gave her courage. "I've been wanting to try the room service menu at my hotel," she blurted as she skirted past him, careful not to touch him.

When she didn't feel him follow her, she turned back. He was standing still half in, half out of the doorway, staring at her with eyes so deeply, brilliantly blue they shone even in the shadows. They weren't half-mast anymore. They were wide open, aware of exactly what she was implying.

Blushing, Emm moved toward her car. "If you'd rather stop somewhere closer, I understand." Her voice was too high-pitched, and he probably thought she was an idiot. She was about to melt into a puddle of humiliated goo on her seat, but in a few strides he closed the gap between them and gently shut the car door she'd left open. He caught her elbow to press her against the side of the car with the entire long length of his body.

"I don't want any more misunderstandings between us, so I'll just ask—are you inviting me for more than lunch?"

The sun was behind his head so she couldn't see his expression, thankfully, for she was already trembling, half sorry she'd obeyed her very unruly impulses. She had never felt so at war with herself. She stared at the pulse beating in his throat, but she'd started this and she wouldn't back out now. All she could manage was a nod.

He seemed to sense her unease, for he only lifted her hand and brought it to his mouth to kiss it, back and then front. Her fingers tingled, as if she'd been shocked by a taser. Her knees went weak, both at the sexual chemistry bubbling between them and at her own daring.

He whispered into her palm, "I accept. Shall I drive? I'll bring you to your car before I go back to the office."

Again, she could only manage a nod.

The short drive to her hotel involved zero conversation but rampant speculation on both sides. She saw his quickened breathing, the slight flush on his high cheekbones, and she knew that inside, he was almost as worked up as she was; he was just better at concealing it. The elevator ride was equally boring, at least on the outside.

She had to fumble several times to get her door open until finally he took her key card and opened it for her. He closed the door behind them, then slowly, decisively, he reached behind him without looking and put the chain in place. "Eat after."

She nodded. She was so nervous, hunger had fled, and besides, now she could see his face and eyes, she was wondering if she'd been premature. Oh, he wanted her, no doubt about that. She could see the bulge in his pants. But still, he stayed where he was, looking at her. Waiting.

Suddenly, she realized why. He didn't want to scare her, had picked up on her skittishness. She had begun this, but she had to indicate her willingness to explore the sexual promise that had sizzled between them since they'd met outside his ranch on a long and winding road . . . was it only a few weeks ago?

Emm felt the dampness beading between her legs, but still she stayed frozen; whether heaven or hell awaited, she truly didn't know. And never would if she didn't take three short steps.

His breathing evened out a bit and his voice was deep, low, but still controlled when he asked simply, "Why are you doing this, Emm? Are you having second thoughts?"

She took such a big breath her breasts rose and fell. When his gaze lowered, her heart skipped a beat at the almost tangible caress. She debated hedging, but she owed him honesty, and she'd have regrets aplenty back in Baltimore without adding lying to the memories. "Because after I leave here, I don't want to spend the rest of my life wondering what it would have been like."

At her raw honesty, he took a compulsive step toward her. She couldn't help it, she backed away. He caught his lower lip between his teeth and bit down so hard she saw the full lip go white. "Don't torment me if you've changed your mind." He leaned against the door again, as if he needed the support.

He was tormented, too, and that realization broke through to her. Things had gone too far between them to turn back. She also knew that even obviously aroused, he'd leave her alone if she asked. Perhaps there was no future for them beyond this afternoon, but what came tomorrow was decided by what began today. For once she'd do what she wanted to, right or wrong, prudent or foolish. She spanned the short gap between them until they would have been almost nose to nose if she hadn't had to tilt her head back to meet his eyes. He'd left his hat in the car, so his thick hair was tousled, as if inviting her to mess it up further.

Emm gave him what she hoped was a seductive smile, but she was clumsy when she went to unbutton his shirt. It didn't help that her hands were shaking.

Still standing against the door, he clenched his hands at his sides, as if only then could he control his need to ravish her. But as he eyed her awkwardness, he gave her a smile that was so tender it almost brought tears to her eyes.

Then he said something totally unexpected. "I apprehend the ruses of sexual conquest are not in your hitherto vast lexicon?"

Emm's hands froze. Sweet nothings, lies, and even the promises men and women exchanged at such moments could not have moved her like his teasing statement. It spoke volumes of his innate under-standing of her character, for him to use such "big words" to both tease her gently and put her at ease. Not to mention the fact that both his diction and etymology were perfect, unlike the other men she'd dated . . . She had to swallow the lump in her throat and bury her face in his soft chest hair, hoping she could master the urge to cry.

Then Emm, the PhD, the history and science lover, the verbose and the loquacious, could manage only two words: "Thank you."

With a husky chuckle, he lifted her chin and swooped toward her mouth, giving her the gift of laughter and himself.

But there was one more thing . . . She covered his mouth with her hand and looked up at him, her eyes so dilated they were more black than blue. "Just sex."

"Texas friendly, ma'am. So I won't bite . . . much," Ross replied, his deep voice still tinged with laughter, like a promise on her mouth.

With the first touch of male to female, all the controlled stillness that had kept him leashed erupted into fluid movement. He yanked her to him at the same time, lowering his head to encourage her ten-tative fingers to explore all she wanted. She was pleased that even this first time, when usually men had to feel their way in pleasing her, Ross had read and encouraged her wish to bury her fingers in his thick hair and learn the perfect shape of his skull. But in giving her that leave, he took his own. At the same time, his knee nudged her legs apart so he could tilt her lower body into the hard vee of his. He broke the kiss for a second, only to slant his head at the perfect angle to hers.

This time, his lips took her. There was no other word for that complete possession.

He'd been tender and patient in his kiss before, letting her learn him. Not this time. This time, he kissed her open mouthed, his tongue urging her mouth to open for him and accept the demanding thrust of what was to come. Simultaneously, he rubbed his hips against her, tilting her so far over the arms clasped around her waist that she would have fallen if he wasn't supporting her. The tingling that had begun in her hands forked through her body, centering between her legs in an almost painful throb. Helplessly, she opened to his explorations, submissive in a way totally foreign to her. Her mouth opened wider still, and her tongue began to duel with his, presaging what was to come in a way almost as arousing.

Still, it wasn't enough . . . She wriggled, her hips moving in tandem with his, trying to press every molecule in her body to its counterpart in him. As if she belonged to him, as if all the primal rights between men and women since time began ruled them in this twenty-first-century hotel room. He didn't quite wear a bear skin and carry a club, but he was all Texas arrogant male by way of wealthy New York Yalie, and the complexity of who he was fit her own duality perfectly.

She'd intended to take some control—it was her invitation and her hotel room after all—but her knees were so weak she could barely stand. Laughing even more throatily against her mouth, he lifted his head and picked her up in his arms. She expected to feel the soft mattress against her back, but he surprised her again by instead whirling her around in a circle three times, holding her carefully, exulting in the weight of her and the joy to come.

And she laughed back, body, mind, and, though she feared to admit it, soul. This was the joy she was made for, but only he had ever called forth such total intimacy. The room spun, and his face became the center of her world. He was gloriously, righteously male, luxuriating in his possession of her. And again, in this wordless way, she realized how much he'd wanted her, that he'd feared never seeing her again, too, so he was extending the moment of possession like the precious thing it was to him, setting their intimate world symbolically spinning even before the sex act.

His boyish joy was infectious. Any semblance of shyness or hesitation was left scattered on their private whirlwind.

Her feet knocked the bedside lamp.

The papers on the small table fluttered in the whoosh of air to the floor.

His boot caught the chenille spread, which fell in a heap to the carpet. It also upset his balance enough to make him stumble, but like a good Texas Ranger captain, he had a great sense of direction—straight onto the bed.

He was even in control enough to land on the bottom so he didn't crush her. And so it was that Mercy Magdalena Rothschild, for one stolen afternoon, learned at almost forty what it truly meant to be a woman for the first time, in the arms of a man who fit her perfectly in every way. She looked down at his laughing face, totally unaware of how dark her own eyes had gone. Her smile faded. She straddled him, scrabbling at her blouse.

His laugh broke off abruptly. She pulled at the fabric, her fingers too shaky to manage the small buttons, so he gallantly offered his help by ripping off her shirt. She reached behind her back to unlatch her bra. It fell, and she tossed it across the room, sighing as she finally felt free, in every way. She'd expected to be shy this first time, but instead she sat very still and let him look.

Wanted him to look.

He cupped her full breasts in his tough rancher hands, learning texture and weight. "I knew you'd look like this, peaches and cream, my favorite. How do you taste?" He put one hand behind her waist and lowered her down to his mouth, his free hand cupping the opposite breast, stroking her nipple with one delicate finger while his mouth learned the hardness of the other. Her heart felt like it exploded in her chest, but it only pounded beneath the suckling, as if even it knew this man was meant for her. Her nipples had always been very sensitive, and she had to pull most of her lovers back from being too harsh, but Ross, the first time, seemed to read her well. He suckled softly, releasing her just as pleasure became pain, only to cover her breast again with kisses and once, shockingly, the gentlest scrape of his teeth, heightening the sensations of the moment and the pleasure to come.

Then she was squirming, trying to reach for his pants while still leaving her breasts hanging free to his mesmerizing touch. His golden laughter was muffled against her bosom. "Need some help?"

"No. I'll do it." She slipped to his side so she could unzip his pants. While she worked at that taut front, he more skillfully unzipped her skirt, running both hands around the soft curve of her stomach to her back, which arched at his touch, bringing her breasts tight against the side of his chest. Only then did she realize his shirt was unbuttoned. She didn't recall doing that . . . and when did he lose his boots?

The next thing she knew, her skirt was gone, leaving her in a skimpy pair of black lace panties, which she'd selected quite deliberately this morning. In fact, she'd planned this entire encounter, but not for the first time Ross had turned her assumptions and her world upside down. While she was still fumbling at his zipper, he lifted his hips, easing the strain at his crotch, unzipped his pants and kicked them down and off, simultaneously shrugging out of his shirt.

Then, both attired only in underwear, they paused, thoroughly appraising with their eyes the territory their hands itched to conquer. Emm was so busy reveling in the look of him that she barely noticed how thoroughly he absorbed her with his eyes, as if he'd been on the verge of starvation and only she was sustenance.

He was, quite simply, beautiful. His arms were lithe and muscled, his shoulders were as wide as they'd felt, and his chest was centered with a scattering of dark hair. His torso angled down to a lean waist and long, powerful legs that had been made, she saw now, to stride into her life and sweep her away to this moment.

She put one hand flat on his chest, feeling him flinch at her touch, but she knew it wasn't because he didn't want her to, but because he wanted so badly for her to touch him now, often, in any way she liked. She saw the need in his flared nostrils and midnight sky eyes. She accepted the wordless invitation. She scooted in front of him on her knees to put both hands on his shoulders and let them drift downward.

He was hers. She'd enjoy him.

This would be a long, slow, luxurious building up of memories for the alone time to come. "Be still," she commanded, her voice hoarse. And she was woman enough to want to tease him back, a little. She saw sweat break out on his upper lip, but he kept his hands limp at his sides and let her palms skim over him.

He felt so good. Smooth skin sprinkled with a light dusting of hair, but everywhere she touched he was hard. She couldn't resist teasing him by tickling his hard ribs. He spasmed, his nipples hardening. Laughing her own version of female triumph, she lowered her mouth and laved his nipples, one side, then the other. He tasted so good; she was so involved in her exploration, it took her a second to realize he was tugging at her underwear.

She lifted up and let him pull them off, lying back to let him look. It was his turn to learn her like a blind man, except he had the double pleasure of sight. His hand drifted over her, barely touching. When she squirmed to get closer, to deepen the contact, his lips quirked, but he only transferred the light caress to her other side, arm to waist to hip to ankle. A delicate caress that was more torment than pleasure.

She reached for the cock straining at his underwear, but to her shock he caught her hands, held them above her head and lay on top of her. He buried his face in the nook of her shoulder, breathing heavily, but his hips began to move of their own accord, thrusting against her. "You can't touch me there, not yet," he finally whispered.

She was moved, realizing he was trying to stop himself from going so fast. "How long has it been for you?" she asked.

"Months. Years since anyone I cared about. How long has it been for you?"

"Years since anyone I cared about."

He lifted his head to delve into her eyes. Blue on blue, limitless horizon to boundless possibility. In that moment, in that mutual offering, she knew. She didn't just want this highly complex, highly moral and totally unsuitable man. She loved him . . . Emm choked back a sob and pulled her hands away.

He let go as if scalded, and she realized he thought she'd changed her mind.

No, far too late for that.

She'd take this once and only as if it were forever and often.

When he released her, she thrust her fingers through his hair, pulling hard enough to sting, but he obediently lowered his head to hers to seal their bond with a kiss. And she tried, with all her overflowing heart, to tell him with the touch of her mouth the words she didn't dare express. She sipped and nibbled and explored with an unfettered passion that was as much an invitation as an overture.

And he read it, and responded with the world's most enthusiastic RSVP. He kicked off his underwear, grabbed a condom, and ripped the package open. But she caught his hand and shook her head. "I'm fine, and I know you are. I want to . . . feel all of you." She tentatively but eagerly gloved him with her hand, or tried to. But she had small hands . . . and he was not.

He arched, perfect, hot, and heavy in her hand. He leaped to her touch, groaning, and then there was no time for tenderness or finesse. Only the passion that had almost come too late.

He parted her legs with one hand, adjusting his angle with the other, and in one slow, long stroke, he ended the separation between them forever. Her head fell back against the pillow, her mouth opening in wonder at the amazing feel of him reaching deep, and deeper still, until he reached the tip of her womb. Then he pushed deeper, as if he, too, couldn't get close enough. Hard but soft, steel but silk, a perfect fit. They both stayed still, luxuriating in the warmth and closeness. Their eyes locked again.

For once she didn't automatically react against the male arrogance in his gaze. He might as well have stated *you're mine*. Her only reflex was instinctive—a tightening of her muscles upon him. He sucked in a harsh breath, and just like that, she brought the whirlwind into bed with them. Lifting her hips up as if he couldn't get deep enough, he thrust in and out. She tried to push back, but he had her pinned, so she let her instincts take over again and flexed upon him as he entered, releasing as he exited, only to plunge back again hard enough to shake the bed. And soon, too soon, her mind didn't prompt her body to flex upon him for her body took over. . . .

She was groaning, then, her eyes fluttering closed. As she felt the building pressure, she reveled in her own pulsations, knowing it brought them both closer to release. He went to the brink with her, his breathing harsh as he lifted her hips and held her wide to his invasion. That was all it took. She arched her back, crying out. He made a choked sound, half curse, half prayer, and stabbed deeply, arrowing home as if he belonged there, to bathe her in the fulfillment of their mutual climax. Simultaneously, she blew apart into a billion pieces. She cried out, for the spasms that gripped her had never been so hard or so pleasurable.

Only when he covered the sounds of her climax with his palm did she realize she was almost screaming. Then he replaced his hand with his mouth to claim the sweet gift of her surrender, his heart hammering against her.

He collapsed, letting her hips go, and she lay like a rag doll beneath him, gasping for breath. Slowly, slowly, they came down, but for a long moment, he stayed nestled inside her, as if loathe to break the intimacy. But finally she shifted a bit uncomfortably under his weight, and he levered himself to her side, pulling her head onto his chest.

She had to break the moment or burst into tears, so she teased him. "The girls must love it when you tase them. You don't even need a stun gun. . . ." As he chuckled, she propped herself on an elbow, playing with the light whorl of hair around his nipples. The dark hair was speckled with gray, but that only made him more appealing to her. He was all man, yet sensitive enough to care about and empathize with who she was, both as a woman and as a person.

He caught her hand when she drifted lower in her exploration, brought it to his mouth and kissed it, whispering, "That's nice to hear, but brevity is the soul of wit. I can give my opinion of you in one letter."

Emm's sense of the ridiculous was stimulated. She wrapped her fingers around his kiss, treasuring it for the long, lonely times. She rested her cheek on his wide chest. "Now you have me wondering. One letter? I'm that easy?"

"No, never easy." He lifted her chin so he could kiss her mouth. "Here's my opinion of you." He murmured into her lips, "Mmmmm-mmmmmm."

The humming of that drawn-out, delicious letter murmured against her sensitive mouth tingled in a delightful way that electrified her, scalp to toes. Just like she said, no Taser needed. At the same time, she melted, warmed by the nicest compliment she'd ever received.

But when he pulled her on top of him and ran his hands over her backside, molding it with his rancher palms, she tensed. "We can't. Don't you have to go back to work? It must be almost four . . ."

"Mmm, work." And for the first time in twenty years, decorated Texas Ranger Captain Ross Sinclair missed a deadline.

After Ross left, Emm tried to work on her other cases, she really did, but she found herself staring into space with a foolish grin. She was a bit sore between the legs even after a long hot bath, but she welcomed that proof that she hadn't dreamed the most fulfilling sexual experience of her life. She knew it had been too luminously enlightening for that feeling to be one-sided.

Which begged a larger question: Since neither just business nor just sex seemed to work between the two of them, what now?

In his office on the edge of downtown, Ross was wondering the same thing while he stared blindly at yet another open file. He should feel guilty for taking advantage of the sister of a victim, but the guilt would not come. She'd initiated things in a way that settled his few remaining doubts about her sexuality. Yet she'd also showed a certain shy wonder at the look and feel of a very aroused man, enough that he was also confident she didn't sleep around much. She obviously loved holding little Trey, his closest confidantes liked her, and she had all the education, intelligence, and class he could wish for both as a Ranger and as a Sinclair.

But there was still a huge problem . . . He knew her desperation to find her sister and niece had increased. Their lovemaking would only complicate things because, consciously or not, she'd expect her lover to also be her champion of justice, an untenable situation for a Texas Ranger, and one reason he'd hesitated to pursue her.

But it was too late now for regrets, if he had any. Which he didn't.

He would have to choose: Emm or the case.

Ross sighed heavily, then picked up the phone to make the call he'd been dreading. Being appointed the head of a multijurisdictional investigation that crossed international borders was a coup even for a decorated Ranger captain, and it would raise eyebrows throughout the agency when he asked to be removed. While Emm wasn't a suspect—strictly speaking, she wasn't even a victim—he was emotionally compromised, had been even before the unbelievable hours in her hotel room. He had no choice but to do this. He might as well have *conflict of interest* emblazoned on his forehead in scarlet letters.

Ross dialed the number he knew by heart. The head of the Texas Rangers was someone he'd met a few times but didn't know well. He could try his own boss first, division chief for West Texas, but this decision would ultimately have to be made by the head of the Rangers, and Ross always believed in cutting red tape. Especially when his own head was on the line . . . not to mention his heart.

CHAPTER 10

Later that day, over a thousand miles away on a secluded hilltop in Mexico City, in her room, which was attached to Arturo's, Yancy carefully finished her makeup. She wore more than usual: heavy eyeliner, glittery silver eye shadow, and even sparkles glued to her fake eyelashes. She looked at the ethereal chiffon dress spread on the bed. It glittered from short hem to cap sleeves with diamantés. No cheap sequins for this event—each brilliant was sewn, not glued, in place, and the dress had been custom made. At the fitting, she'd thought she looked like the whore he'd been trying to make her, but when she slipped into the tight black gown and wriggled it up her hips, the dress fit perfectly. Her spike-heeled Jimmy Choos looked as if they were studded with diamonds. When she stood in front of the full-length mirror, she was stunned at the complete ensemble.

Somehow, she looked both wanton and elegant. The dress flared slightly at the knee, seeming to float around her when she walked, as if she carried the elements of stars and night with her like an exotic goddess. Arturo had insisted she wear only the best for this party, for she'd be meeting all his current business partners and two he hoped to sign a deal with in the next few days. Like most warlords of his ilk, he was taking increasing advantage of globalization and was in the process of setting up distribution channels for his wares stretching as far as Australia.

She knew that was one reason he favored her despite her age . . . how many women in Mexico could boast a partial Rothschild family connection? He expected her to be his best asset, for beautiful women, especially beautiful American women of aristocratic birth, were the prime possessions of crime lords everywhere. And she'd proved both astute and loyal, or so he thought.

His mistress was expected to dress the best, talk the best, even seduce the best when called for. And before this night was out, he'd warned her, she might be expected to do exactly that if either of his new potential partners asked nicely enough. Such sharing was not uncommon at gatherings like this, and he had a room set up for it, complete with champagne on ice, strawberries, and soft music.

When he'd laid out the rules, she'd nodded submissively, wishing she could tell him he could only whore her out if he could find her. Before the stroke of midnight, like some maladjusted Cinderella, she'd leave her exquisite diamanté shoes as her only legacy, taking with her the jewels she'd need to barter and the only other thing she valued—her daughter. However, Yancy was also savvy enough, after being a drug lord's mistress for almost six months, to know she might need more than jewels to bargain with if she had to go to the Mexican police.

She had discreetly made notes in a tiny diary she kept hidden in her room, unable to use the only cell phone he allowed her because it was often searched at random. She'd recorded names when she had them, descriptions, dates of meetings, and any overheard conversation she gleaned as to routes and methods, which usually wasn't much. But she'd heard enough to know that something new was in the works, with what she believed were Chechen connections. She suspected his new associates were offshoots of the Russian mob because of their accents and tattoos. And these men, even more than any of the Mexicans she'd met, scared her.

Arturo, as brutal and selfish as he was, still had his own peculiar set of values and family obligations. He was good, in his way, to anyone who was loyal to him.

These men, the way they looked at her, made her feel not just like a whore but like chattel. They'd use her sexually or gut her with the same finesse . . . if one of them asked for either her or Jennifer, she might have to move up her schedule. She broke off her reflections when Arturo entered the room, carrying a small black velvet box. He stopped cold at the sight of her. His eyes flared with lust and he kissed the tips of his fingers, even bowing his head slightly in homage.

She smiled, for he'd never been so deferential, and did a slow 360-degree turn just for him. "I was worried this was too tight, but it fits perfectly. I'll have to compliment the seamstress when I see her."

He walked into the room and indicated she face the mirror. She complied. He opened the velvet box and told her to bend her head. She felt him attach something around her neck, and when she stood straight again, her eyes widened. She whispered in English, "My God."

The necklace he'd fastened had an enormous diamond in the middle, with more diamonds scalloped all the way around to the clasp in smaller, graduated sizes. She'd been to enough extravagant fêtes in Baltimore and DC to recognize platinum when she saw it. The jewels had been soldered on in such a way that they shimmered when she took a breath, as if she wore shooting stars around her neck. She felt the heavy weight and guessed the center stone must be at least ten carats by itself. She reached out to touch it. "Is this . . . rented?"

He shook his head. "It's a deposit on my investment. Only the best for Los Lobos."

Of course. Like any successful tycoon, he thought only in terms of assets and liabilities. She was literally wearing proof of his business prowess, her beauty offsetting the jewels, not vice versa.

He gave her dangly earrings that were also enormous flawless diamonds suspended on smaller diamond waterfalls, which she attached. With the diamanté pins holding up her hair and the shimmery bronzer she'd applied to her shoulders, legs, and arms, the only place she didn't sparkle was her mouth, which was a deep, luscious red.

But as she looked at the glittering stranger in the mirror, the cold, rational part of her brain that had saved her thus far took over. This would simplify things. She wouldn't have to try to slip out with her small jewel case after all. What she was wearing would bribe half of the corrupt cops in the city.

"But I will let you keep it if you help me close my deal tonight. I'll make up the cost in a month if all goes as I plan." He turned her into his arms and kissed her deeply, thrusting his tongue into her mouth as far as he could reach.

She managed to stay still and even squeeze him back, as if she enjoyed this, but she wanted to bite down on the fleshy protuberance. It was all she could do not to kick him with her stiletto. He expected blind adoration from her in return for even being allowed to wear these probably million-dollar baubles. Because it was expected, when he released her, she managed a smile. "They're beautiful. Thanks for letting me wear them. But after the party, you need to return everything. They would buy a lot of security. . . ."

He looked a bit gratified at her assurances, but then his gaze narrowed and his hands on her shoulders tightened enough to hurt. A harsh tone entered his voice. "I want you to stick close to Jesús and see what you can find out and observe. I think he's selling me out."

Yancy's alarm was genuine. "Why do you say that?"

"We lost almost a thousand pounds of merchandise to the Knights Templar. He's the only one other than me and Tomás who knew the entire route of the shipment."

Yancy turned to him and straightened his bow tie, pretending deep concern. Her lush mouth even trembled a bit. "They're the worst . . . If they're trying to take over, aren't you in danger?"

He smiled at her cynically. "You'd lose your meal ticket and your protector, *sí*?"

She backed away a step, pretending deep offense. "You've been good to us, and I'm grateful. I'm honestly trying to help." She met his eyes steadily, and he relaxed a bit.

He hesitated, and then led her into his capacious bathroom, which was on the outside wall of the house. "No one else knows about this but Tomás. We are setting a show tonight for the Chechens, to impress them that here in Mexico, we know how to be elegantly continental."

This certainly explained the elaborate party, Yancy reflected, complete with covered dishes and a planned cigar-and-brandy remove into the study while the women gossiped in the salon. Her attention snapped back to Arturo.

"But if something should happen, I want you and Jennifer to be able to get away. Go to the safe house I showed you." He pulled his cell phone from his pocket and stabbed in a code. The red light on the digital whirlpool tub, which she'd thought was linked to temperature, turned green. He then pressed the whirlpool jet button on the big fiberglass tub three times, waited, then pressed it again three times. A click sounded, as if a lock were being opened. He stood aside.

To her amazement, the tub slowly rose sideways with a humming sound, and she realized it was on a hydraulic lift. He leaned down and flipped a switch. Dim lighting showed a small but navigable circular staircase winding down into darkness, with wooden studs on each side. She realized the staircase was inside the walls. She eyed the long mirror on the wall at the end of the tub. Ingenious. It wasn't just for decoration. It hid a cavity that must have been built with the house. This staircase obviously wound down two complete floors.

"I'm seriously impressed," she said sincerely. "Where does it end?"

"A tunnel beneath the compound wall that ends beneath the big tree across the road. This is one reason I bought the house." He pressed the jet button again three times, and then again three times, and the cavity slowly closed as the tub took its normal position. The light turned red again.

He eyed her and spoke slowly and deliberately. "And there's an alarm that hooks directly into the security panel. If I don't deactivate it with my cell phone, it will go off, so no one else can use the tunnel without my authorization."

Message received. Yancy nodded her understanding. "I won't tell anyone or go near it unless something awful happens."

He gave her a quick kiss on the cheek. "Help me catch Jesús and seal this alliance and I'll enter the code into your phone."

He was very good at the carrot-and-stick routine, she thought irritably, but she only smiled, as if gratified by his generosity, amazed by his arrogance, that he thought it was okay to abduct women and force them into sexual slavery and then expect their adoration . . . but now wasn't the time for anger. The location of the staircase gave her another bargaining chip, but if all went well tonight, she'd never need that code. She appraised her image in the mirror, looking for flaws, but found none.

He nodded approvingly. Then he held out his arms for her to appraise him. "How do I look?" he asked.

Like a peasant trying to be a billionaire by wearing a Savile Row tuxedo, she wanted to say, but she nodded, as if impressed. "Like a king."

He nodded his satisfaction. "And your daughter? She is . . . ready?" He meant was she composed enough. Jennifer had been in tears more often than not lately, and Arturo knew this from his son, who was beginning to lose interest in her.

Yancy was well aware of his thoughts and said calmly, "The last time I saw her she was fine, but I should probably slip into her room and check before I go downstairs." She touched up her lipstick again as he watched indulgently. She'd learned early on that the more valuable Arturo found her, the better he treated her and, by extension, her daughter. . . .

He used a Kleenex to wipe his reddened mouth. "Everything else is ready?"

"Yes. I checked with the kitchen and the housekeeper before I came up to dress, and they're on schedule with the menu and the flowers. And the valets you've hired; will they be enough?"

"*Sí*. We may have to park some cars outside the compound, but I have men on guard."

At the landing, they parted. He went downstairs and she turned toward Jennifer's room. To her relief, the guard stood aside when she appeared and the door was unlocked.

Standing before her own mirror, struggling into a skintight royal blue silk gown that brought out her blue eyes, Jennifer still had the usual dazed look. Yancy's concern mounted as she went to her daughter and softly kissed her cheek, careful not to muss her reapplied lipstick or Jennifer's heavy rouge. "You remember tonight is the night, don't you?" she whispered in her ear. "When the men go into the study for their cigars, we're supposed to retire with the women for margaritas and mojitos in the salon, but I want you to act drunk and pretend to throw up so I have an excuse to take you to your room. I've paid someone to help us escape in the trunk of a limo—"

Jennifer nodded woodenly. "Yes, Mother. When do we get to go home? I'm bored here."

Yancy whirled her daughter around and shook her slightly. "Listen to me, dammit! How many Xanax did that bastard give you? What else?"

Jennifer was so unsteady, even the slight shake almost made her fall. "Sleepy," was all she said, yawning.

Tears added their brilliance to the diamantés in Yancy's fake eyelashes. Jennifer had been either an emotional wreck or virtually comatose of late, and Yancy knew Tomás had upped her Xanax dosage. She suspected he was feeding her other drugs, anything to keep her quiet and quiescent. Obedient arm candy for this event.

Yancy bit her lip and then cursed herself; now she'd have to touch up her lipstick again. Her gaze lit on Jennifer's jumbled dressing table and a stretch rhinestone bracelet that would look good with the small diamonds in which Tomás had bedecked Jennifer. Yancy grabbed it up and stretched it. It seemed pretty sturdy. Yancy slipped it on Jennifer's bare arm and lifted her daughter's chin to look deeply into her eyes. "Remember how I taught you to pop a rubber band against your wrist when you were sleepy or nervous or had to remember something?"

She shook Jennifer again, once, hard. When that had little effect, Yancy pinched her, hard.

Jennifer's head lolled back, then snapped erect, her eyes focused. "Yes, Mom."

Yancy snapped the bracelet on Jennifer's arm. "I want you to snap this every time you get the chance tonight. Every time it pinches your wrist I want you to remember, repeat after me, 'Throw up with my first margarita in the salon after dinner.'" She made Jennifer say it six times until she was satisfied she would remember.

She relaxed a bit. "Okay, one other thing." She had to swallow hard, but there was no way to dress this up. "Arturo and Tomás have new . . . business associates. Chechen scum, but it's possible they may want to . . . spend the night with you. If it happens, just do whatever they say, no matter what. Hopefully, they won't want to . . . retire until after cigars, but if they do, you have to keep them happy. We can't have a scene right before we finally escape. Clear?"

Jennifer's lips trembled and the glazed look was coming back, but she nodded briskly.

"Just keep it together tonight and I promise you, tomorrow we'll wake up in the US Embassy and we'll be home within a month."

"Home," Jennifer whispered. She popped the bracelet, and the glazed look faded a bit. She nodded more firmly.

"Go downstairs, then, and pretend to be happy."

Jennifer walked downstairs with some of her usual grace, though she was still a bit unsteady.

After she touched up her lipstick, Yancy also walked downstairs, stepping carefully in her high heels. Arturo greeted her at the bottom and even offered his arm. She rested her fingertips on it and took a last satisfied look around, as if she were, indeed, chatelaine of this mansion. Soft instrumental Spanish music played from the expensive built-in speakers. Flowers cascaded down from the arched entry and were massed in crystal vases between burning candles on the entry tables.

A heavy antique silver salver gleamed in the middle of the huge dining table in the formal dining room, which seated twenty-four people. More crystal vases overflowing with flowers and glowing candles were interspersed with the silver. Yancy had arranged most of the vases herself, and she'd helped the chef draw up a menu that had gained Arturo's final approval. Only one element spoiled the tableau:

Armed men were everywhere, as usual, but tonight they were suited, and only a few openly carried machine guns. Most merely had bulges under their armpits.

Her hand on his arm, she followed him to the doorway, where the first guests were arriving. Anyone seeing the urbane if not handsome Latino and the gorgeous natural blonde on his arm would have assumed they were married, independently wealthy, graduates of elite universities. Successful Mexico City businesspeople welcoming a roster of international guests.

Which, in a way, was true, except the business all were involved in was uniquely lucrative. And uniquely dangerous.

Every woman wore glittering jewels and every man wore a tux. Yancy had attended fancy dinners with Emm and her Rothschild stepfather, but she'd never felt as if she fit in, with her off-the-rack dresses and cheap shoes. But tonight she sensed Arturo's macho pride in having her on his arm, and he courteously introduced her to anyone she hadn't met, which included most of the guests.

Yancy smiled brightly at a new arrival. Jesús. As a key distributor of both meth and cocaine, he was at the house often, and Arturo had already sent her to Jesús's bed as a reward for beating his quotas. But she'd also read his blatant ambition and invited him several times to her bed when Arturo was away. She'd dated such men before, identical in morals and ambition; they just wore Wall Street suits when they stabbed someone in the back.

Yancy hadn't figured out if Jesús was an undercover Mexican cop or just playing the two rival cartels against one another, which she knew was a very dangerous game. He was, Arturo had thought, totally loyal, at least until tonight. Apparently now Arturo suspected he had divided loyalties, which was disastrous news to Yancy, because Jesús was their ride out of the compound. She had to do damage control for one more night.

She'd flattered his ego and played up her hatred of Arturo enough that Jesús was enamored of her and had agreed to help her and Jennifer escape, especially as she'd promised him a hefty reward from the Rothschild side of the family and a portion of the money raised when she sold her jewels. He intended tonight to be his last appearance as one of Arturo's trusted lieutenants, so he had little to lose. Arturo would already be out for his blood.

But she and Jesús merely smiled perfunctorily at one another as he lifted her hand to kiss it. Yancy stuck the tiny piece of paper he slipped in her palm between her breasts as she turned aside to bend, as if to straighten the strap of her shoe. Arturo glanced her way as she slipped the glittery strap higher. Something flickered in his eyes that disturbed her but then she was greeting another guest. Arturo's cold dark eyes followed Jesús as he went to help himself to champagne, but a second later the drug lord was smiling at his new associates.

The older and shorter Chechen's eyes were fixed on her bodice when she straightened up. Had he seen her hide the scrap of paper? Her heart skipped a beat, but she only forced a seductive smile, offering her hand as both men eyed her up and down and then back. Both kissed the air above her hand. One said something to Arturo in Russian, which, to her shock, he answered, albeit slowly. She had to greet another arrival, but the hairs rose on the back of her neck at this added proof of Arturo's utter dedication to ruling the world of drugs. He was barely literate, so learning Russian must have been a real challenge for him, and it was also a scary sign of how much this alliance meant to him. His life's ambition was to be included in *Fortune*'s list of billionaires, like his predecessor, El Chapo. Except Arturo didn't intend to be captured . . . no matter how many people he had to kill or palms he had to grease.

As the festivities wore on, with extreme effort, Yancy managed not to fidget with her bodice to see what time she and Jennifer were to slip out of the house to the courtyard; Jesús would plead tiredness before the cigars and retreat to his limo. The way the younger Chechen all but stripped Jennifer with his eyes and slapped Arturo's son on the back made time, always a precious, vanishing commodity, more priceless than the jewels Yancy wore.

She figured she had about three hours before Arturo ordered her to the upstairs room or, even worse, Jennifer. Or . . . and this time she grew dry mouthed at the thought . . .

Both of them.

Back in Amarillo, Emm reveled in the slight soreness of her lips as she waited at the hostess desk for Curt. She was so tired after the session with Ross it had been an effort to show up as expected, but she'd dragged herself to the appointed dinner, knowing it was too important to miss. She fixed a false smile upon her face as she greeted Curt at the reception area. "Thanks for meeting me." He took her arm as the hostess led them to a nice booth near the back. It was dramatically lit, and Emm realized the woman thought they were a romantic item.

They traded small talk at first, but Emm slowly ratcheted up her questions from bland to pointed. "I thought your penthouse was gorgeous when I came to your housewarming party. What else have you done to it?"

After Curt described his extensive renovations, she added, "That must have increased the market value quite a bit. You bought at a really good time, so I imagine your equity is substantial."

Curt looked away. "Yeah, I had to pull a home equity loan to afford everything."

That was easy enough to check. "So how do you like your new Carrera? It's the turbo model, isn't it?"

He nodded woodenly, eyeing her more closely. "You're . . . chatty tonight."

"I love my new car, just thought we'd compare notes. What did it cost you, again?"

"Again? I don't believe I ever told you." Curt drummed his fingers against the tabletop. The waitress had cleared everything and they were having coffee.

"Why are you being so cagey? I'm just making conversation." Emm stirred half and half into her cup.

"Yeah, well, you're being nosy."

Emm smiled wryly. "It's uncomfortable when it comes back atcha, isn't it?"

He relaxed a bit and smiled reluctantly. "Guess so. Goes with the territory. To answer your question, I paid almost 150k for the Carrera with all the royalties last year from my new best seller. I saved them for that purpose. I'd always wanted one, and I'm not getting any younger."

Emm looked suitably impressed. "I agree there's no substitute for a high-performance car and the rush you get behind the wheel. Dad wouldn't tell me exactly what mine cost, but I know it was over 100k." She folded her napkin over her plate. "So you don't have any insight to share on the cartel's methods? Anything that could help locate Yancy and Jennifer?"

"I already told you, no." His voice rose again. "You didn't have anything to share either, so it looks like this was a—" He broke off.

"Wasted conversation? Then at least I can get the bill. But we made the appointment, and I keep my side of the bargain. Just like Yancy would."

He flinched at the name, as if he couldn't help himself. She knew he'd been wildly in love with Yancy, but her half sister had found Curt too hidebound to stay with him long-term; plus, she said he was equally boring in the sack. From the look on his face, he was also recalling their breakup. But as she'd finally pierced his tough reporter hide, she had to take advantage.

She stirred her cup again. "I didn't realize you still had feelings for Yancy."

Curt shoved back his thick blond hair with a frustrated hand. "Neither did she. I tried to dissuade her from threatening Brett Umarov because I know he's dangerous, but she wouldn't listen."

Emm frowned. "What are you talking about?"

"She didn't tell you?"

"Tell me what?"

Curt sighed. "Brett is probably one of Los Lobos's top distributors on the East Coast, and Yancy threatened to go to the DEA about him if he didn't help her find Jennifer. She believed he was involved in her daughter's disappearance. I believe he's been moving cocaine and heroin for the cartels for years, hidden in his band equipment on his tours. The DEA has brought him in several times and searched his bands and equipment, but they've never found anything substantial, just personal stashes. They ducked the charges because all of them have clean records. At least until now."

Feeling sick to her stomach, Emm shoved her cup away so hard, coffee splashed into the saucer. "When did this happen?"

"A few days before Yancy disappeared. I thought she told you, thought that was why Brett has been dragged back in for questioning. I figured you told Sinclair. "

A furious flush stained her cheeks. "If you knew all this, why the hell didn't you tell the police?"

"I tried to tell that Ruiz fellow. But he blew me off, said they'd already interviewed Brett and found nothing."

"You said you heard Brett had been questioned again . . . Who told you that?"

Curt scowled. "You know I can't reveal my sources. I've been investigating the Mexican cartels for years and I have to give my sources absolute, total anonymity because of how dangerous it is for them to talk to me."

"Uh-huh. What about protecting the woman you claim to love?"

Curt surged to his feet, a flush coloring his own broad cheekbones now. "She broke up with me over a year before she was grabbed. She didn't even return my calls when I tried to keep in touch. But still, I tried to be there for her. I warned her not to threaten Brett. I even went to the police when she disappeared—"

"So if I ask, I'll find this official report on file, right?"

Curt froze halfway around the table, his napkin still clenched in his hand. He tossed it on the table. "Are you calling me a liar?"

"Curt, you're a reporter. You bend the truth for a career." Emm tossed her own napkin on the table. "Well, this is one time you won't slant your way out of a scandal. I think you know more than you let on. And I know you're living very well on a reporter's salary at a time when every daily in the country is cutting costs."

Curt leaned across the table toward her, saying through his teeth, "You don't talk to me like that, you rich little bitch!"

Emm gathered her purse over her shoulder and looked him straight in the eye. "You're right; I don't have to talk to you at all anymore. The Texas Rangers are on the case. You're hiding something, and even if I can't find out what it is, they will." She turned on her heel and walked away, aware of the pure venom aimed at her back.

Emm's eyes burned with tears as she drove back to her hotel. That had been a useless exercise, except for the information about Yancy threatening Brett. She'd be sure she told Ross and Abby tomorrow during the interview. They could check the evidence to see if Curt had really called Ruiz, as he claimed. As for Curt, she was more convinced than ever that he was hiding something, and it wasn't just his sources.

Back in Mexico, the lavish dinner sat heavily in Yancy's stomach, though she'd eaten lightly. Arturo had placed his Chechen guests in places of honor, one on his right and the other on his left. Because she was seated at the other end of the long table—fortuitously enough, next to Jesús—she had no idea what they were discussing, but she was certain it wasn't the food or the flowers. The older one kept looking toward her, while the younger one had fixated so intently on Jennifer that even her daughter's handicapped sense of awareness was on alert.

She was trembling where she sat, and Yancy read her urge to flee. *Just a little longer, baby.* She tried to send her thoughts across the table, but Jennifer was practically shredding her linen napkin, oblivious to everything but her own panic and despair.

Yancy had little choice. It was midnight. Despite the rigid timetable they'd all agreed on, she had to move up the schedule or Jennifer would blow everything. Giving Jesús an infinitesimal nod agreeing to meet him at twelve thirty, a time she'd confirmed on a bathroom trip that had ended with her flushing the incriminating piece of paper down the toilet, Yancy stood and smiled brilliantly.

She clapped her hands. "Everyone, thank you for such lovely company on a lovely evening. I hope everything was delicious?" At the enthusiastic *sí* from every quarter, she smiled even more brightly, pretending not to notice that some people had to gulp down the last of their Mexican flan with dulce leche sauce, and that Arturo was frowning from his end of the table.

"If the ladies would please join me in the salon for after-dinner cocktails, I believe the gentlemen will have brandy and cigars in the study." Yancy led the way out, followed by the somewhat bewildered ladies.

Arturo forced a smile for his two most important guests and also led the way to his study.

Yancy waited until the waiters had taken all the drink orders before she sat down on the sofa arm next to Jennifer, who had collapsed against the couch. She saw from the fixed look in her daughter's eyes and mouth that she was fighting tears. As the drinks were being served, Yancy grabbed a strong margarita for Jennifer and offered it. Jennifer took it, her hand shaking so much it spilled slightly.

Yancy sliced her a look, trying to cover Jennifer's nervousness by raising her own mojito. "*Salud.*" As the women sipped their cocktails, Yancy sliced a sideways gaze at her daughter. When Jennifer just sat there, shaking, Yancy leaned over her as if to whisper in her ear but used her body to shield the way she snapped the stretch bracelet against Jennifer's wrist. Jennifer's blue eyes sharpened a bit.

Leaning forward, she took a deep sip. Then, cradling her stomach with her free hand, she leaned forward, gagging. Yancy put her glass down on the table and grabbed up an ornate cloisonné bowl to hold it in front of Jennifer. She was not surprised when Jennifer's pretense became real. She vomited into the bowl.

With moues of distaste, the women closest rose and got out of the way. Yancy accepted an older woman's handkerchief and wiped her daughter's mouth when she was done. "I'm so sorry, ladies. I need to get her to the bathroom and help clean her up. Forgive me."

Yancy nodded sharply at a hovering waiter, who took the soiled bowl away.

Yancy put her arm about her daughter's shaking shoulders and led her past the stairs toward the back of the house. They stayed in the guest bathroom for a good ten minutes, Yancy genuinely concerned as Jennifer vomited again into the toilet. "Did you take the pills I gave you?" she asked sharply.

Jennifer nodded. "I feel dizzy."

Too many drugs, too much alcohol, too little food. At least that's all she hoped it was. Jennifer was so scattered, Yancy wasn't sure she trusted her when she said she'd taken the morning-after pills. Yancy tenderly wiped her daughter's face with a wet hand towel. "Can you keep it together another hour or so? Then we'll be out of here."

Jennifer took a deep, shaky breath, both hands cupping her obviously still nauseated stomach, but she turned first for the door. "What now?"

"I'm taking you outside for some fresh air." Which was exactly what Yancy told the hovering servants. As they passed, she eyed the closed study door, hearing raised male voices. Good; they were embroiled in tough negotiations. Or an argument; even better.

Yancy walked Jennifer down the back steps to the bench in the rose garden. She looked at the time on her cell phone. Her ally in the security kiosk had given her a five-minute window: 12:20 to 12:25. He was going to pretend a flicker in the power, long enough for her and Jennifer to climb the back fence where she'd scaled it before and meet Jesús and his driver as they exited the compound. The many security cameras fixed on the road and the wall would be dark just long enough. . . .

Five more minutes. Yancy kept wiping her daughter's brow with the handkerchief. This wasn't an act. Jennifer was both clammy and nauseated. Yancy hoped she'd be able to make it over the wall. A guard circling the grounds holding a submachine gun eyed them as he passed, but he recognized them, saw Jennifer's distress, and walked on. Yancy heard the crackle of a radio as he receded around the corner, but she couldn't hear what he said.

Time crawled. Never had four minutes taken so long. Yancy

counted two more armed guards. The dogs were loose, but she'd befriended them and they knew her. One even trotted up to be petted. He sniffed Jennifer but seemed to sense her distress and that she was no threat. He wandered off.

Two minutes left to the blackout. Yancy heard the study doors open and then male voices coming into the hallway. Now. No more time. She jerked Jennifer up and led her to the wall. She boosted her onto the lowest part, but Jennifer's heels gave her no purchase. She slipped back down. Yancy knelt and undid the heels, then did the same with her own, leaving them sparkling on the grass.

This time Jennifer made it up and over, though there was a tearing sound as she struggled against the rough wall in her fragile silk. Yancy's dress was looser at the hem, and she lifted it around her waist without a second thought, scaling the wall with the ease of someone physically and emotionally tough. Both women dropped down behind the bushes next to the road, staying in the shadow of the wall. The road was quiet, vacant. No sound of an approaching car. She checked the time: 12:30 exactly.

Her heart hammering against her ribs, Yancy pushed Jennifer down so they were both crouching behind the shrubs, waiting another interminable minute. Still only a moonlit, quiet road, no opening of the electric gate. 12:32.

Yancy debated whether they should take their chances and run, but she knew people were likely to start leaving soon, so they'd be seen unless they took to the wooded hillside . . . with no shoes. Another two minutes and then finally, the gate opened and a black limo eased onto the road in front of the mansion. As it passed them, she couldn't see the driver or the passenger in the tinted bulletproof windows, but the trunk clicked open. Yancy led Jennifer around it and was moving to help her in when the moon appeared from behind the clouds and shone brightly enough for her to see inside the trunk.

Something was huddled inside already. A pile of rags in this expensive vehicle? Yancy bent her head to peer more closely, and only then did she see the dark, wet stain still spreading on the pile of fabric.

She reared back. The pile of fabric was an expensive tuxedo.

Suddenly, the truth hit her. She didn't need to see the face to know it was Jesús, or that he was dead. Somehow he'd either betrayed her or been discovered . . . Every instinct bade her run, but she knew it was too late.

Both limo doors opened. Tomás got out of the driver seat and Arturo got out of the other side. She lifted her chin and met flat black eyes that didn't catch a glimmer of the moonlight. She'd seen that look before, but it had never been directed at her.

Jennifer shrank away against her mother, and Yancy automatically put her arm around her daughter.

"So, you arranged this, *sí, mujer?*" Arturo asked almost conversationally. Two more men got out of the limo, and her heart sank when she saw the two Chechens. Both held machine guns. "How enterprising. Well, what are you waiting for? Get in. Your carriage awaits."

Yancy looked down into the occupied trunk, back at him. "I was playing along, trying to get more information from Jesús."

An ugly smile stretched his sensual mouth. "Good lie, but still a lie." He held up a tiny book.

Yancy's spine wilted when she recognized her tiny log of his illegal activities.

"You were so busy, *querida,* it was easy to send my men to search your room after Jesús told me you were paying him to smuggle you out after the party."

Run, run, Yancy's instincts screamed, but she looked at the two Chechens, who had tightened their grips on their machine guns. She stayed put.

A cynical smile stretched Arturo's full lips as he continued with satisfaction, "My men have had the pleasure of Jesús's company in private for the last twenty minutes. He was as weak as he was disloyal. It was obvious to me in the study that he was enamored of you. Under . . . persuasion, he told us everything. All the times you slept with him, the bribes you intended to make him with the jewels I gave you." He took a small switchblade from his jacket pocket and snicked it open. "We are being watched, so we mustn't disappoint them, no?"

Yancy shrank away, so panicked she didn't give much thought to his last comment, but he only cut a small piece of fabric from the hem of her dress and then did the same with Jennifer's gown. He gave both scraps to the Chechens, who nodded, as if they knew what to do with them.

A gun poked Yancy in the ribs. "Get in," said the older Chechen in his accented Spanish.

Her stomach roiling, Yancy hiked up her skirt and clambered into the trunk, moving as far away from what used to be Jesús as she could. Jennifer soon followed, over Yancy's pleas and protests that her sick daughter be allowed to get into the car. Jennifer retched as she climbed, so unsteady that Tomás had to lift her inside the trunk. He was not gentle. Red marks appeared on Jennifer's arm and leg where he gripped her, forcing her over the lip of the trunk.

Arturo hovered against the fitful moonlight like the shade he was. With rough hands, he jerked off Yancy's necklace and earrings, sticking them in his pocket. Then, with a cold smile at his new associates, he said, "Enjoy them, *compadres*. Use them and then discard them at your leisure, or take them home with you, if you like the taste of treachery. I don't want to see them again."

The trunk slammed closed, leaving Yancy in the dark with her sobbing, retching daughter. The bitter taste of her own failure blended with the copper scent of blood. She felt the stickiness of it everywhere, no matter how she shifted away, along with a few heavier, slimier bits that she didn't want to identify. Only by biting down on her lip to stop herself from screaming was she able to face the knowledge of what would happen to them next.

Yancy Russell, who had been strong enough for many months to carefully plot their escape in the face of threats, abuse, and sexual assault, stared blankly into the darkness, unable to utter a word of encouragement as she listened to her daughter's sobs.

CHAPTER 11

The next day, Emm was at the interview fifteen minutes early. She'd dressed primly for the occasion in her plain white cotton blouse and plain black pant suit, as if denying the wild sensuality Ross had aroused yesterday. She knew it was a lie, Ross knew it was a lie, but maybe Abby wouldn't.

In any case, she completed the masquerade with small gold earrings.

Ross met her in the waiting area exactly one minute before the appointed time. His eyes caressed her up one side and down the other, and his lips quirked, as if he caught the unspoken message. She merely shook his hand briskly and gave him a look back that said, *Just business*. His expression went blank. Without comment, he led her into his office. Abby already sat in one chair. She nodded a greeting with a stiff smile that set Emm on alert. She hadn't known Hermione Abigail Doyle for very long, but she knew her well enough to realize Abby didn't do subterfuge any better than she did herself.

Something had happened.

Ross waved Emm into the other chair and didn't waste time. "Here's the phone and Internet communication file for Yancy." His earlier teasing had been replaced with a stony expression she hadn't seen since he'd stopped her on the road outside Amarillo. That seemed eons ago now.

"What is it?" she asked. "What's wrong?"

"In a moment." He only nodded slightly at the communications file. While she read, he stated the facts of the interview into a small recorder and had her sign a release. Then she flipped through the few pages quickly, but other than more phone calls between Yancy and Curt than she'd ever suspected, she saw nothing unusual that alarmed her. She recognized an area code for Miami a few times, and something tickled the back of her brain, but she realized it wasn't immediately relevant even as she tried to memorize the number for later.

She shrugged. "I'm sure you both know Curt shows up often. Yet they broke up over a year ago, and most of the calls are incoming from him." She looked at each of them in turn, knowing Ross wouldn't be happy to hear she'd confronted Curt herself with her suspicions. She wanted to see if they'd questioned him before she relayed her own information.

When she waited, he snapped off the recorder and answered her question as clearly as if she'd voiced it. "Yes, we brought him in for questioning, and he didn't try to hide the fact that he still cares about Yancy. He told us himself about his calls to her and they seemed relatively innocent in nature. Invitations for lunch, sharing his purchase of his new car, that kind of thing. He said he tried to maintain a friendship with her because she mattered to him."

"Did you know Yancy told him she was going to threaten to turn Brett Umarov in to the DEA for drug trafficking if he didn't leave Jennifer alone, and she suspected he was involved."

Ross and Abby both stiffened. "Who told you that?" Ross demanded.

"Curt did. And he also claimed he warned Detective Ruiz, who took his statement on the matter shortly after Yancy disappeared. Yet, from all accounts, Ruiz let Brett go without a further investigation, even though a search of the band's recording studio turned up drugs in small quantities. "

Ross looked at Abby, who had immediately opened her laptop and brought up a file. She paged through some information, stopped, and scanned a page. She nodded. "There is a report, but it's very abbreviated, states only that the former boyfriend came in to give a statement claiming his former girlfriend had named Brett Umarov as being involved in drug trafficking for Los Lobos. Ruiz stated he sent a junior detective to question Brett, but the man came back saying it was a dead end. End of report."

Ross stared at Emm so long and so harshly that she shifted uncomfortably, feeling as if she was sitting in the hot seat. "Satisfied yet that we're doing our job?" he demanded.

She tilted her chin up at his look, also hearing his unspoken accusation clearly. "Yes, I questioned Curt. He claimed he had to take a second mortgage on his condo to pay for renovations. He also claimed he bought the Carrera with royalties from his new book. That should be easy enough to check. It cost 150k."

At Ross's nod, Abby turned her laptop on the front of his desk so Emm could see it.

She explained, "We just got this yesterday at my request. The publisher agreed to share Curt's royalty statements with, shall we say, a bit of persuasion—and a subpoena—from our friends at the DEA."

Emm scanned the summary report. It showed a healthy 50k in royalties in the last year, but not near enough to pay for such an expensive vehicle, as Curt had claimed. His mortgage record also showed only a first lien, with no second. She leaned back, unsurprised. "So he lied. Twice. What now?"

Ross said, "The problem is, if we bring him in for more questioning he's likely to panic and run, or to alert whomever he reports to in the pipeline that we're probably on to him. While financial records like this indicate a smoking gun, it's not enough to prosecute. We need evidence of the actual laundering because the money trail will lead us to the head of the cartel with enough evidence to storm the compound and, ultimately, win convictions in both Mexico and here."

Ross rounded his desk and rested his hips on the front edge so his knees almost touched Emm's. Perhaps it was silly, given the way she'd yielded to him body and soul—was it only yesterday?—but she scooted her chair back, not wanting to touch him. His mouth tilted up derisively at the corners, and she could see he thought it was silly, too.

But he only said, "Emm, you're going to blow this entire investigation and possibly further endanger Yancy and Jennifer if you don't stop interfering. Not to mention you could be grabbed yourself."

Emm ground her teeth together, but she managed evenly, "I don't care. I've played nice, trying to follow the rules, and every law enforcement agency I've dealt with, including the Texas Rangers, seems too tied up in red tape to make any real progress." When Ross sucked in an angry breath, Emm scraped her chair back and stood. "Curt Tupperman is involved in all of this, and I'm going to find out how and bring you the evidence you say you need." She turned for the door, but Ross caught her arm.

He stuck his face into hers and enunciated each word with cold finality. "If you don't cease and desist, you'll not be watching anyone or anything except your career swirling down the stainless-steel toilet in the ladies' jail."

Emm pushed him back. "Get out of my face. If you try to arrest me, you'll find out I do know how to be a Rothschild when pressed. Nice turn of phrase, the press . . . I wonder how Curt's competitors would like a whisper of this story? I can tell you he's not very popular. I don't think the Rangers would come off very favorably either. Three women, all taken from the Baltimore area, one dead, the other two about to be." Emm tapped her fingers against her chin, as if contemplating. "Come to think of it, my grandfather has connections both at the *New York Times* and the *Washington Post*."

Ross and Emm stared each other down. Check, countercheck, stalemate.

Ross took a deep breath and looked at Abby, who nodded infinitesimally.

He backed off and went to another file buried on his desk. He brought it back around, lancing her with those deep blue eyes that now gleamed with a hint of sharpened obsidian. "If you let word of this leave this office, I *will* have you arrested. This is highly confidential information, but it seems to be the only way I can convince you that we are proceeding as quickly as we can to shut down all of this cartel's operations, including drug smuggling, human trafficking, and, recently, identity theft. They're also trying to branch out into Europe, we think, with the Chechens as partners. Prices for their products are as much as triple on the continent. This Chechen connection will be a very lucrative partnership for Los Lobos if it gets finalized, and it will make them even harder to shut down. There are huge Eastern European mob alliances on the East Coast, which we think may be the reason for the Baltimore-Dallas-Amarillo-El Paso trafficking route."

"So shouldn't Mexico do all it can to stop them now?" Emm asked hopefully. "Before they finalize this deal?" She slumped back into the chair.

Ross pulled a picture from the file. "About twenty-four hours ago, Jesús Cerritos, a known lieutenant of the man we know as Arturo Cervantes, was found dead in a Dumpster in a bad part of Mexico City. In his pocket was a piece of blue silk, along with another piece of black chiffon studded with rhinestones. The Mexican police found traces of vomit on the blue silk and have sent it to us for full analysis. We can get age, genetic type, and some other information from it, but without a matching sample of DNA we can't confirm it belonged to either Jennifer or Yancy."

"Blue is Jennifer's favorite color," Emm said dully. Somehow, she knew the swatches of fabric belonged to her sister and niece. She covered her face with her hands, holding back tears. No one had to tell her the unspoken message of two feminine scraps of fabric found in the pocket of a dead man. It was a message. And while on the one hand, if the fabrics had belonged to her niece and sister, that meant until twenty-four hours ago they were in Mexico City and had not disappeared into Europe's murky underworld, on the other hand, it also meant . . . A distressed sound escaped her clasped hands and she began to cry.

Helplessly, Ross looked at Abby.

Abby put a gentle hand on Emm's shoulder. "There's more. I'm sorry, but you asked to be kept in the loop. Please be aware that you cannot share what we're about to tell you with anyone, for any reason. Agreed?"

With a deep, shuddering breath, Emm lifted her head and wiped away her tears. "I swear."

"I can't tell you how," Abby said, "or all the agencies involved, but our side has had a certain mansion on a hilltop outside Mexico City under surveillance for over a week with the approval of the Mexican government. They're not happy that the border wars between the various cartels are spilling over into the capital and they want it stopped. They've found numerous victims from both the Los Lobos and Knights Templar cartels in the last month, indicating the rivalry is heating up."

"The assassination MO for Los Lobos is cutting out the heart." Ross took up the sordid tale when Abby hesitated. "The Knights Templar generally behead their victims."

The fact that he didn't mince his words despite her distress was proof enough to Emm that he was angry at her refusal to cease and desist. Emm covered her mouth again, but this time she had to swallow back the acid upwash of her breakfast. After a minute, she angrily dashed her tears away. Then she dropped her hands and looked at both serious faces. "And this Jesús—was his heart cut out?"

Both of them nodded.

"About thirty hours ago there was a huge party with international guests." Ross finally, slowly, offered her the picture he held as if he had to but didn't want to. "This picture was taken at approximately twelve thirty a.m. Mexico City time outside the mansion."

Emm accepted the picture. It had obviously been taken with night vision technology, and the images were grainy, but she recognized the proud tilt to that finely shaped head and the strange zigzag part that had been the bane of Yancy's existence. No matter how she tried to comb her hair into a neat upsweep or side part, her hair always settled back to natural dishevelment, something that Emm had told her teasingly added to the wild sexuality that drove men crazy. It was also obvious that both women in the photo had fair hair that stood out against the dark background of the brick wall behind them. Even in her distress, she made a mental note of the details of the wall and its immediate surroundings. But she only whispered, "Yancy . . . Jennifer."

"Are you sure?" Ross asked. He had to clear his voice.

"Yes. They're in Mexico City?" She studied the picture for another long moment. It seemed as if both women were looking toward someone rounding the car parked before them. Both of their postures were very tense.

"They were about twenty-four hours ago. We also got one shot of both Arturo and his son Tomás getting out of the same limousine. So they're either living at this compound or were guests. So far we haven't determined which, because the ownership is through a convoluted set of partnerships we haven't fully traced yet. But he was definitely in the company of two fair-haired women."

"Were you able to confirm they're wearing the same fabrics as the samples you found?"

"As you can see, visibility isn't great, but our analysts say the patterns are consistent with the samples." He still sounded very grim.

"Los Lobos knows you're watching, don't they?" Emm stated. At Ross's jerky nod, Emm cried, "We have to go there, now!"

Ross took a deep breath and caught her hands, as if he'd been expecting this reaction. "Emm, this is the first actual confirmation we've had that Jennifer and Yancy are being held by the Los Lobos cartel. And if we're right, and the scraps of fabric mean what we think they do, then it's likely both Yancy and Jennifer are no longer even in the compound. They've been . . ." He couldn't finish.

"Discarded?" Emm filled in bitterly. "Trash. Expendable. Used up . . ." She would have continued, but her voice broke. "Why do you think Los Lobos sent this message?"

"If they know we're watching, I think they want us to know both women are no longer there. And it may be a warning. That the women will be killed if we seize the compound. If they're still there. This is the only shot we had of the women, so we couldn't tell if they were in the limo when it drove away."

Emm was so anguished that she broke a nail as she gripped the arm of her chair. "We can't just do nothing! They were still alive twenty-four hours ago, but what about tomorrow?"

Ross rounded his desk and knelt in front of Emm to take her hands. He tenderly kissed the broken nail and said into her fingers, "This is out of my hands now. You should know that I've resigned, effective as soon as my division chief finds a replacement."

Her startled gaze leaped to meet his. But his deep blue eyes were veiled as he continued, "I have no control over what the international task force decides, and ultimately the Mexican government will make the call on whether to try to seize the compound or not. They won't do it if they can't confirm that Arturo Cervantes is nearby. It will be a hugely expensive operation and they'll only green light it if they think there's an excellent chance of success."

Emm snatched her hands away. "Meaning Yancy and Jennifer are expendable. Tiny little pawns in the big, bad game of international chess."

Ross sat back on his heels, but his only response was a small nod. "I don't like it any more than you do, but that's the way the system works."

Emm leaped to her feet and ran from the office. Tears streamed from her eyes, making her path down the steps blurry, but she finally fumbled out her keys and got her car door open. She pressed the Start button, wiping her eyes on her sleeve, and roared out of the lot, uncaring that she broke about three laws as she did so.

On the steps, Abby and Ross peered after her.

"She's going to look for them herself," Abby said softly.

Ross raked his hands through his hair in frustration. "Why do you think I asked to be replaced as head of the task force? I'm also taking a leave of absence as soon as the reunion ends so I can chase after her if need be."

Abby looked up at him, her wide mouth stretching into a skeptical half smile. "And what if you have to arrest her for interfering in an investigation?"

"As you know, even off-duty Rangers have that right, when the situation warrants it. And I'll do whatever I have to in order to keep her safe, even if it means tossing her in a jail cell." Ross spun on his heel and stalked back up the steps, leaving Abby walking down in a contemplative mood, wondering what she could do to help. It seemed to her Emm and Ross were made for each other, but her own limited forays into romance had ended disastrously, so who was she to play matchmaker?

On the other hand, she could certainly use her considerable expertise to help keep Emm safe. And the only thing that would make Emm back off was a breakthrough leading to Yancy and Jennifer's locations.

Abby paused when she got to her car to look at the latest e-mail message in her secure account. There it was, the one she'd been waiting for. The undercover DEA operative in Mexico City had found three pharmacies that had recently filled the script for Yancy's unusual hemophilia medication. They'd hacked into each store's database and found evidence that one pharmacy had supposed US ownership, so large sums were being wired back and forth between Mexico and the United States. It smelled like money laundering to the operative, as it did to Abby.

A bit more digging yielded the fact that a maid at an estate outside the city had filled a huge variety of prescriptions, among them Yancy's favored hemophilia medicine, Effluenatasis, Xanax, and the morning-after pill. The maid had been followed once, when she'd come to pick up an entire bag full of scripts, back to the estate where she worked. Nothing could be seen behind the walls, even with the latest technology, for they were too thick, but the link had been deemed strong enough to warrant electronic surveillance.

Which was how the task force had finally been able to get pictures of Yancy and Jennifer in their finery; they'd sent a drone high overhead with the blessing of the Mexican government. After immediately forwarding the e-mail to Ross for his inclusion in the database, Abby started her car, wondering if she should go straight to Emm's hotel. She decided it was best to let Emm calm down before she told her they'd tracked down Yancy's prescription at the same mansion where they'd taken the picture of the two women.

Besides, she had more digging to do.

The night after the interview, Emm ignored her phone calls and increasingly urgent texts from Ross to meet him for dinner. Even though it was still early, she wore her teddy as she folded her arms over her knees and stared into the darkness. Her room service sandwich and soup sat untouched on her nightstand. She knew Ross was worried about what she'd do, and well he should be. Her duties here were almost done. If tomorrow she was able to convince the Sinclair family to redevelop both buildings instead of tearing them down, her first assignment would end a success.

Then what? Logically, she should return immediately to Baltimore, write up her final recommendation, and get her next assignment. Her boss probably wouldn't be happy if she asked for a leave of absence so soon after being hired, but he'd accept it if she used her sister's health as the reason.

Tomorrow was the first day of the Sinclair reunion, and it was the only free time the partygoers would all be unoccupied and together to hear her PowerPoint presentation. She'd worked on the presentation for over a week now, trying to perfect it, for she'd known what the complete survey would say just from following the engineer around: The buildings were both structurally sound. And only yesterday, he'd e-mailed a detailed report that showed exactly that—borings, elevations, steel beams, building sections, foundation, soils survey, and all. He'd agreed with her that the crumbling base around the bigger structure was only a cosmetic curtain wall and easily enough repaired, though it would be costly because it would require a skilled hand mason. Virtually the entire interior, from the doors to the stairways to the wood floors, even to the old elevator, could be repaired and preserved to save the historic character.

As challenging as the project had been, her thoughts were only for Yancy and Jennifer. She wished she could save them so easily. While she'd initially felt a jolt of relief that both were alive, still in Mexico City, given the careful placement of the fabric from their dresses, it was obvious their days were numbered.

Emm appraised the sequence of events and the various players, trying to deduce the best way to get into Mexico City. Finding the mansion would not be difficult; she'd appraised the wall behind the limo and it was pretty distinctive, brick with ornate wrought-iron pillars that looked more English than Mexican. Massive, on the hills outside the city. Google Earth was a handy piece of software ... but what good would it do to breach the compound as an historic expert interested in Mexico City architecture only to find them gone?

No matter how she looked at it, Curt Tupperman was her best potential lead. She believed him when he said he still cared about Yancy. She suspected he was involved somehow with Los Lobos, though at this point she was sure of nothing. However, whether he was an investigative reporter or a criminal, she had few options. He could help her get access to the compound where Yancy and Jennifer had been sighted, and that was all she cared about.

She also knew something Ross and Abby apparently didn't: Curt had a small interest in a private jet network. He'd told Yancy when he swept her away to Aruba for a long weekend while they were dating that as costly as it was, given the peripatetic nature of his work, it ultimately saved him time and money because he often had to travel on a moment's notice. Ross and Abby also didn't know Yancy had a good friend on the company's executive board. Someone who could pull up all reservation records.

In the quiet of her reflections, Emm recalled that Miami area code and why it had stuck in her memory. Emm even remembered the woman's name: Louise. She'd actually e-mailed her sympathies to Emm when she'd heard the news about Yancy's abduction so soon after Jennifer. Emm turned on the light to check her watch. Eight p.m. her time, nine p.m. Miami time, where the company was based. Emm grabbed up the pad next to her bed and scribbled several phone number combinations. She stared a moment at the numbers and was pretty sure she had the last four right, but she wasn't certain about the first three. She wrote down several combinations, picked up her cell phone, and started dialing.

As she waited for someone to answer, she made a mental checklist. After she spoke to Louise to find out if Curt had made any recent reservations, or had flown to Mexico around the time of either kidnapping, she'd pack. Tomorrow, immediately after the reunion, she'd approach Curt again and try to get him to go with her to Mexico City. If he refused, she'd book a flight on one of the majors.

Even as the scholar coolly, systematically went through her phone list, the soft, tender, lonely Emm was crying inside.

After tomorrow, she would never see Ross Sinclair again. But she'd have at least one happy memory to pull out and enjoy as she got old . . . For that, she couldn't be sorry.

When she got back to Baltimore, hopefully accompanied by Yancy and Jennifer, she'd stay so busy that the desolation lapping at the shadows would recede back where it belonged. At the edges of her life, kept at bay by a career she loved and a fractured family that needed her.

Ross slammed his desk phone down, frustrated. He drummed his fingers on the top of the desk in his study, debating just showing up at Emm's hotel, but he knew where that might lead, and his family arrived in the morning. He'd also seen the e-mail and final analysis from the engineer and skimmed the write-up carefully enough to realize both how comprehensive it was and that Emm had been right in her initial analysis. She was going to recommend they first be fined and cited with possible huge fines and then felonies if they tore either building down in defiance of a federal stay . . . He'd already checked the statutes.

The family would not be pleased. Sighing, he printed out six copies, one for each member of the LLC they'd formed to develop the building, but as he did so he wondered if Emm would still show up to try to persuade them to save her buildings. Her buildings. For some reason, he liked the ring of that.

His doorbell dinged. Ross went to the door himself, thinking it might be one of his guests, arriving early. He was surprised when he opened the door to see Chad standing there. He wore a jacket and his badge, so he was dressed for business. "Hey, Chad, what brings you here so late?"

"Can I come in?"

Ross stood back. "Of course." He led the way to his favorite spot, the two chairs before the fire, which was still crackling in the spring chill. He poured them each a drink and sat down, waiting for Chad to begin.

As usual, Chad didn't mince words. "They want to make me head of the task force, and I had to ask how you felt about that. You know I'd never take your job behind your back."

Ross nodded, unsurprised. He swirled his brandy, searching for a tactful way to say this. There was none but the plain truth. "I asked to be removed, actually."

Chad tilted his hat back, as he did when he was confused about something. "Why in God's name would you do that? Pulling off this investigation would get you to Austin."

"If I wanted to go to Austin. Which I don't."

"Okay, but that's still an extreme reaction unless . . ."

Ross tossed back the rest of his brandy. "Unless I have a blatant conflict of interest."

Chad took off his hat and cradled it on his lap. "Ah, I see." He peered more closely at his former boss's shadowed face. "I take it Ms. Rothschild is the conflict?"

Ross nodded, hoping his flush couldn't be seen in the dim lighting. "I'm going to ask her to marry me at the end of the reunion." He smiled, as if mystified a bit at his own haste. "If nothing else, that will get her to shut up for five minutes."

Chad laughed. "Don't count on it." He sipped his own drink more judiciously. "Isn't your family likely to be opposed?"

"Yep. At least my mom and my aunt will be. If Emm had won a Nobel Peace prize *and* a Pulitzer and personally owned the Rothschild trust fund, they'd still be opposed. Why do you think I'm rushing things?"

Chad grinned ear to ear. "Fait accompli, in your fancy-schmancy, Yalie parlance."

"That 'aw shucks' BS may work with Jasmine—"

"Actually, it never did—"

"But it doesn't work with me." Ross stood and offered his hand to his friend. "You're the first to know about my resignation from the task force and about my marital plans. I don't have to ask you to keep them quiet. Even from Jasmine."

"I'll try, but Jasmine reads me like a book. She knows I drove here to talk to you and she's going to ask me what happened."

Ross grinned. "So can you read her yet?"

Chad smashed his hat back on his head. "I'm working on it. Ask me again in about, say, fifty years. . . ."

Ross's laughter followed him toward the door. But before he exited, Chad turned back to Ross. "And if we have to go into Mexico? Do you want to be in on that operation . . . in an advisory capacity?"

"Yes, but only because I know the data so well. I'm also taking a leave of absence, so I'd have to be included on that basis."

Chad nodded, unsurprised. "And Ms. Rothschild?"

Ross scowled. "She has the bit between her teeth to find her sister and niece. I'm worried about how far she might go."

"I figured as much." Chad opened the door. "Okay, I'll be sure you're included on the task force if we do go in."

"Thanks, Chad."

On the door sill, Chad paused to look at his mentor and friend. "You know, Jasmine and I probably wouldn't be together now if I hadn't kidnapped her and asked you to arrest her."

This startled a smile from Ross. "Are you suggesting I follow suit?"

"I'm suggesting you don't let her get away even if you have to hog-tie her to your bed." With that plain speaking, Chad nodded and closed the door behind him.

The sound of Chad's words echoed more loudly to Ross as he climbed the stairs to his room than all his fears put together.

So what would he do if Emm refused his proposal? Ross smiled grimly, reaching for the handcuffs he kept handy next to his bed. Not for the obvious reason; merely so he could grab them quickly with his badge and gun. He'd had no likely candidates to take to his room. Until now . . .

CHAPTER 12

The next morning, Emm's eyes were bloodshot from a restless night as she prepared for her first official presentation as a historical trust officer. She knew the entire Sinclair family, probably including Ross, would not like what she had to say, but he'd seen the survey results by now, so he couldn't quibble with her original analysis. They'd been too busy with . . . other things to discuss the buildings, but the Sinclair trust members needed to be aware that she was recommending to her bosses that the buildings be preserved. While their renovation would potentially be more challenging and less lucrative than a ground-up multistory building, the community and tax credit benefits were huge. More importantly from the perspective of Amarillo's downtown revitalization, the preservation of one building often led to the restoration of others.

When she'd run through her PowerPoint for the third time and was secure in her ability to convey her passion without notes, she turned her laptop off and eyed her messy room. Inside her still slumbered somewhere—under the just-business professional—the idealistic little girl who'd adored Sleeping Beauty and Cinderella. She wanted to believe Sinclair was her prince who'd come, perhaps almost too late, to rescue her from her dreary existence, but she was also a modern woman who knew that one toss of the bedsheets did not a long-term relationship make. Especially with a man in his early fifties who'd never been married and was obviously skittish about women.

Reluctantly, she did as she ought, not as she wanted, and packed most of her stuff. Whether Sinclair asked her to stay or not, she had to be ready to leave for Mexico City because nothing, not even her own hope of future happiness, could get in the way of finding Yancy and Jennifer.

Telling herself the tears in her eyes were from determination, not despair, she left her room key and a generous tip for the maid on the bed, lugged her bags into the hallway, and wheeled them to the elevator.

She got a complete copy of her lengthy bill so she could be reimbursed for her expenses by her employer and then nodded at the bellhop's offer of assistance. "Can you store them for me for a few hours until I can get my plans settled?" she asked.

He did so, leaving her free to walk out carrying only her purse and briefcase. She'd already set up a luncheon appointment with Curt following her presentation. She intended to wheedle, beg, and, if that didn't work, threaten Curt into flying to Mexico City with her. She knew Ross and Abby would be on high alert the minute they found her gone, and they had the connections to trace her reservations on a commercial airline.

But a private jet listed only under Curt's name? They'd never find her in time to stop her from going to Mexico City. As to what she did next, she'd stayed up half the night as she used Google Earth to pinpoint several potential candidates for the mansion she'd glimpsed in the photo. The wrought iron was custom and very distinctive, and after spending hours searching, she'd only found three structures on the outskirts of the city that had the same style of fencing.

She had a plan, at least the beginning of one. Its execution would depend on whether Curt was with her or not . . . which was another reason he had to go with her. She spoke some Spanish, but he was fluent, and if he truly had nothing to hide and still cared for Yancy, once she told him about the bloodied fabric samples and the photos, he should be willing to help.

Her conscience pinged her as she recalled her promise to Abby and Ross not to share that information, but Yancy and Jennifer's lives were at stake . . . Besides, feeding him enough information to hang himself would aid, not block, the investigation. If he was really a money launderer for one of the wealthiest, most ruthless crime lords on the face of the planet, she could be in danger, too, just as Ross had feared, but it was a risk she had to take.

When she arrived at Ross's ranch a bit before nine a.m., expensive cars of all types, even a Rolls or two, crowded the circular drive in front of the house. She had to very carefully parallel park between a Mercedes and another BMW even to find room for her car. Taking her laptop and file full of handouts with her, she climbed the stairs. She was reaching for the bell when the door burst open and two teenagers in new jeans and spotless boots almost knocked her down the steps as they ran outside.

Laughing a "Sorry, miss," they hurried down to the outbuildings, where she now saw tables set up with white-and-red-checked tablecloths. Saddled horses were tended by several cowboys in traditional chaps and hats.

The roundup, it seemed, was about to begin. Emm gingerly stepped inside Ross's vast foyer. It, too, looked different, with red, white, and blue bunting strung from beam to beam and wrapped around the balustrade leading to the upper floors. A huge cowhide rug was centered on the flagstones.

Emm smelled appetizing aromas. She knew José must be cooking a huge breakfast spread, probably had been since well before dawn. Ross had told her something of his family retainer, that he insisted on doing most of the cooking himself with catering to fill in. He worried José was getting too old for such a task, but the old buzzard, as he affectionately called his friend, was adamant.

Emm heard voices coming from the study, but the heavy door was closed and the gender was indistinct, though she could tell that at least some of the voices were raised in anger. Feeling like the famous Roman messenger, the bearer of bad news to the emperor, Emm stifled her urge to barge into the study and salute with one hand raised, palm out, and declaim, "We who are about to die salute you!"

Smiling wryly at her own quirky sense of humor, which tended to surface at inappropriate times, Emm set her file and computer down and went in search of José. He'd know the agenda and where to direct her. She'd only been in the kitchen once, however, and she took a wrong turn and ended up in the luxurious secondary master suite downstairs. She peeked inside the room and did a double take at its occupant.

A statuesque brunette stood next to the bed in a silk wrap that barely came to her knees. She was unpacking the open Louis Vuitton suitcase on the silk spread.

Muttering a "sorry," she was about to retrace her steps when a feminine voice said, "Why, hello; you must be Mercy Magdalena Rothschild. A lovely name, by the way."

Politeness forced Emm to pause. "I'm sorry; I'm not very familiar with the house and I wasn't sure where to go because it sounds
like R—Mr. Sinclair is busy."

The woman turned from the bed, holding a very expensive set of
scanty black lace matching lingerie—Emm could just see the La Perla
tag in the bra—and a bustier, garter belt, and black stockings. Not the
attire for a family reunion, Emm thought with a sinking heart. And
hadn't Ross told her all the family but his mom and dad and aunt
stayed in the outbuildings he'd had constructed for these visits? She'd
wanted a tangible sign of his affections or lack thereof . . . well, here
it was.

She'd obviously made the right choice in packing without even
telling him.

Emm forced a smile. "Sorry again. I'll just wait next to the fire.
I'm a bit early."

Again the woman spoke as she tried to turn away. "Oh, please,
stay. I'm an old friend of Ross's from Yale. Elaine Gottlieb." She nodded at the chair across from the bed. "Eugenie and Clara have invited
me to hear your presentation, and I was just changing for it. Won't
you visit with me while I dress?" She took out a pair of jeans sewn
with diamantés and added a shirt—Emm had to gawk a bit in disbelief—with pockets and pearl snaps. By the looks of them, real pearl
snaps. Oh, dear lord, if the woman pulled out fur chaps, Emm knew
she'd gag. Still, half-rapt, half-repelled, Emm sank into the chair as
instructed.

Luckily, her coffee stayed down, because Elaine turned aside to
pull the jeans up very long, perfect legs that made Emm cross her
own stumps in self-defense. Even if Elaine did look a bit too shiny
and new in the clothes, she was a gorgeous woman without a wrinkle
in her skin. She looked more like thirty than her late forties, and her
long dark hair had the shine of a seal.

Elaine said, "We have some buildings in Baltimore we've been
thinking of renovating. My dad wanted to tear them down, but I
talked him out of it. I really respect what you do."

"Thanks," Emm managed.

"Would you be willing to take a look at them next time you're in
town and give us your professional opinion?"

"It would only be a guess. The tax credit process is quite involved, and the buildings have to meet a detailed checklist of criteria to war-rant inclusion in the National Register."

"So I've heard, but you can smooth the way a bit, can't you?" Elaine buttoned her shirt. "My father is friends with half the senators and congressmen in DC, so I'm sure we could help your career."

Emm realized this woman had, from the first taste of her baby bottle, been fed a steady diet of cream of the crop. She literally knew no other way to operate but by asking for, and granting, favors. Emm's coffee threatened to come back up as she wondered how Ross could make such sweet, soulful love to her one day and invite this snob into his home the next. An old lover to boot; Ross had let her first name drop during their cuddling when she'd tentatively asked about his previous lovers.

And based on the clothes Elaine had packed, she was an old lover who expected to take up where they'd left off years ago.

Unable to even pretend politeness anymore, Emm rose. "R—Mr. Sinclair has my e-mail address. Feel free to e-mail me particulars and I'll see what I can do. Now, if you'll excuse me, I need to review my notes." Emm fled.

Elaine called after her, "You will come to our wedding, won't you?"

She was half-expecting the catty invitation, but when it came, Emm bit her lip so savagely she tasted blood. She went into the guest bath she'd used a couple of times before and did what she could with her puffy lip by applying more lipstick. She heard Ross's voice call-ing her. She wiped a tiny dot of mascara from her eyelid, a remnant of the single tear she couldn't control, took a deep breath, and opened the bathroom door. At least one thing was settled: One way or an-other, she'd be leaving Amarillo. Today.

She entered the vast living area. "I'm here. Is everyone ready to listen?" She smiled brightly, too brightly, because he gave her a strange look. He opened his mouth to say something, but Elaine en-tered, walking a bit stiffly in what were obviously new boots.

"We're ready, darling. We were just having a little chat while I dressed. Emm's going to look at some of our buildings, isn't that nice?" She linked her hand around Ross's arm. She whispered some-thing to him, and she was so tall he didn't even have to bend his head to hear.

Emm pretended not to notice as she got her laptop and file. "Where do you want me to make the presentation?"

"I have equipment set up in the study," Ross said. He pulled gently at his arm, forcing Elaine to release her grip. The woman merely sailed on her long, elegant legs into the study.

Ross hung back, offering to take Emm's laptop, but she waved him away.

"Emm, it's not what you think," he began.

She wanted to whirl on him and demand what it was, then, and why had he had sex with someone who hoped to be his new girlfriend when his old girlfriend was arriving the next day, obviously intent on sharing his bed, too? True, they'd made no promises to each other, and she did initiate things. But he'd snookered her into believing he was a man of class and discrimination, even said it had been a long time since he'd made love to someone that mattered.

Obviously, I don't matter either, Emm concluded.

But she only pretended not to hear him and forged ahead. Ms. Gottlieb might come from great wealth and power, but Emm had Rothschild blood in her veins, and for once, she'd use it to intimidate. Ross would remember her in the years ahead, as she would likely remember him.

Fondly? At this point, she didn't give a flip either way.

The minute she entered, the buzzing conversation stopped. She felt six pairs of eyes appraise her coolly. She noted that the four men, ranging in age from late seventies to thirties, relaxed when she smiled at them. But the two very well-preserved women, perfect size sixes garbed in custom black jeans, fringed shirts, and boots, eyed her critically. Emm knew from her research into the family that they were sisters. Well into their seventies, though they looked fiftyish, and arbiters of both style and society in their East Coast domain. Ross had been a surprise baby, and perhaps for that reason both his aunt Eugenie and his mother Clara were fiercely protective of him.

Normally, they would have intimidated Emm with their regal noses all but sniffing at her, but given recent events, she was too raw to care. She'd never see these people again, so she'd do her job and get the hell out. Ross came in and closed the door. He introduced her, and she thought his father looked a lot like him. His hair was entirely silver, but his bearing was erect, and he had the same vibrant sparkle of intelligence and curiosity in his blue eyes.

The niceties out of the way, Ross nodded her toward the audiovisual array he'd hooked to a wall screen that had obviously been built for presentations like this. Emm had used such equipment before, so it only took her a second to hook up her computer with the Power-Point presentation she'd prepared. When she was ready, she handed out the six copies of the survey she'd printed and began to review it section by section.

They were only a few pages in when Clara tossed her papers aside in irritation. "We're not engineers; just summarize for us, please."

Emm met the glacial blue eyes that were the exact shade of Ross's. She said very precisely, "The conclusion of the structural engineer R—Mr. Sinclair retained is that both the Hoover and Draper buildings are structurally sound. If you'd care to have his findings reviewed, I perfectly understand. Or you can get a second opinion by another preservationist. But neither will change my recommendation to the Parks Service that both buildings be preserved, not demolished."

"Huge surprise there," Elaine said sotto voce.

Ross glared at her, but Emm's eyes never wavered from Clara's even more glacial stare. "I had a presentation planned that details the many benefits of historic preservation, the criteria for inclusion in the National Register, and the possible monetary benefits, but I'm happy to e-mail my entire presentation to R-Mr. Sinclair to disseminate among you, if that's your preference."

"Yes," both Clara and Eugenie said simultaneously.

Ross said gently, "Why don't you tell us in broad terms a layman can understand why you feel so strongly the buildings should be saved?"

His father echoed, "Yes, please."

Emm hesitated, but she may as well go for broke. "Historic buildings are the orphans of the metropolitan environment. Quite often isolated, with no other similar buildings nearby, they usually suffer years of neglect before some enterprising soul recognizes their worth. But I would challenge you to imagine New York City without the Empire State Building or the Woolworth Building, Dallas without the Kirby, and now, Amarillo without the Draper and Hoover buildings." Emm watched the two older women and was relieved to see even they looked thoughtful.

Pressing her advantage, Emm put it in bottom-line terms. "Fully restored, they will not only give your family a growing cash flow but will show the community that the Sinclairs care about the legacies they leave and are good stewards of the built environment. Just think of all the dump space saved by not demolishing these buildings and instead turning them into productive anchors for downtown, an example for other property owners to emulate."

By the time she finished, Emm saw she'd come close to convincing all the men. Clara and Eugenie had softened a bit.

She'd done her best . . . Emm collected her equipment. Hiding her own sigh of relief, for never had a presentation unnerved her the way this one had, Emm nodded regally. "Thank you for your time." She turned toward the door.

All the men murmured polite thanks, and Clara, Eugenie, and Elaine echoed them, if artificially.

But Ross protested, "But you're not leaving, are you? I wanted to include you in the festivities—" He gently caught her arm.

"I have a prior luncheon engagement," Emm said, taking a step toward the door so he'd be forced to release her arm. She couldn't bear his touch right that moment, not in this room where she so obviously didn't belong. Elaine Gottlieb, however, family member or not, obviously did . . . and she'd been invited to this private financial gathering, which spoke volumes to Emm of Elaine's position in the family.

Emm exited, trying hard not to run, but Ross followed her into the hallway.

"I'll come by your hotel tonight, if I can. We need to talk." Ross reached for her hand, but Emm pretended not to notice as she grasped the front door lever.

Biting back tears behind a perky smile, Emm bubbled over her shoulder, "Sure, I'll look forward to it!" This was the first and last time she'd lie to him. He'd find her long gone. . . .

"Emm, my mom and aunt don't realize how cold and arrogant they can be. Once you get to know them . . ."

"I'm sure. I have my own share of family members like that. No problem. Thanks for listening to my presentation." Safely outside the house now, Emm became the professional again. It was best to end all contact with him as it began: just business." More calmly, she said, "After I complete my recommendation to the office that the buildings merit restoration, I'll e-mail you a copy and forward you the signed original for your records. You want me to send it here or the office?"

"Here."

She nodded, hefted her laptop strap over her shoulder, and started down the steps, letting momentum and the tap of her heels drown out his soft, "Wait." He hovered on the steps, but his father bypassed him and caught up with Emm before she was able to open her car door.

For her ears alone, he murmured, "I'm sorry for my wife's and sister-in-law's attitude, but they're accustomed to getting what they want, and they're very protective of Ross."

Emm smiled at him perfunctorily. "That was apparent. I'm sorry if I spoiled your reunion, but I had to give my honest, professional opinion or I'd be negligent in my new job."

He nodded. "I understand that. Tell me, are you any relation to Edgar Rothschild?"

"He's my grandfather."

"I saw the box of cigars you gave Ross. You have exquisite taste." He eyed her up and down approvingly. "If we decide to continue with the redevelopment, would you be willing to talk with us about leading it?"

Emm knew only the need to escape before she burst into tears. He was being very kind, but this final leave-taking would be much easier if he'd been as cold as his wife. It was easy to see where Ross got his empathy. She managed, "I can't operate as your developer as long as I'm employed by the Parks Service, but that's very kind of you."

She opened her car door, nodding at him in thanks a final time. As she got into her BMW and carefully maneuvered between the other expensive vehicles, she knew he still stood there watching her, so she waved and drove off very sedately.

She grabbed her sunglasses out of her bag. Later, she wouldn't even recall the trip into town. It was the sun, bright and intrusive, she told herself, that brought tears to her eyes. They blurred her vision so much that she swerved off the road once and had to pull over to grab a tissue. Back on the road again, she glanced at the clock. She should reach Curt's hotel right on time for their luncheon appointment.

But as she drove carefully back into town, much slower than was her wont, she couldn't totally quell the tears as she envisioned Ross and his new bride in his mansion. Elaine obviously had much more money and class than some poor little relation of the Rothschild dynasty. Elaine would be a better mistress of the growing ranch, and Ross's aunt and mom obviously liked her.

Besides, Emm didn't want to stay in Amarillo. Not really. Too dry, too desolate, too hot, too cold at night. Too . . . She tried to focus on the bright day, but as the long, winding road led her away from Ross's door this time, the lovely sunshine illuminated only a very dull future.

Inside the study, Ross glared at everyone present but focused the bulk of his ire on the three women. Even his mother had the grace to shift under his fury, but she burst out, "She has no right to stop us from utilizing our own property—"

"She has every right. That's her job. And she has a PhD in historic preservation. Her initial analysis was spot-on, if you read the detailed survey. She knows what's she's doing."

"If she's not in collusion with the engineer . . ." Eugenie's insult faded away as Ross's fury turned in her direction.

"Very well; if we can't agree on the proper way to proceed with the development of these buildings, I have a solution." Ross went to his desk and pulled out the checkbook attached to his oil and gas accounts. His father entered just as Ross started writing a check.

He was puzzled and went to look over his son's shoulder. His eyes widened. "Now wait a minute, son. We need to talk about this." He glared at all three women. "The three of you were quite rude. I only hope this doesn't get back to Edgar Rothschild."

Ross tore the check from the book and stalked over to his mother, thrusting it into her face. "This is the current per square foot valuation of each structure, per the tax rolls, which you have records of. I want to buy both buildings outright."

For the first time, Clara's gaze softened. She barely glanced at the generous sum. She moved Ross's arm away from her face and clasped his wrist. "Ross, you know we don't want the money. It's the principle involved—"

"You mean the principle that states I own a majority share in the trust and have the right to buy the buildings at my discretion? Or that I'm managing member and am ultimately responsible for the details of the development? Well, I've made an executive decision. Mercy Magdalena Rothschild is going to develop these buildings, with or without the trust's approval."

Elaine gasped. Ross's cold gaze turned on her. "Elaine, I don't want to be rude, but you should have notified me you intended to come—"

"I wanted to surprise you," Elaine protested. "Your mother and aunt invited me—"

"And I would have asked you to please stay away if I'd been warned. If I'd had any doubts about my feelings for you, this has settled them, so I thank the three of you for that." Since his mother refused to take the check, Ross tucked it in his father's shirt pocket. "Now, please let this be the end of the debate over the buildings so we can all enjoy our two days together. I'll have my attorney draw up the appropriate contracts and forward them to you next week."

Ross went to the door and opened it. "José has breakfast ready, and his biscuits can only be appreciated piping hot." Though he didn't know it, he looked very like his mother at that moment as he eyed his family members one by one, daring them to argue. They trooped to the door, but his mother exited last and looked up at him.

"Ross, I'm only trying to protect you from an opportunist. I had this girl investigated before we came, and her part of the Rothschild family is penniless. They only have what they earn. From all accounts, her father is . . . in sales. He's not very close to his family, and I've heard this girl's older half sister is, well, scandalous. Elaine is a much better match for you."

Ross's eyes lost their icy sheen, becoming incandescent as his pupils expanded in anger. "I don't want Elaine. I want Emm. Deal with it. She's going to be my wife—if she'll have me after this fiasco. And if you don't make amends with her, it will be her decision whether you ever darken my door again. Now leave me the hell alone before I say something I'll really regret."

And Ross marched out, leaving his mother staring after him open-mouthed.

Emm was still crying when she reached town, and she had to drive around for a bit to calm herself before her luncheon with Curt. She repaired her makeup in her car mirror, took a deep breath, and entered the restaurant. He was tapping his fingers on the tablecloth when she entered. She was glad of the low lighting.

She plopped down in the booth across from him. "I'm sorry I'm late. I've just come from the Sinclair homestead, where I gave my presentation on the buildings to Ross's family."

Curt's reporter's ears pricked up. "How did that go? I've heard the older females of the family are . . . trying."

Emm laughed shortly. "That's a more charitable way than I'd put it." She sipped her ice water, unaware she was still trembling slightly until her teeth chattered a bit against the glass. She set it down, taking deep breaths.

Sympathy softening his face, Curt shook his head wryly. "We don't always want what's good for us, do we?"

"No, but in this case I think what's good for me tastes bitter but will be efficacious in the end. We'd never . . . have worked out anyway. What would I do in Amarillo, Texas?" She took a sip of hot tea as soon as the waitress delivered it. The warm mint steadied her enough for the shaking to stop. "But enough of my love life, such as it is. We've been friends for a while, so I'll be crystal clear. I had an ulterior motive for inviting you here." She reached across the table to cover Curt's restless hand.

He stiffened. "And what's that?"

"I need you to fly to Mexico City with me. Today, if possible."

"What?"

"I know you have a charter jet service, and that's perfect for this particular . . . outing. We need to get into the city quietly, and we'll probably need to get out even more quietly. The private jet will be much harder for anyone to track. Both outgoing and incoming, preferably straight back to Baltimore."

Curt was already shaking his head. "I haven't the faintest idea where Yancy is; you know that. All this speculation about my affairs is just that, and I'm not happy you think I could be even peripherally involved in something so distasteful as human trafficking."

"At this moment, I don't care whether you're involved or not, though the brutal truth is if you are, it would certainly give us easier access. I'm not doing this in collaboration with any authorities," Emm said grimly. "In fact, if Ross knew what I'm contemplating, he'd probably throw me in jail for obstruction."

"Emm, this is not only dangerous it's suicidal—"

"Yancy and Jennifer will be dead in a few days if we don't go."

That shut Curt up. After a moment, he said slowly, "How can you make a definitive statement like that? For all we know, they're both somewhere in Europe by now."

"The DEA, CIA, FBI, yadda yadda yadda, WTF is a better name for every damn one of them as far as I'm concerned; anyway, they have their uses. They've had a certain compound outside Mexico

City under surveillance for a number of days. I wasn't supposed to share this info, so you absolutely have to keep it between the two of us, no inclusion in your book. But Ross showed me photos of both Yancy and Jennifer, wearing evening attire, standing by a limo outside the gate. Snippets of their dresses were found in the pockets of a dead Los Lobos lieutenant who was supposedly feeding information to the Knights Templar. His heart was cut out."

Curt absorbed this, his handsome face now grayish as he listened. Finally, he said, "So you just want to drive around outside the city hoping to find them? And this is an armed compound? How would we get in, even if we stumble across it?"

Emm snapped her cup down in her saucer so hard the china clanged. "Please, give me a bit more credit than that. I spent hours on Google Earth. The ironwork and brick wall in the background of the photo are very distinct—a European, not a Spanish or Mexican style. I only found three homes that match."

Curt blinked rapidly. "Are you insane? Even if we pick the right one, do you think we can just waltz into the compound of one of the world's most ruthless drug lords and ask to see his mistress?"

Emm smiled and rummaged in her purse. She offered him two cards, one his own, which she'd saved in her card case, and her own as historical preservation consultant—the title she'd used before landing her most recent job—with a Maryland address. She knew better than to offer anything with even a whiff of association with the US government.

She tapped the cards, her voice lowering to be sure no one heard her. "I've been doing my own research. And the last Mexican high lord of crime, El Chapo, who was apprehended several years ago, actually gave interviews on occasion. We live in a digital world, and the latest cocaine czars like Arturo Cervantes need notoriety to oil their international connections and spread fear. I believe he'll happily let us inside if we present ourselves properly and promise to keep certain incriminating details vague. What do you think it would do to your book sales to have such inside . . . well, forgive the pun, dope on your story?"

Finally, Curt looked intrigued.

Not far from the compound under discussion, but in a much seedier area of Mexico City, Yancy yanked yet again at the handcuffs that held her securely to the iron bedstead by one arm. She was nude, had been for the last couple of days. The two Chechens had taken turns with her. At first she'd fought and bit, which had only led to her being cuffed and brutalized. She pretended to be comatose when she could, and that had helped some because they hadn't pestered her now in over twenty-four hours. They'd even sent a girl in, apparently of Chechen descent, because she spoke neither Spanish nor English, to bathe and feed her.

Like cattle, Yancy thought bitterly, being prepared for market. But she knew she needed all the strength she could muster, so she forced herself to eat whatever they brought. And with every bite, her rage at Arturo grew. She didn't know how, she didn't know when, but she would help bring him to justice if she died trying . . . He was the poisonous head of the snake. While there would always be other bosses ready to take over, none of them were as resourceful and ruthless. Just disrupting the flow of funds and drugs Los Lobos funneled around the world would give the authorities time to rescue some of his human trafficking victims before another head of the hydra grew powerful enough to take over.

But as she ate with one hand while the frightened girl cleaned her with a rough washcloth and a bowl of soothing warm water, Yancy had to gag down the last of the stale tacos with a filling that was indistinguishable, but didn't taste or feel like meat. While on one level of her brain she knew the poor quarters and supplies were a frightening indicator of her value to the Chechens, at the moment there was only one human trafficking victim she was concerned about. When they'd arrived, Yancy had heard Jennifer's screams down the hall, but in the last twenty-four hours the deadly quiet had been even more terrifying than her daughter's pain.

Yancy swallowed the bile of her own fear. She pointed down the hall, lifted a hank of her own dirty but still fair hair, and used a word even those not fluent in Spanish sometimes understood. *"Niña? Muy bonita?"* Yancy mimed sleeping by folding her hands and resting her cheek. She nodded down the hallway.

The girl's eyes flickered but she only shrugged and collected the water and the rag.

Yancy pulled viciously at the cuffs, which the girl had never undone. Her wrist was raw and she knew if she kept pulling she'd begin to bleed, so she forced herself to desist. When the girl turned to the door, Yancy begged, "Please, help us."

The girl's shoulders sagged a bit, but she exited without a response.

Yancy was alone in the dark, left to her own initiative. She should be used to that, she thought vaguely. But this time, she was fresh out of ideas.

This time, when the tears came, she couldn't stop them.

CHAPTER 13

Back in Amarillo, Curt still waffled. "Emm, we can't do this without help. Neither of us even knows how to shoot."

Emm leaned across the booth to spear Curt with her eyes. "Oh, for heaven's sake, even if we were both Marine snipers, we'd be idiots to try to shoot our way into a compound that's probably stocked with every machine gun known to man and plenty of drug dealers willing to use them. This situation requires negotiation and finesse, something we're both good at." When he stared at the napkin in his lap, she softened her tone. "Okay, you say you still love Yancy. You say you have no other interest in the cartels except as fodder for your stories and your next book. I need your help in Mexico City to find them, and eventually you'd have to go there anyway, wouldn't you, to collect information for your book? Why not now? Help me save Yancy and Jennifer. I have nowhere else to turn, at least not to anyone who can move in time."

Curt finally looked at her. "What, are you going to hold me at gunpoint and force me to order the jet?"

Emm said simply, "No. I'll sell my car if I have to, but one way or the other, I intend to be in Mexico City by tomorrow night."

"I can't talk you out of it, whether I go or not?"

"No." One word, but rife with determination.

Curt sighed and picked up his cell phone. "I don't know if they'll pick us up in Amarillo. We may have to go to Dallas first. We have to deal with our cars, but let's go get your luggage first."

Emm leaped to her feet to kiss his cheek. "Lay on." She almost added, *Macduff*, but given the outcome of that particular tragedy, she held her tongue.

* * *

Ross paced his hallway that night, aware of his mother's concerned gaze but uncaring. He'd been trying Emm's cell all day, and she hadn't returned his calls. He understood her well enough to know that she felt used and discarded after seeing Elaine in his home. And if he'd come across her old lover being included in intimate family events, he'd likely have concluded exactly the same thing. Every instinct in his body demanded that he go to her hotel to explain in person, but he was host of this damn jamboree.

"Ross, please come and eat some of this delicious barbecue," his mother pleaded from the doorway that led to the outside tables and festivities. LED lanterns manufactured to look like old kerosene ones lit the scene, more gaiety added by strings of colored lights and the country-western band Ross had hired for the evening.

Ross was still angry with her, but he managed stiffly, "In a minute."

Helplessly, she turned back to the merrymaking.

Ross pulled out his cell phone yet again, but this time he dialed Abigail Doyle.

By the time she was able to get away from an intelligence-gathering meeting led by Chad Foster, Abby was bleary-eyed with tiredness, but she'd promised Ross she'd check on Emm. Ross hadn't been specific, but if the presentation on the buildings hadn't gone well, that was reason enough, along with Emm's fears for her sister and niece, for her to refuse Ross's calls.

When she arrived at the hotel, Abby went straight to the elevator, not bothering with calling Emm's cell phone, which Ross had told her Emm had turned off. When she arrived at Emm's door, it was almost eight o'clock. She knocked firmly. She heard someone stirring inside, and then the door was flung open. A handsome young man in a suit blinked at her. She blinked back, noting two still latched suitcases near the door. "Excuse me, is Emm Rothschild available?"

He looked mystified. "I just checked in. Did you ask at the desk?"

Her heart sinking, Abby apologized and hurried back to the elevator. When she reached the desk, she had a hard time getting the clerk to tell her much until she flashed her business card and said she was there at the behest of Ross Sinclair, and that Ms. Rothschild was a material witness in a case.

The clerk pulled a stapled packet from the checked-out box on her counter and appraised it. "She checked out this morning and fetched her bags, which we'd held for her, several hours ago," the pretty young brunette clerk said crisply. "She didn't mention where she was going, and I didn't ask." She moved to turn away, shoving the packet back into the box. She didn't see a small pink memo fall from the packet and curl beneath the desk, nor did Abby.

Abby slapped her hand down on the desktop to forestall her. "Please make a note of my phone number. If you hear from her again or get any messages, please be sure you call me with that information. It's possible she may be the victim of foul play. And one more question—was she with anyone when she took out her bags?"

The brunette hesitated, then nodded. "Some tall blond guy. I've seen him before. I think he's a reporter. Now if you'll excuse me . . ." She turned back to her work. Abby had already turned away, almost running. In the meeting she'd just conducted with the heads of the various agencies involved, she'd shared her latest data, painstakingly assembled by various informants and intelligence sources. The evidence was not in Curt Tupperman's favor. In fact, it had been so glaringly incriminating—including many calls between his cell phone and Brett Umarov's, a man Curt claimed not to know, and many more deposits going back over two years, totaling over a million dollars—that Chad had convinced the Texas attorney general to issue a warrant to bring Curt in for questioning. Given the way Curt traveled the state, they needed statewide jurisdiction. The authorities were looking for him now.

If Emm was jetting to Mexico with a man she thought was her friend, she'd find out too late that Curt Tupperman didn't love Yancy. Despite what he said, he had zero motivation to help find her.

Curt Tupperman was probably the man who'd had her kidnapped.

Emm tipped the transport agent generously. "Your driver will be careful with my car?"

The agent looked offended. "Of course. And we are well insured."

"Okay. My dad will be your contact in Baltimore. Please text me when it's safely delivered."

The agent nodded wearily. "Yes, ma'am, I assured you we would. Mr. Tupperman as well."

Curt, hovering over her, winked at the agent. "Hers still has the new car smell. But mine is pretty damn special, too." Emm was so busy reviewing the papers a final time that she didn't notice Curt reaching for the outside pocket of her bag as he chatted amiably. Or that he dropped something into the trash can next to the desk.

With the assurances that both vehicles would be driven to their destinations by hired drivers who were trained to take extreme care, Emm and Curt got into the waiting taxi outside. Emm didn't know how he'd done it so quickly, but Curt had convinced his charter service to send a jet from Dallas to pick them up at the private strip of a wealthy local rancher he knew. In an hour, they'd be on their way to Mexico City, on a flight too hard for the agencies to track. At least not in time to stop them. The jet service still had to file a flight plan, but they were going direct to Mexico City.

Curt had to sit in the front because half of the backseat was loaded with bags. Emm's fit in the baggage compartment, and she was surprised to find Curt had brought so much stuff with him to Amarillo. For a moment she wondered if she was making a mistake going with him to Mexico City, but even if he was somehow involved with the cartel, surely he'd never really hurt her. He wasn't the type.

Besides, in the war between caution and concern, concern for Yancy and Jennifer won hands down. If she hesitated, all she had to do was think about that photo and the two torn fragments of their evening gowns.

Whatever his intentions, Curt was her fastest way out of the country. And since the morning's little chitchat with Elaine Gottlieb, Emm refused to dwell on Ross Sinclair's reaction when he found her gone. Whether he reacted as a lover or a Texas Ranger, when he got her last-minute SOS, he'd take appropriate action.

The next morning, Ross ignored his family's protests and drove into town to meet Abigail. She'd called him early to tell him she had bad news about Emm but they needed to discuss tactics in person. When he arrived at the DPS headquarters, he wasn't surprised to see Chad's car, even this early on a Sunday. But his twinge of unease about Emm became a kick to the gut.

Bracing himself, because he already had an idea of the news, he knocked on the large office they used as a conference room. When he entered, he saw it was full of high-level task force leads: the DEA,

Border Patrol, Homeland Security, the FBI Agent in Charge he'd worked with before, a woman by the name of Rosemary. And, of course, the Texas Ranger head of the task force, Chad Foster.

After a brusque hello all around, Ross pulled up a chair and fell into it. "She's gone, isn't she?" he said.

Abby explained her exchange with the desk clerk at Emm's hotel. "I didn't call you yesterday because it was very late after I followed up on the logical leads. When I left, I immediately checked all the flights to Mexico City. She wasn't on the manifest of any of them. However, I traced her car to a local transport agency when her license plate popped up as recent activity. She apparently hired them late yesterday to drive her car back to Baltimore."

Now Ross's unruly heart was a tom-tom in his ears. "So when she left, she didn't intend to come back . . . How the hell is she getting to Mexico City? I can't believe she'd go any way but by air. Do you think she used a false ID?"

Abby shook her head. "When I didn't get any hits on her name, I went to the airport and surveilled the security backups. She wasn't on the only two flights that could connect with Mexico City."

"And Curt Tupperman? Have you brought him in yet?"

Abby looked at Chad.

Chad shook his head grimly. "He's checked out of his hotel, and his car came up on the same database as Emm's."

Ross paled. "So you're pretty sure she's with him? Did you track her phone?"

Everyone else looked away, but Abby stared at him unwaveringly, nodding. "Yes, but unfortunately it was static. This morning we found it in the trash at the auto transport agency." Abby nodded at the evidence bag on the table.

Clearing her throat at his expression, she offered Ross a short list of two names and two private airfields. "However, when we couldn't find Ms. Rothschild on any of the commercial flights, I alerted the FAA to watch for any private flights heading to Mexico City, and late yesterday there were two originating in the Amarillo area. Do you know these men?" She recited the names on the list, glancing up at Ross. Both extremely wealthy oil and gas ranchers had private airstrips long enough for large private jets. He knew both men slightly. Amarillo's moneyed interests were a small, intimate group in which he'd always been included, if sometimes reluctantly.

Ross dismissed the first one. "Raoul has many interests in Mexico and travels on a weekly basis between here and there. He's as forthright and honest as they come. But Jimmy Patton . . . he was on one of my golf outings with Curt, and they were buddy-buddy." He scowled blackly. "The sneaky bastard has Emm. . . ."

Ross leaped to his feet to pace. "How could she be that fucking stupid? He's part of the money-laundering end of Los Lobos, I'm sure of it!"

Abby said gently, "In my brief acquaintanceship with Ms. Rothschild, I'd say there's very little she won't dare when someone she loves is in danger. I would also be extremely surprised if she didn't have serious suspicions about her supposed ally and prepare accordingly. She is the one who identified him first as a suspect. . . ."

Ross rubbed his aching forehead, opening his mouth to say he needed access to a jet, immediately, but a knock at the door forestalled him. A junior FBI agent hurried in, carrying a printed e-mail marked "secure server" at the top. He went straight to the FBI Agent in Charge, Rosemary Reed, a svelte blonde who looked more like a model than a dedicated G-man. "Ma'am, the Mexican authorities just notified us that Ms. Rothschild and Mr. Tupperman's passports were stamped at a private executive airport outside Mexico City."

"When?" asked Rosemary sharply.

The agent checked the e-mail. "Two hours ago."

Ross looked pleadingly at Chad, who nodded. "Confirm that the registration number of the jet is the same one that left the Patton airstrip and see if Mexican customs will hold it until we arrive." The young agent hurried back out.

Ross looked at his friend. "I realize it's a bit irregular, given I resigned from the task force, but I need to be on this operation. I . . . know her better than anyone else."

Chad looked at each task force member one by one. Rosemary eyed Ross's drawn and pale features, opened her mouth, then closed it and nodded reluctantly. It was apparent to all the lead agents that Ross Sinclair was definitely not objective in the matter of Emm Rothschild's possible alliance with a man now wanted by at least five federal agencies, but they kept their reservations to themselves. In over twenty years of brilliant and unblemished service to the State of Texas, Sinclair had always been a stickler for details. The fact that he'd resigned from the task force because he knew his feelings were compromised convinced all of the men in the room that he was still a professional law enforcement officer, not just a man in love.

But Rosemary eyed Ross critically as they began making a plan of action that would have to be coordinated with Mexican authorities.

Under the circumstances, Ross didn't take time to go back to the ranch to pack. He called his dad and asked him to organize things as the reunion ended and to convey his regrets, telling him curtly only that he had to make an emergency trip out of town. He picked up a few things in Amarillo and stuck them in a DPS pack, along with his state-issued Sig Sauer P226 .357 and his own custom Ed Brown hand-made 1911 .45 with rosewood grips. He also had two extra clips for each pistol. Others would be carrying shotguns and machine guns.

Would it be enough? Given Mexico's strong anticarry laws, the Mexican authorities didn't like them bringing in weapons, even for a joint op, but they'd allow it this time because of the huge firepower they'd likely be facing, and the fact that there were likely American hostages involved.

But then Chad knocked and entered with a full set of protective gear on one arm, wearing another set, and Ross's sense of urgency increased. "The latest from DC." Chad pounded on his own chest as hard as he could. "Some type of hybrid material. They say it will stop damn near anything. I wanted to try my own out before we go and thought you should, too."

Chad set the gear down on Ross's desk. Ross nodded at him to close the door. Chad complied, looking resigned, as if he knew what was coming.

Ross said, "As former head of the task force, I think I'm now up to speed on the latest intel. Please assign me just to this operation instead of you. I have to go; she's my woman. You don't. You have a family."

Chad scowled. "I was half-expecting this from you, but you're not my daddy, so back off."

Ross frowned right back. "I never said I was, but with all the personnel on this op, we don't both need to be there, and it would be smart to have someone manning everything from central control. That way if we need to request more Mexican troops or get more equipment trucked in, or need to scramble for more intel we didn't expect, you can coordinate all that."

Chad made a rude noise. "Yeah, right, while y'all get the collar on the meanest SOB in Mexico City, I'm minding the kitchen. Not hardly."

"Dammit, Chad—"

"No. That's final. I'm responsible for this op and I can't supervise remotely. I do promise to stay out of the way of the Mexican Marines. The president just gave us his approval to include them, but they're supposed to lead the raid. It is their country, and we have to be careful not to step on any toes." His voice softened a bit. "Besides, Jasmine would never ask me to stay. She knew I was a Ranger when we got together, and she's not clingy. It's one reason I love her so much. She doesn't try to change me."

Ross bit back the logical response: *Yes, but what about little Trey?* Instead, he turned to the new gear. As Chad helped him try it on to be sure it fit properly, Ross's thoughts fixed yet again on Emm. He was pretty sure she wouldn't have made the trip without a detailed plan, but what could that possibly be? She didn't even know where the compound was, much less how to get inside, and even if she did, it was likely Yancy and Jennifer had been moved.

He knew from bitter experience that planning only carried so far. And even if Curt was by some miracle just an investigative reporter, Emm's life was in extreme danger.

As the taxi drove them into the hills above Mexico City to investigate their first target, Emm searched frantically in her handbag for her cell phone.

Curt looked concerned when she leaned down and felt beneath the seat. "What's wrong?"

"I can't find my phone. I didn't have time to activate it for international reception before we left, but I know they can track it, just in case we need the cavalry."

"Don't worry about it; mine's activated," Curt assured her. "I come to the City pretty often."

She'd seen him use it only once and thought it looked pretty antiquated. It was probably a burner phone he'd purchased with cash. Someone at his income level didn't need to do that unless he was worried about being tracked.

Emm's heart began hammering in her chest and they hadn't even reached the compound yet. Dread and fear grew with every hairpin turn. She was very careful with her cell phone, and at the end of the flight she'd checked for it so she could activate it once they reached Mexican airspace. Curt had been up front talking to the crew, so he hadn't seen the suspicious, despairing look she'd sent his way as she realized her phone was gone. She hadn't seen him take it, but the exterior pocket on her purse fit the phone exactly, and she had to tug to remove it. No way it just fell out.

Now, as she'd tested his reaction, he'd responded exactly the way a guilty man trying to keep her on a leash would respond—reassuring her that she didn't need it, rather than wanting her to have her own backup. As they rounded yet another curve, going higher in the hills, Emm only hoped that her last-minute cry for help had been received.

Because it looked like she would need it.

Still, as she spied a hulking red-brick compound on the hillside above, she pretended surprise and rolled down her window. "That's it! How lucky we found it first . . ." *Lucky my ass*, Emm thought . . . yet another block on the towering pile of evidence that indicated Curt Tupperman was on the take from one of the world's most powerful drug lords.

Curt nodded enthusiastically. "Okay, we agree on the script?"

"Yes; you want to do a human interest story on some of the surprisingly positive side effects of the drug trade in Mexico, such as funding village schools and lifting many people out of poverty. I'm your girlfriend, an expert on historic buildings, and I'm cataloguing all the European-style mansions built in the City since the turn of the century. I just wonder if I might have a quick tour." When he nodded enthusiastically, Emm wanted to slap that mendacious grin off his face. To hide her disgust, she rummaged in her purse and touched up her makeup and lipstick, thinking frantically.

She did have a plan, such as it was. If she succeeded in getting a tour of the mansion, she'd watch for any personal items that might belong to Yancy or Jennifer. If she confirmed their presence, she intended to come clean to Arturo Cervantes and offer a huge ransom for both women. Kidnapping was a lucrative side business for many of the cartels after all, so she'd be speaking his language. And when he saw her card and realized she was a Rothschild, he wouldn't doubt her ability to raise the funds, even though she knew it was a lie. But first, she'd demand proof of life . . . and by the time they actually took her to Yancy and Jennifer, she hoped Ross and the cavalry would arrive.

If they didn't get the message in time, well, she'd have to improvise. And she and Yancy would finally see the true Curt Tupperman based on whose side he took.

She was jolted back to the present when the taxi stopped. Curt leaned forward to pay the driver and asked him to wait.

Emm took advantage of the moment. As she put her makeup back, she unzipped a small pocket inside her purse and activated the tiny GPS tracking device she'd purchased, just in case, from Amarillo's only advanced electronics store, prior to her luncheon with Curt.

Then, as Curt opened her door and she got out, the mansion loomed above them, blocking the early morning sun. Suddenly it didn't seem beautiful anymore. Emm wished she'd taken time for one more purchase—a gun—even if logically it could only increase the danger to her since she didn't know how to shoot and didn't have a prayer of winning a gunfight.

The truth was, it would have given her great comfort as that big wrought-iron gate rolled open like the gates of hell.

Back in Amarillo, the task force members were in the process of boarding a big DEA jet saved for complex tactical operations when Abby's phone pinged with a message. She was boarding last, burdened with three laptops, each for a different purpose, and she hadn't heard it ring in the roar of the jet engines.

She struggled up the ramp, glad when a young FBI agent with an improbably cherubic face took the laptops from her as she boarded. His name was Al, as she recalled. He nodded shyly at her thanks, giving her the opportunity to listen to the voice mail she'd just received. Her eyes widened, and she was so excited that she didn't realize everyone else was belted in and ready for takeoff.

Ross called out at her expression, "What is it?"

"When she checked out, Emm left a message for us," she said, going to a different function on her phone. "They didn't find it until this morning, after the janitor cleaned last night. It had fallen beneath the desk." She brought up the scanned attachment to the e-mail and showed it to Ross. The big smile that stretched her angular face, making it almost pretty, was the happiest expression Ross had ever seen her wear.

He looked down at the message and read off for the others: "'Ross and Abby, by the time you read this I'll be in Mexico City. If I meet Arturo Cervantes or his son, I'm going to offer to ransom Yancy and Jennifer and will stall the negotiations as long as I can. Here's the GPS tracker ID I brought.'" And she gave the coordinates to her device, signing it Mercy Magdalena Rothschild.

Ross slumped back in his seat next to Chad, never so relieved as he was at this moment. Nothing would stay a drug dealer's murderous instincts better than an offer of a huge ransom from a Rothschild . . . As they taxied toward takeoff and Abby belted herself in, Chad leaned over to whisper in Ross's ear, "Told you she was a good fit for you. Now she's too valuable to kill. She's one smart cookie."

"And she could be added to the merchandise if things go sour."

Chad agreed, "Exactly. But that's what she wants, isn't it? Maybe she'll find the two women just in time for us to track them all and save the day." When Ross nibbled at his lip, obviously still worried sick, Chad added, deadpan, "She'll be okay. Or as someone said, 'I do not believe in using women in combat. They're too fierce.'"

Ross finally smiled, as Chad had hoped. "Patton? Omar Bradley?"

"Margaret Mead. I've been reading her so I can keep up with Jasmine, and I figure if anyone understands the species, it's a female anthropologist." Chad winked and went back to his own laptop.

Ross looked at Abby, knowing he didn't have to say a thing, but he still held his breath as she opened her laptop and entered the coordinates. The rest of them relaxed just a bit as they took off. Despite his impatience, Ross gave it some time, knowing that even with the plane's advanced satellite technology, the tracker software would take a moment to synch with Emm's location.

But the second they reached cruising altitude and the pilot allowed them to unbelt, he whipped off his seat belt and knelt next to Abby's seat. "Did you pick up the signal?"

Abby looked at the little blip on her screen, and her face was drawn again when she looked back at Ross. "Yes. It's in the hills. Very near the compound and getting closer."

Ross took a deep breath. "Great. Well, at least we have strong evidence of her whereabouts." He went back to tell Chad.

While he talked to Chad, the other task force members discussed the new development. They'd already made contingency plans for a likely hostage situation, but now instead of two potential American citizens, they might be dealing with four . . . Still, there was a potential bright side: Maybe Arturo Cervantes would be distracted with the negotiations enough to give them time to get in place to storm the compound. Maybe this interfering woman all the others had been viewing as a liability would really be an asset.

As they walked inside the compound, Emm stayed true to her role and snapped a picture of the exterior of the building with the camera she'd purchased from a drugstore on the way. The suspicious older man who met them in the courtyard didn't seem to recognize Curt. He snatched her camera away, growling at them. Three more men hovered over them with machine guns at the ready, but they relaxed a bit when Curt gave them his card.

Emm's Spanish wasn't as good as his, but she understood enough to realize Curt was citing a mutual acquaintance and explaining why they'd come. Emm heard her name, "Mercy Magdalena" only, and was relieved he hadn't revealed her surname. The second they heard that, they'd know why she'd really come. For that reason she intended to give her card only to Cervantes senior.

After the underlings gave both Emm and Curt a quick, professional search, finding nothing in the way of weapons, the head guard unhooked the radio on his belt and said something into it in very rapid Spanish Emm couldn't follow. A more measured response came back and, to her vast relief, they were escorted inside the soaring foyer. In other circumstances, Emm would have loved the gorgeous architecture, which was indeed a wonderful blend of European and Mexican elements, but then their two guards, still heavily armed, shoved them inside the study off the foyer.

Finally, Emm came face to face with the monster who'd been behind the kidnapping not just of her family but of so many innocent young girls. She wanted to spit and claw at him, but she instead took a deep, calming breath and waited, like an obedient female, looking around as if fascinated.

Cervantes spent a moment grilling Curt, and then her name arose. Curt nodded at the camera the guard held and said something more. Cervantes relaxed, but only marginally. He gave a commanding look at his guard, who indicated to Emm that she was to open her blouse.

Her eyes widened as she became the focus of all the males in the room, including Curt. When she resisted, he said out of the side of his mouth, "We have to show them we're not wired. Just open your blouse and turn around slowly." The men took her jacket and his, turning them inside out and looking for anything electronic.

Curt lifted his shirt, even pulling his pants up to the knee. Emm's fingers shook but she did as told, wanting to run when she saw all the intense dark eyes fixed on her as if she were prey. Which was all she was to men like these . . . She spun around, looking over the heads of each man as if she were alone, and then she pulled her blouse closed, buttoning it with shaky fingers.

Cervantes's full mouth curved at her obvious unease. He said something to his men, which Emm caught as *"bonita"* and something less flattering. Emm shrank against Curt, as if afraid, which was not a difficult emotion to portray. Next, they demanded to search her purse. Emm had been afraid of that, and she'd done what she could to disguise the tiny tracking device. She handed her purse over. The guard fingered through it, including the envelope bulging with cash. Cervantes lifted an interested eyebrow, but when the guard held the envelope up hopefully, Cervantes shook his head. The disappointed guard put the money back, searching each cavity, finally unzipping the side pocket where Emm had hidden the device. She held her breath, carefully tucking her blouse back in her long skirt so they couldn't see her tension, but the guard's questing fingers moved away as if scalded when he brought up the two tampons she'd put on top of the device. He dropped them back in and handed the purse to the head guard. When Cervantes nodded, they gave the purse back to her.

Finally, Cervantes seemed satisfied. He waved them into chairs, but his four guards took stances on each side of him and behind Curt and Emm. Only then did Cervantes allow Curt to pull out a pad and make a few notes. Emm waited her turn, content to let the clock tick, as Curt conducted an apparent interview. From what she could see, Cervantes did not seem to even know Curt, so maybe she'd been too hard on her former friend.

As Emm half-listened, she couldn't help wondering if Abby and Ross had gotten her SOS. If they hadn't, well, she'd cleaned out her savings account and had plenty of Yankee greenbacks to barter for information and transportation. But for now, the ball was in Curt's court. She was glad to see that Cervantes seemed more relaxed. He gestured with his hands while he described in rapid Spanish what sounded like a traumatic boyhood, but Emm couldn't keep up. She began looking around the study, already cataloguing the locations of windows and another door she could see far down the hallway.

All in all, it was going pretty well so far.

At least they hadn't been shot.

At least Cervantes seemed to buy their ruse.

Or he didn't and was toying with them while he debated whether to cut their hearts out . . .

Deeper inside Mexico City, Yancy had yanked so hard at the handcuffs that her wrist had finally started bleeding. After Arturo had given her the new prescription, she'd only had time for a few doses of her meds before they took her, and now Arturo was so angry with her that he obviously didn't care if she lived or died. He hadn't alerted the Chechens to her illness, or sent the meds along. So she'd been without them, what was it, almost three days?

The wound had been trickling for over an hour, but it also made her wrist slick. Yancy barely paid it any mind because the continued silence down the corridor tormented her. She'd tried calling to Jennifer, but that had only resulted in a vicious blow from one of the Chechen thugs. She'd seen neither the tall, thin, younger Chechen nor the smaller, stout, older one for over twenty-four hours now, and she assumed that was a bad sign.

They were probably arranging transport for them. Or worse . . .

With little else she could do, Yancy began screaming, kicking at the iron bedstead. "I want to see my daughter!" She screamed a good fifteen minutes, until she was almost hoarse, before she got a reaction.

The same thug came back in, using his machine gun butt to slam her in the stomach. Yancy curled up in a ball. She cried out, cradling her stomach with her free arm. A bruise began to bloom. He ran a hand over the tattoo on her spine, but when she shrank away and someone called for him, he reluctantly went back out, tossing a harsh command on the way out.

She didn't speak Russian but got the message: *Shut up or die, bitch.*

Yancy was winded and hurting, but if she gave up, Jennifer would die. She raised herself against the bedstead and slammed her back against it, jolting it against the wall. The old iron headboard was rusted, and for the first time Yancy realized it wasn't stable because the frame bowed under the force.

Experimentally, she slammed against it again. It made a terrible racket, but so far the thug hadn't come back in. The metal bed slat she was latched to bent slightly at the bottom, where rust had eaten at the weld. With renewed vigor, she shifted her weight against it again and again until, with a groan that didn't make too much noise, the slat separated from the headboard. It would have gouged her, but she was expecting it and dodged aside in time.

She slipped the handcuff off the unattached slat and was free.

She stood so fast that the room swam. She was nauseated from the punch, sore everywhere, including between her legs, but she had one thought—get to Jennifer. She ripped the thin blanket off the bed and wrapped it, togalike, around her nudity. She was bleeding, bruised, and smelly, but at the moment she didn't care. She'd get one chance at this . . . She slipped to the door and listened. Somewhere, classical music lilted down the hall, but other than that, she heard no signs of life. Glad they hadn't bothered to lock the door, she eased into the corridor.

She realized she was in an abandoned hotel when she saw all the numbered room doors and the exit sign above a stairwell. As she moved in the general direction in which she'd heard Jennifer screaming, she passed the stairway and tried the door. It was locked; no surprise. The only way out appeared to be the elevator, which was obviously guarded in the lobby.

She listened at each door but heard only silence. From one she heard moans that raised the hairs on her neck, for they sounded sexual in nature. She obviously wasn't the only sex slave here. Instinct screamed at her to run, but she'd never leave without her daughter. Most doors were locked, but one finally yielded, and when she opened it, she saw enough to know exactly where she was. Messy, stained sheets, tawdry underwear flung on the floor, a see-through robe on a hook. A big box of condoms, mostly empty.

She was in a brothel. And a very low-end brothel at that . . . They didn't intend to move her. They'd already sold her. She was too old, and too much trouble, so they'd cut their losses.

If she didn't find Jennifer, and fast, she'd only leave this place in a body bag and Jennifer, still young and valuable, would disappear forever.

CHAPTER 14

On the hills outside the City, inside the compound's luxurious study, Emm Rothschild watched the lively way Arturo Cervantes, Mexico's oldest and most ruthless drug lord, conveyed his story. He'd been wary at first of answering questions in any depth, but Curt, as a seasoned, nationally known reporter, had interviewed princes and popes. Adding a wary drug lord to the list wasn't much of a challenge.

Emm read over his shoulder and saw that he was, indeed, making copious notes that would aid in his story. Nothing incriminating; more of the history of Arturo Cervantes and how he did, indeed, support not just an army of men but their families. He'd put more than one poor boy through private school and into university.

The morning waned into afternoon as Curt's pad grew full. A waiter brought tea and scones and finger sandwiches. Emm would have laughed at the pretension if she hadn't been so tense. She was too nervous to be hungry, but she forced herself to eat, not knowing when she'd get the opportunity again. The clock struck five p.m. as Cervantes obviously grew restless. Curt thanked him and then led Emm forward. Emm heard something about *"casa"* and more that sounded like her credentials.

Cervantes's intense stare fixed on her. Emm's skin crawled at the way he looked her up and down. She saw the appetite in his eyes, and it had nothing to do with food. But she only accepted the camera they finally returned to her after a direct order from Cervantes. Then he swept his arm before them, and Emm realized the great man intended to give her the grand tour himself. She gave a pleading look to Curt and he moved to follow them, but Cervantes made a staying move with his hand and two guards blocked Curt. Ruefully, he sat back down in his chair, shrugging at her slightly.

She knew that look—*your idea. Good luck* . . .

Emm's heart skipped a beat, but she had little choice, given everything that was at stake. She followed as he showed her around the ground floor, her shoulder purse wrapped securely over her shoulder. She found herself oohing and aahing at the huge house, which looked like something from the Mexican version of *House Beautiful*. She saw several flower arrangements, drooping a bit now, that looked like a style Yancy favored, but that was hardly conclusive. In the kitchen, however, she saw a recipe for *tres leches* flan that someone had pinned to a board on the refrigerator. While Emm stalled, pretending to focus the camera on the long granite kitchen counter, in reality she was reading the handwritten notes through the lens. Someone had quadrupled the recipe and calculated the new ingredients by hand. Her heart pounded against her ribs, for she recognized that untidy scrawl. Yancy's handwriting was horrid and this looked exactly the same, with the backward slanted *l*s and *t*s. Still, it wasn't definitive.

But when Cervantes led her upstairs, he bypassed his room, allowing her to look into the second one very close to his. She peeked inside, seeing the feminine decor and the makeup vanity. She lifted the camera, rhapsodizing in her schoolgirl Spanish that the room was lovely. She pointed—could she see inside? He hesitated but let her in. Attached was a bathroom and Emm said, *"Baño?"* and made an embarrassed face. He eyed her carefully, shrugged, and gave her a regal nod of acceptance.

She went inside and did actually use the facility, but when she turned on the water to disguise the noise, she did a quick search of the medicine cabinet above. Nothing distinctive except . . . She pulled the pill bottle out. It had Cervantes's name on it, but then she read the name of the medication.

Effluenatasis. Yancy's new hemophilia drug, rare in Mexico City, rare even in the US, it was so new . . . Proof as definitive as she could want.

Torn between relief and fear, she was putting the bottle back when the door opened gently behind her. Arturo Cervantes watched her close the medicine cabinet. He said in broken but distinguishable English, *"Sí,* I thought so. She no here." He smiled, his grin bright and toothy in the vanity lights.

Glad somehow that the charade was over, Emm took the card she'd saved in her pocket and offered it to him. He glanced down, obviously unsurprised at the name. She offered her hand as the overture to what she knew would be very tense, and very critical, negotiations. Not just Yancy and Jennifer were in danger now. So was she . . . "Mercy Magdalena . . . Rothschild. Yancy's *hermana. Mucho gusto.*"

Back in town, Yancy shook off her horror at where she was and what it meant and plunged inside the next open door. To her relief, there were clothes hanging inside. Slutty clothes, but she was used to that. She didn't risk pulling on underwear, but the tight fake leather skirt and tank top were better than a blanket. Even the stiletto shoes fit, but she needed to be light on her feet, so she kicked them off and looked for something easier to walk in. There was nothing. With every move the handcuffs rattled, and she knew that no matter how she tried to disguise them, they'd give her away.

She sat down, pulling at the one still latched around her wrist. Her skin was slick with blood. She bit her lip as the wound opened further. But she kept twisting her wrist from side to side, pulling . . . pulling . . . and finally her thin wrist slipped free. She wanted to toss the cuff across the room but instead wrapped it in a pillow case from the bed and shoved it as far beneath the bed on the dirty carpet as she could reach.

She rummaged through the rest of the room and to her delight found a black lace mantilla. In a Catholic country, even prostitutes went to Mass; they had plenty of reason to cover their heads, too. She pulled it down over her face and anchored it to her blouse with a couple of pins to keep it in place. She blinked, her eyes adjusting, but finally she could see through the heavy lace well enough to brave the corridor again.

She despaired as she tried more doors, certain she was already past the room where Jennifer had lain screaming, but then she heard the elevator ping and ducked inside the last empty room. She cracked the door and watched two Mexicans dressed like gang members pass. One carried a small automatic pistol, and they eyed both ends of the corridor warily, as if they didn't want anyone to see what they did next. The other used a key to open one of the locked doors across the hall. A rustling of what sounded like sheets, and then the taller one exited with a bundle of sheets over his shoulder. As he passed, Yancy saw long blonde hair swinging limply almost to the floor.

She had to cover her mouth and bite her palm to stifle her own groan so she could listen.

If she'd had any doubt about who it was, the brief conversation between the Mexicans settled it. "What do we do with the body?"

"Same quarry as usual."

"What happened?"

"The Chechens gave her drugs to shut her up and she used them all. Waste of a pretty *mujer*. Tomás was finished with her and said I could have her next."

And then they were in the elevator, leaving Yancy with a buzzing in her ears and, finally, no more fight. She slipped down the wall to the filthy carpet and buried her face in her knees, sobbing. Uncaring that the sounds she made could bring someone to investigate.

Then blood dripped down her arm to the floor. She used the blanket to dab at it, but it only welled up again. It wasn't a huge wound, but she knew from past experience that she needed a specialized shot from a hospital to stop it. Within a day or two, she'd be past the point of no return.

Her eyes hazed over as the ugly red tinted her world. Red blood, red roses in the garden, her red lips as she kissed a man with a greedy, grasping red tongue, hungry for more, always more . . . Her grief hardened into a cold, pure hatred.

Arturo.

He'd done this to them. Kidnapped her, subjected her to his filthy abuse for months on end, letting his son brutalize Jennifer and turn her into an addict too weak to keep fighting to live.

Everyone was terrified of him. But she wasn't. Not any longer. Because now he had nothing to threaten her with. If she didn't get medical attention soon, she'd be dead in a day or two anyway, and she wasn't sure she cared anymore.

No one was coming. She was alone.

What did she have to lose? She went to the scummy sink, the only plumbing in the tiny room, and turned on the faucet, scrubbing away the residue of tears and blood from the last few days. Her mouth was sore and split, but she slathered on the red lipstick she found there to cover it. Then she used a bit of powder to disguise the bruise on her cheek. She washed between her legs and under her arms, spraying on a heavy dose of perfume. Then, wrapping the mantilla more closely about her face, she slipped into the stilettos and down the hall to the elevator, wearing a black jacket over the wound to disguise the blood.

She'd used her feminine wiles for many months to survive.

She'd only have to use them a few hours longer. . . .

On the threshold of the bathroom, Arturo Cervantes shook Emm's hand, and if she'd been outside looking in, she would have been bemused at this bizarre propriety between a murderous drug lord and a supposedly pampered society girl. But she was all too involved, and scared right down to her designer pumps. Even her quirky sense of humor couldn't find anything funny in this scenario. Especially when he pocketed the card and smiled. A smile that reminded Emm of a knife balanced on its tip, ready to cut or clatter away, depending upon the next fifteen minutes—and her deceit and negotiation skills. She skirted past him as she obeyed Arturo's still polite gesture, indicating she should precede him down the stairs. Emm was eager to reach the study, to have Curt's company again. What she had to say now would take fluency on both sides.

And a prayer. And luck. Voicing the soundless prayer, and glad she still had her grandma's four leaf clover, Emm entered the study. Shadows were gathering outside, so they'd been here most of the day. Surely time enough for Ross to arrive if he'd taken an agency jet.

If he'd received her message.

At the secure government portion of the enormous airport in Mexico City, while workers unloaded all the equipment, Chad and the other task force leads gathered around the Mexican Marine general who'd been tapped to spearhead the raid.

Ross watched as Chad explained the new wrinkle. The general brigadier, who sported four silver stars and a gold eagle insignia, scowled but bit off orders to his subordinate. Ross's Spanish wasn't as fluent as Chad's, but he thought he understood well enough that the general was telling his men to take the infrared imaging equipment so they could try to figure out where each person was inside the compound. Their spotters had confirmed that Curt and Emm had arrived in the morning, in a cab that still waited outside the gates.

Ross was itching to get started, but he tamped down his impatience, well aware he was a guest in another country. He was just happy they'd let him keep his guns, even if they inspected them carefully and noted what he carried, including model and ID numbers, in a file. They'd done the same with all their weapons. With the virulent drug wars in Mexico, too often lost or seized weapons ended up in the hands of the cartels, so he couldn't blame the authorities for being extra cautious.

When the general was finished, Chad came over and briefed them. "We're going in three vehicles—two panel vans with the lead truck armored. The road has a sharp ess curve right before the compound, and we're going to shut off our lights and coast until we stop probably a quarter mile away. We'll have to hoof it up the hillside from there, but it's our only chance to surround the place unseen. They have state-of-the-art security beginning right past that curve, so once we crest the hill, we're committed and have to move quickly. I asked about interrupting their power, but the general says Cervantes likely has generator backups, so it wouldn't gain us much and would probably alert them. We'll just do it as a diversion as we move in."

Ross cleared his throat, his heart hammering. "And Emm? How are we going to protect her?"

Chad looked a bit uncomfortable. "She's your responsibility," he said. "They've been planning this op for weeks and one woman, no matter who she is, may have to be expendable if Cervantes tries to use her as a shield." Chad offered tablets to Ross and the others. "But he did give us a schematic of the mansion, and they've had the place under surveillance, too. He says this exterior wall—" Chad zoomed in on part of the ground-floor plan—"is the study where Cervantes conducts most of his business. If the infrared imaging shows several bodies in that room, we can assume that's where he's holding Emm and Tupperman and make one of our entries there at the same time the marines go in the front and rear."

Chad looked at each of the task force leads from the various agencies. "Remember, assuming we get the chance to do a search, our priority is any information we can get on who the splinter groups are back home. Who heads them, how the drugs and women are being smuggled, the trail of funds—"

"Particularly look for the names of Curt Tupperman and Brett Umarov," Ross inserted.

They nodded, now all grim professionals. Even Rosemary wore the new body armor, though she looked thinner still in the heavy equipment, like a model playing soldier.

Ross hesitated, knowing Chad might not like him butting in, but he had to do this. For Emm . . . And Chad was so new to the task force, he probably hadn't had time to get fully up to speed.

He pulled out a file from his pack and handed around pictures of Emm, Yancy, and Jennifer. In happier times, true, but it would be enough to identify them. "Here are pics of the hostages. The two Russell women, if they're here, have probably undergone months of abuse, so we need to be ready with medical attention."

Rosemary nodded at her medic. He held up his bag and tapped the mike in his ear. "Just say the word and I'll storm up the hillside." He'd been instructed to hold back until summoned as he wasn't a field operative or combat specialist.

Almost as an afterthought, Ross added a stock photo of Curt. "Tupperman, we think, is one of their top American contacts, but we're not sure. Just take him into custody, but don't trust him. We'll sort it out after we have the situation secure."

They all nodded and got into their assigned transports.

Chad had pleaded for, and received, permission for him and Ross to ride in the front armored truck. As they began the long trip from the airport, Ross was relieved to get a text from Abby, who was in the rear panel van, saying that the tracker was still live and hadn't moved. The over-the-counter electronic device wasn't sensitive enough to pinpoint Emm's exact location, but Abby knew she was still at the compound.

Inside the study in the compound, Emm forced herself to meet Cervantes's obsidian eyes. They'd turned on all the lights as it was now dark outside. Curt was translating, as needed, between the two of them. The thought crossed her mind that he might censor some of what she said for his benefit, but she had little choice but to trust him at this point; he was the only ally she had.

She carefully formulated the words she'd mentally rehearsed. "Yancy is my sister, as I said. Half sister, but I love her dearly and she's my only sibling. I've already cleared this with my father—" she was getting pretty good at lying, Emm thought, for her voice didn't even falter—"and we're prepared to pay richly to get her and Jennifer back."

Cervantes snapped something. Curt paled slightly but translated,

"He wants to know why he should trust anything you say when you invaded his home under false pretenses."

Emm pulled the envelope from her bag. "A deposit in good faith. Fifteen grand." She extended it and one of the guards took it, counting the money. "If he'll allow me to confirm Yancy and Jennifer are okay, to see them with my own eyes, I'll contact my father and have him wire half of whatever ransom we all agree on to the account of his preference. We promise not to go to the police or any other agency, either here or in the States. Once we have Yancy and Jennifer safe, that will be the end of it. We'll arrange our own transport out of the country, and when we've boarded the plane, my father will wire the other half."

As he listened to Cervantes, who used his hands again as he talked, Curt sighed. "The women are very valuable. Especially the younger one." He listened, swallowed, and added, as Cervantes looked Emm up and down, "And if he adds you to his inventory, you won't be a threat and he'll still make a lot of money."

Emm had been ready for this one. "He can do that, but my father and grandfather know where I am." Another lie. There had been no time, and Emm barely knew the wealthy side of the family. "My great-uncle has many businesses in Latin America and knows many people. Including governors and other business owners. Yancy is not a Rothschild by birth, so they looked the other way. But I am . . ." Emm lifted her chin as that gaze raked her again, hoping, for once in her life, that she looked as regal and snotty as people always said.

Cervantes laughed and made an aside to his men. Curt looked away rather than translate. Emm said through her teeth, "What did he say?"

Curt muttered, "He said all women are alike between the legs. And he thinks you just haven't been mounted enough."

Cold sweat broke out on Emm's brow, but she lifted her chin a bit higher and said coolly, "And you can tell him that despite the insult, he needs to recall that the Rothschilds have made billions with our business acumen. We deal fairly with partners. He can check that independently if he likes, along with this—Mayer Rothschild, who founded our banking dynasty in the late seventeen hundreds, was orphaned at twelve and grew up in the ghetto. He, like Señor Cervantes, was a self-made man. His five sons took his teachings around the globe, leading to the empire we have today in finance, publishing, wines, and many other ventures. My grandfather would respect a man of Señor Cervantes's determination and ability, as do I. I am not afraid . . . and I've dealt with him truly and fairly. But no matter what, I love my sister and niece very much. I am resolved to leave Mexico only with my sister and niece safe beside me. I can be Señor Cervantes's asset—or a very big liability." Emm bowed her head before the despicable man in a gesture of both respect and challenge. Wouldn't Yancy be proud of her desperate new ability to bluff? They played Texas Hold'em together when they could, and Yancy usually beat the socks off her . . . once quite literally when she'd demanded Emm's Christmas socks as part of her winnings.

She was relieved when Curt finally said, "How much? He wants to know how much you offer."

Yancy got to the lobby easily enough, but as she'd feared, it was full of guards. And also as she feared, it wasn't easy to exit. When the elevator pinged, she peeked outside the still opening elevator door. A scowling guard started toward her, so she pushed the close button on the elevator and tried the lowest button. Nothing happened, so she figured the basement level was off limits and pressed the fourth-floor button again, trying not to think of Jennifer, of somehow saving her body from being thrown on top of many others like waste in some rock pile. She held grief at bay only with cool calculation.

This entire disgusting building was based on a very tawdry form of free enterprise, but prostitution had always been about money. Therefore, if she wanted to leave in one piece, she needed to be on the arm of one of the johns who funded this business. Part of the enterprise, not an escapee.

She went back to the room she'd entered before and left the door cracked so she could hear better. She also took the time to do a more thorough search, hoping she might find some sort of a weapon. Thirty minutes later, she heard a door open down the corridor and a male voice. She'd found a long and sharp nail file of sturdy steel, but it would be pathetic against Arturo's army.

Still, she stuck the file in her jacket pocket and sashayed out into the corridor. She caught up with the businessman in a wrinkled suit who had pressed the elevator button. He looked at her nervously, shying away a bit, but Yancy only ran her hand down his arm and then down his hip. She lifted the veil and widened her lovely green eyes. He stared into them, fascinated.

"I'll give you whatever you want if you'll let me leave with you in your car," she whispered seductively, still caressing. "I am one of the most popular girls here."

She felt the frisson that went through him, but he looked around uncertainly. "I have no more money."

"I don't want money. I want to go to—" and she named the main street near the compound. When he still hesitated, her hand drifted closer to his groin. She brought his hand to her firm breast.

"That's all? I want . . ." and he named several disgusting acts.

Yancy lowered her veil again but nodded to hide her revulsion.

This time, when she entered the lobby, she was latched onto the arm of one of the brothel's best clients, who had his own arm around her, his free hand caressing her breast. They whispered to each other as they slowly made their way to the exit.

She heard the guards debating her identity as they passed and held her breath as her john opened the front door, but they exited unmolested. Then she was seated in a nice Lincoln sedan and driving through very crowded streets toward the compound.

They hadn't gone far when the john pulled to an empty side street and stopped. He demanded a blow job. Yancy hesitated, eyeing the keys. She moved closer to him on the wide bench seat, as if to comply, but she whipped the nail file from her jacket pocket and held it to his carotid artery, leaning over him as if to whisper sweet nothings.

Instead, she said, "Get out or I swear I'll give you a mark to remember me by. You disgust me. Do you know some of the girls in that place have been kidnapped?" She pressed the sharp edge into his throat. Swallowing harshly, he fumbled for the door. He tried to grab the keys at the last minute, but she cut his neck enough for him to bleed. He bleated and reared his head away. Blood dripped onto his shirt and he screamed, covering his scratch. But his gaze fell to the blood flowing now from beneath her black sleeve. He looked at his hand, at the few dots of his own blood, then back at her wound. His expression changed from anger to horror as he realized it wasn't his blood. Frantically, he reached for the car door and fell onto the pavement outside.

She drove off, well aware that the first thing he'd do was call the police and report his car stolen. Good. She hoped he made all the papers when he described who took the car. Even better, she always liked a police escort when she was going to kill drug dealers . . . Yancy laughed, but strangely her voice sounded broken. However, she still had the presence of mind to pull over long enough to search the car. She found a thick wad of napkins and tied them around her wrist as she drove with her free hand. It wouldn't stop the blood but would help with the mess.

The center of attention in the luxurious study, Emm tried a low number first, like a true monied Rothschild. "One hundred thousand."

Cervantes scoffed a laugh and bit off a nasty remark. Curt said, "He can make that on Jennifer in six months. He wants five years' worth of revenue or he isn't interested."

Emm did some quick calculations. "He wants a million just for Jennifer?"

The drug lord smiled broadly. His English was apparently good enough when it came to hard, cold Yankee dollars. He nodded. *"Sí."*

The cold sweat had extended to Emm's hands, but she only said coolly, "And for Yancy?"

Curt interpreted. "Half that. Take it or leave it."

Together, that would be 1.5 million; a lot of money even for a Rothschild heir. Emm debated negotiating longer to give Ross more time, but the truth was she was frantic to see Yancy and Jennifer. She needed to start that process. There was something about Cervantes's attitude that made her uneasy, aside from his obvious lack of scruples. He was hiding something.

"Very well. But I'll only call for the funds once I see for myself that Yancy and Jennifer are okay. Are they here?" She watched his response very closely.

He shrugged, pulled out his cell phone, and made a call. He said something hesitant and indistinguishable, but it sounded like Russian. Emm and Curt exchanged a look.

So it was true. He was working with Chechen gangsters.

Cervantes listened. He scowled at the response, gave one harsh command, and hung up abruptly. He stood, stretching, and bit off an order to his lieutenant. The gun lowered.

"They'll be brought to you shortly," the lieutenant said in English, and Emm realized he'd understood every word she and Curt had exchanged. "While we wait, Señor Cervantes would invite you to dine with him." He listened to Cervantes's genial description of the menu and smiled at Emm. "Argentinean beef. Rare."

A delaying tactic? Emm wasn't sure she could eat a bite, but she only nodded graciously, aware she had to be true to the role she'd created. "You're having Yancy and Jennifer brought here?"

Cervantes nodded, but she wasn't sure she believed him. She looked outside. The moon was rising. She'd forgotten her watch and had no idea of the time. Except that it was late.

And getting later . . . fast.

Where was Ross?

Outside on the hillside, Mexican Marines, heavily weaponized in body armor and guns, snaked up the slope until they could peek above it. Further down, the US agents remained crouched and waiting for their okay to advance.

Chad held a lethal tactical shotgun, the barrel too short to be legal for anyone other than law enforcement, and packed a machine pistol on one shoulder, his pistol on his hip. Ross held his issue weapon at the ready, with his custom .45 loaded and waiting in his holster.

The Mexican Marine captain leading the squadron of elite special forces lifted his fist and began counting, his fingers rising in a countdown. One, two, three . . . he was reaching for four when car lights split the ess curve.

They all had to go flat as a Lincoln rounded the last dogleg. Ross and Chad crawled up the slope, careful to keep their heads as low as possible. The car drew to a stop in front of the compound, blocking the entrance. A veiled woman wearing spike heels, dressed like a hooker, got out to meet the angry guard who exited to berate her for blocking the driveway. She sashayed to meet him, her hips swinging, not intimidated when he poked her in the stomach with a machine gun. She said something to him they couldn't hear, dropping the veil. More guards poured out as every exterior floodlight snapped on.

The marines and Texans all cursed and ducked down at the same time. They waited a moment, but the loud, excited exchange indicated the guards were too involved, and probably blinded by the lights, to see them. They peeked over the slope again. The woman advanced into the light, saying something, and offered a small and shiny object that looked short but sharp, from her pocket as they frisked her. The oldest guard used his radio and got an immediate response. They grabbed her arm to force her inside the gate.

She stumbled, and Ross caught her profile illuminated in the bright lights. "Holy shit, it's Yancy Russell," he hissed to Chad. Chad passed the word to their colleagues and the marines. A brief conference ensued on whether to delay the raid or not. They all looked down the slope at the general, who had maps and radios spread on the hood of the armored truck, which they'd parked beneath a huge tree. Abby stood next to him, speaking into a phone, and Ross realized she was trying to get drone assistance for the infrared imaging. They hadn't been able to get close enough to the structure to use the equipment they'd brought, so if they invaded now they'd be going in blind. Because she was a consultant, they hadn't allowed her near the tactical side of the operation, but they wanted her there for data collection at the end.

But the general and his men were growing impatient. . . .

As they debated, Ross caught something shiny that looked black in the lights as Yancy was yanked inside. It was coming from her wrist, dribbling behind her in thick dollops on the pavement. "Shit, she's bleeding," he whispered to Chad. "She has hemophilia. Emm will be frantic." He gave his friend a pleading look. "We have to go. Now, before they have time to get organized. The minute Emm sees her bleeding, all hell will break loose. Looks like Jennifer isn't with her."

Nodding his agreement, Chad went down to talk to the general. The ensuing seconds were the longest of Ross's life; he tensed to top the slope by himself if need be but restrained himself, waiting for the general's answer. Acting on his own would only get both him and Emm killed . . . maybe Chad and Yancy, too.

Besides, he'd resigned as task force chief. This wasn't his call.

CHAPTER 15

Inside the study, Emm watched as all hell seemed to break loose. A crackle came from the radio. Something about *"mujer Yanqui."* And then, blessedly, Emm heard Yancy's name. With a cry, she leaped to her feet.

Cervantes bit out an order and one of the guards yanked her back down, pressing her in the side with his machine gun. She subsided but had to bite her lip until it bled to contain herself. However, the study door was still ajar, and she could see the large foyer when the door was thrown open.

Out of the corner of her eye, she saw Curt reach for his pocket. The guards were all focused on the door, so she was the only one who saw him press a button on his cell phone. Their eyes locked briefly.

She didn't need to see any more to know he was messaging someone. His gaze flickered back to watch the drama in the foyer, but not fast enough, and she knew him well enough to read his eyes. As usual, he was playing both ends against the middle. He'd played along only until he could set his own agenda in motion. What that was she had no idea, because none of these men seemed to recognize him. Had he used an assumed name?

Feeling sick to her stomach, with the gun still poking her, Emm could only watch and wait, every instinct in her body screaming at her to run to Yancy's aid.

Guards poured in first; then the oldest guard, obviously the shift leader outside, dragged a tall woman in black inside the door, slamming it shut. She flipped her long, dirty, tangled blonde hair over her shoulder and turned to face Cervantes.

"Yancy," Emm screamed.

Yancy turned toward the sound of her voice, so she wasn't ready for the fist that slammed into her cheek. She went sprawling.

Cervantes shook his sore hand and bit off a curse at the woman at his feet, kicking her for good measure. Yancy sat up, spitting a retort Emm couldn't catch, but it was obviously virulent. She rose to her knees, reaching for the pistol in the belt of the guard nearest her, but he dodged away, kicking at her hand. Yancy cried out, cradling it, and they all saw the dripping blood.

Even the gun poking her wasn't enough to stop Emm then. She shoved the guard away, leaped to her feet, and ran toward the door.

As the guard lifted his weapon to fire at her back, the lights in the entire building went out. At the same time they all heard a small explosion coming from the basement area. For a split second, total stupefied silence reigned as the room was pitched into darkness.

There was a macabre flash, and everyone dodged away from the brilliant, disorienting light. As the emergency generators kicked on, shattering glass, splintering wood, and small explosions seemed to rock the entire huge house from every direction.

Then the guards were shooting at doors and windows. Half-blinded from what she realized must be flash-bang grenades, Emm groped into the hallway far enough to put her arms around Yancy, and hold her tight as she pulled her sister flat against the cold floor. Yancy began sobbing, but only Emm knew it because pandemonium ruled as the gunfire intensified.

Armed and armored soldiers seemed to pour inside from every opening. Arturo's huge army suddenly seemed very small. Guards began falling. Emm lifted her head; even over the cacophony she heard a familiar voice.

"Emm!" It was Ross. He held a handgun at the ready and shot a drug dealer in the arm who was aiming at the two women. The drug dealer's machine gun dropped to the marble floor as his elbow splintered through his forearm, blood spurting. He fell, screaming.

Emm barely noticed. She smiled brilliantly in Ross's direction, still blinking, trying to focus. "I knew you'd come," she said simply, still sheltering Yancy under one arm. But she'd raised herself high enough that she was in the line of fire. A bullet flew past her, singeing her scalp and leaving a terrible pain in her head and a viscious ringing in her ears. She shook her head, trying to clear them.

Ross crouched and fought his way toward her, stepping over several fallen men, two guards and one marine, returning fire from several angles as he came.

The next thing Emm knew, she was being jerked from the floor, providing a human shield for Arturo Cervantes as he backed her up the stairs, a .357 pistol pointed upward at her side at a lethal angle that led straight to her heart. She tried to fight, but the pistol prodded harder, and her head felt like it was going to come off her shoulders, so she went limp and let herself be pulled. Blood oozed from the graze, trickling down the side of her head and face.

Ross froze. Chad Foster came in behind him so fast he bumped into him. Ross was so tense he barely moved at the impact, but he had enough presence of mind to press Chad's raised shotgun toward the floor.

The gunfire was sputtering off as more armed marines rounded up the guards. Several had locked themselves in the study and shot through the door at their enemies, but the outcome was inevitable.

To everyone but Arturo Cervantes. He had Emm almost to the landing now.

Ross's gaze flickered to the side toward the DEA lead agent, who was crouched behind the curve of the stairway, aiming carefully at Cervantes's head.

But Cervantes had survived in a brutal world so long partly because of his tactical ability. He pulled Emm flat over him on the upper landing, obviously expecting an assault from his blind spot. The shots went well above his head, pocking the plaster walls. And then, with his brutal peasant's strength, Cervantes half-crawled, half-slithered, pulling Emm's light weight with him until he could stand, around the shield of the walled corridor.

Half the force stormed up the stairs after him, Ross in the lead. As Ross rounded the corner, Cervantes landed a lucky shot as he slammed his bedroom door. Ross took the slug in his helmet. They heard a hydraulic humming and what sounded like a very sturdy bolt shooting home.

Ross dropped to one knee as stars swam and his ears rang. For a moment, he swayed, about to pass out; then a familiar hand clutched his shoulder. Chad stooped to check on him, testing the dent in the helmet and drawing a deep breath of relief when his finger couldn't go all the way through.

"Give it a minute," he said loudly into Ross's ear. "Thank God it was only a .357."

A minute? Emm doesn't have a minute, Ross wanted to say, still struggling to stay conscious.

The next few minutes would have to be explained to him later.

As the marine captain, Rosemary, and the head of the DEA reached the bedroom door, Rosemary shot several times at the latch, and both men kicked the door, but they winced and backed away, nursing sore toes. The marine captain compressed all his considerable weight in one huge assault on the door, but it didn't budge a millimeter. He rubbed his shoulder.

The DEA chief bent to check out the lock and shook his head grimly. "It's reinforced steel. It must have dropped from the ceiling. We'll need a torch."

Rosemary said, "Surely he's trapped . . . Who has a floor plan?"

The captain, who obviously spoke some English, pulled a paper blowup from a zippered pouch. They all huddled over it.

Ross's ears were still ringing, but his gaze had cleared enough that he saw one of the FBI agents run up from the foyer. He said something to Chad that Ross couldn't hear. Chad ran back down the stairs.

Ross hauled himself to his feet, holding on to the wall, willing the deafness and nausea to recede. He painfully moved forward to appraise the door, realizing what was wrong with one glance. He said sharply, though he barely heard his own words, "We need to regroup and send someone to man every upper-floor window and possible egress!"

The marine captain was already on his radio.

Taking a deep breath, Ross was girding himself for what looked like a hostage scenario with Emm as the hostage, when he realized Chad was assessing something downstairs. Ross slowly walked back to the landing, still unsteady, and saw Chad kneeling next to a stretcher. Even from here, that long blonde hair was a ghastly contrast to the blood still dripping onto the expensive marble. He saw Chad leaning over Yancy, listening, as the medic set up a small portable drip into Yancy's wounded wrist.

He made it down the stairs, though he was still dizzy and almost lost his footing twice. He had to hold on to the banister. Slowly, the nausea was subsiding, but it was a good thing he hadn't eaten in over twelve hours. He made it to Yancy's side and knelt next to her, seeing that she was clutching Chad's arm with her bloodied hand. He moved closer, trying to hear, too, and caught, "Escape ... hatch. Bathtub, master ... bedroom."

Chad leaped to his feet, obviously intending to run upstairs to warn the others, but Yancy tugged at his pants leg. He knelt down to her again.

She was struggling for words because the medic had put her on painkillers and a fluid drip to help with blood loss. The man looked away when Ross tried to meet his eyes. Ross had seen that look from medical personnel before—they had to get her to a hospital, quick. He knew enough about hemophilia to realize the medic wouldn't have anything to help in his field kit, and that if she'd been bleeding for a day or two, she needed a shot and probably a liquid drip of the latest hemophilia med or it might be too late to stop the bleeding at all.

Chad knelt down next to her again. Ross leaned in.

"Outside ... big oak tree. Tunnel leads there. Stop him." Her voice broke, and tears seeped into her dirty blonde hair. "He killed my ... daughter." And then she couldn't talk anymore as the drugs took her.

Big oak tree? Holy crap, that was where Abby and the general were waiting.

Ross teetered where he stood, torn between storming outside and staying upstairs to see if they could somehow break in. But he suspected Cervantes would bolt like the rat he was, and he was taking Emm with him. He and Chad exchanged a look. Chad ran for the door, reaching for his radio, but it was missing from his belt. He cursed, taking the exterior steps in three strides. Ross followed. They both skirted the long road, aiming straight for the steep hillside. They looked around for backup as they ran, but the few of their men outside were guarding doors and windows as instructed, and gunfire still peppered occasionally from all quarters.

They were on their own.

Emm's headache had died down a little, leaving room for fear to take its place. But she knew better than to show it. Every time she stumbled or faltered, Cervantes pushed her between the shoulder blades with the pistol. They were in a dimly lit cavity Emm figured led outside somewhere because the curving stairs seemed to plunge forever into darkness. Lights lined the walls, but they weren't bright enough to illuminate much more than the steps, so she had no idea where they were going.

She knew Ross was frantically looking for her, and she was still worried about Yancy. At the moment, however, survival was her only priority. To keep her sanity, she concentrated on one step at a time. She placed each foot carefully, holding on to the thin metal railing as she went.

Following closely behind her, the gun still pressed into her ribs, Cervantes growled into his radio. Static, and then Russian voices answered.

Emm couldn't understand a thing, but she knew if he succeeded in using her as a shield and got away, she was dead. Her headache was clearing. The blood had stopped, though she felt stiffness on one side of her face and head.

As she walked—slowly, as it still hurt—she knew, Ross or no Ross, she had to make a move before she let Cervantes take her. It was obvious what he did with kidnapped American women.

Outside, Ross ran, his steps firmer as he went. He also checked his clip. Three shots left. He switched it with his full one, saying a prayer for Emm as he ran. He'd heard sirens earlier and saw several emergency vehicles blocking the gate. As he swerved past them, he was relieved to see Yancy's stretcher being loaded into one of them. Good. She'd be at the hospital before they'd finished mopping up.

The hillside was littered with scrub and rocks that pricked them even through the armor, but he and Chad still went prone, poking their heads up while they assessed the scene below. They both bit off a curse at what they saw. "Goddammit, why didn't I prepare for this contingency?" Chad groaned.

Below, the general and Abby were being prodded at gunpoint toward a Jeep that had obviously come cross-country in the dark. Three men held machine guns on them, two of them in wrinkled but expensive suits that shone with silk fibers even in the bright moonlight. The third one was a younger Latino who resembled Cervantes.

"That's Tomás Cervantes. We were so damn busy rounding up the father, we forgot about the son," Ross bit off quietly.

Abby and the general were both bound with zip ties, their wrists in front. By the looks of him, the general had been roughed up. His holster was empty. Abby's shirt was missing a couple of buttons at the top and her hair was a bit mussed, but other than that, she looked as calm and rational as usual.

When Tomás surveyed the hillside, his head turning in their direction, they both ducked back down. Chad tried his cell phone several times, then cursed and powered it off again. "No one's live again yet—they're still fighting. If we do this, it's just the two of us."

Ross nodded grimly. "I can't ask you to go in without backup, but I have no choice. She's my woman, Chad."

Chad grinned, his teeth white against the black powder and grime on his angular features. "I'm just happy to hear those words from you. 'Bout damn time. Besides, one Ranger, one riot, right? We can handle some drug-dealer scum between the two of us." Chad peeked back over the slope, watching Abby. She was saying something they couldn't hear, very calmly, to Tomás, her Spanish apparently fluent. He lifted the butt of his machine gun as if to clout her, but when she steadily met his eyes, he dropped the gun and used his voice instead.

Ross smiled, amused even in these extreme circumstances. "Atta girl... We time this right and we'll have backup." They visually searched every square inch of ground around the oak tree, but if there was a tunnel, it was very well hidden.

Ross switched to watching Tomás and saw that he was now focused intently on a hillock of raised dirt and grass next to the tree. Ross inched back up, resting his Ed Brown, with its night sight, on the slope to steady his aim as he focused on that spot, too.

Tension rippled through him like an electrical current as the two Chechens shoved the general roughly into the back of the Jeep. They were obviously expecting their leader any moment.

Emm... come on, baby. Show yourself. Your sister's safe. Mission accomplished. Time to wrap up these assholes.

Inside the dank, dark cavity, Emm's questing toes finally felt something mushy. Ground. She stopped abruptly, disoriented, for the lighting was even dimmer here. The pistol pressed into her back again, and she almost turned on Cervantes, but the time wasn't yet right. She moved forward slowly, carefully, following the impatient hand that gestured to the side. Finally, she saw the ladder attached to the tunnel and began to climb. She heard a rush of air and knew he must have released a latch because a widening opening appeared above her head, starlight and even a smiling bright moon peering down.

She climbed faster, hoping, praying Ross and Chad were on the other side of that hatch.

As Chad and Ross watched, Tomás jerked his head at the two Chechens and then went to stand at the side of the tree, tensely staring down. The Chechens poked Abby in the ribs, but she was an experienced operative and knew better than to get into that car, especially when the grounds were filled with US agents. She said something in Spanish, but they answered in Russian, poking her harder in the ribs with their machine gun barrels, hard enough to send her off balance as they tried to force her into the Jeep.

"I'll take the tall guy in the suit," Chad whispered.

"I'll take Tomás," Ross said. If he was right that Abby was about to make a move, she was closest to the plump Chechen.

She pretended to stumble against the side of the car. Ross saw her gaze sweep the hilltop. He took the chance to wave his arm and thought she must have seen him, even in his camouflage. She seemed to bend over, winded. Ross also saw her reach to the back of her leg for the small pistol he knew she kept there.

As she did so, Emm's head appeared from a hole in the ground. Tomás slung his gun on the strap over his shoulder to roughly pull her into the open.

Cervantes also clambered out of the hole. His son helped him up the last step and then turned his gun on Emm. Cervantes said something sharply. Tomás let the barrel sag toward the ground. He ran toward the Jeep's driver-side door, and Ross knew they were about to force Emm into the car, too. But her gaze had gone toward Abby, seeing her bent toward her ankle.

When Cervantes pushed her between the shoulder blades, she whirled on him. She'd shifted her weight back on one foot and turned to grab his arm, trying to force it up as she grappled for his gun, swinging around, using her entire body weight for leverage.

"Now!" Ross climbed to the top of the slope and scooted downward on his rear and back. Chad did the same, right next to him. The slope was steep enough that gravity did the work of pulling them down, and they could brace their elbows against their chests and sight carefully as they slid. A cascade of rocks and disturbed vegetation heralded their arrival.

They fired, but it was still dark; they were moving on their backs and their targets were at least fifty feet away. Their first couple of shots missed the mark, but stealth was no longer an option.

All four drug dealers looked up. Machine guns turned in their direction. Abby straightened, having used her bound hands to slip her small pistol from her ankle holster. The stout, short Chechen got off a few rounds that sprayed dirt and pebbles next to Ross, but then she'd fired at point-blank range into his meaty thigh. He screamed and fell to his knees. She smacked him over the head with her gun butt and he went down.

Ross had ignored the shots striking uncomfortably close and focused on the one thing that could save them all: accuracy. He needed to think not of his own mortality, or even Emm's struggle, at this moment. He needed to think only of his front sight. Ignoring the rocks and thorns piercing even through his heavy pants, ignoring the grunts and insults coming from Emm's direction as she fought Cervantes for his pistol, Ross narrowed his gaze on a tiny, bright dot, iridescent in the moonlight—his front sight. Even when bullets sprayed around him, he focused on the little dot centered on the piece of forehead he could see above the Jeep as Tomás braced his machine gun on the roof and fired at them.

Bracing his elbows on his chest to steady his aim, he squeezed off a shot. He was rewarded with a spray of red mist and other heavier matter as Tomás's head exploded. He fell behind the Jeep, the machine gun sliding harmlessly off the roof.

Without a pause, Ross next moved his aim toward Cervantes. They were slowing now as they neared the bottom of the slope, allowing them to aim more carefully.

It also made them easier targets.

Ross tried to aim at Cervantes, scared to death Emm would lose the struggle with the drug lord, but Cervantes and Emm kept switching places as they fought.

Chad had missed the tall Chechen the first couple of times, allowing the man to chitter slugs at them. One glanced off Chad's heavy chest plate, ricocheting into the night. Chad was disoriented for a second, but another shot pinged off a rock right by his ear, bringing him back to his senses. He took a deep breath and did as Ross had done, wagering his life on his front sights. As he squeezed off another shot, he saw the Chechen aim a fusillade at Ross. He heard Ross cry out. Chad's next shot caught the Chechen in the neck. He went down, also dropping his gun, but Chad was a few seconds too late. Ross had been hit.

As they both slid to a stop at the bottom of the slope, Chad moved to turn toward his partner, but meanwhile Emm had finally lost her precarious grip against Cervantes's brutal power. Abby had turned her small pistol in Cervantes's direction, so she didn't see the half-dazed Chechen on the ground when he reached for her ankle to pull her off balance. Then she and the Chechen were grappling for her weapon, but Abby, without compunction, kicked him in his thigh wound. He screamed and shrank away. This time, when she clocked him, she used his fallen machine gun butt. He went down and stayed down.

While she was fighting the Chechen, Chad leaped up and rounded the tree so he could have a clear shot at Cervantes, who was turning his pistol on Emm. She fell to the ground as if defeated, but when Cervantes pointed the gun down at her, she grabbed up a small, sharp rock and rammed it upward into his ankle. He cried out, his gun hand wobbling, and Chad was able to shoot to wound, not kill. He caught Cervantes in the gun arm, and the pistol finally fell to the ground.

It landed right next to Emm ... She looked around for the first time, seeing Ross lying still, blood trickling under him into the dirt. She grabbed up the gun and scrambled to her feet, pointing at Cervantes. "You sorry son of a bitch," she said, and her finger tightened on the trigger.

Cradling his wounded arm with his other hand, Cervantes cast a quick glance toward the Jeep and must have seen the remnants of his son. Grief distorted his face for a moment, and then he snarled, *"Chupa mi verga, puta fea."* And then, in English, "Shoot."

As Emm's finger tightened, "Emm, no," came a weak plea from Ross's direction. "I don't want to lose you to the Mexican court system. We need him alive."

Chad had reached the two of them, and he gently pulled the pistol from Emm. "I have the asshole. See to Ross." When Cervantes turned to flee, Chad used the butt of the .357 to pistol whip him a couple of times, forcing him to his knees. Chad cuffed him. He looked around, seeing Abby had the rest of the situation under control.

She'd obviously found a knife and sawed through her own bonds, and was now doing the same with the general's, who'd climbed back out of the Jeep. When the plump Chechen on the ground stirred, the general reared back his leg and booted him in the forehead. The Chechen went limp again. The general spat on him.

Meanwhile, Emm had run to Ross, still sprawled at the bottom of the slope. She pulled frantically at his body armor until she'd bared his t-shirt. His shoulder wound was still bleeding. She pulled Ross's shirt up and used it as a bandage, pressing hard to stop the bleeding. The other slug had grazed his side, leaving a raw, oozing line but no bullet hole.

Chad forced Cervantes up the slope. "I'll send the medic. Lie still, Ross." And to Emm, "He'll be fine."

When Cervantes dragged his feet, Chad kicked him in the butt. "I'd purely love to plug you, so keep it up!" Cervantes didn't know all the words, but he knew the tone . . . reluctantly, he climbed.

Abby smiled at the pair on the ground as the general tied up the wounded Chechen. More sirens blared up the hillside, and they knew the situation was, finally, under control.

Ross's hand, grimy and dotted with a few sprays of blood, reached shakily toward Emm's head. He stroked down over the side of her hair, which was stiff and standing up, darker than the other side, with the blood from her scalp wound. "We'll start a new style," he teased. His voice was steady, as strong as ever.

Satisfied he'd be okay, she sat back on her heels and gave him a brilliant smile back. "What's that? Zombie chic?"

Ross ignored her protests and levered himself to a sitting position, wincing a bit but looking steadier every minute. He fumbled inside the jacket she'd removed and unzipped an inner pocket. "No, how to propose in extreme situations."

Emm went very still.

Abby knew she was decidedly de trop and turned to open the back of the Jeep to begin searching it. The general gave the pair a curious look and climbed the slope to assess his men. For the moment, the couple were alone, or as alone as they could be surrounded by dead and wounded men.

Ross pulled out the small box he'd brought along, just in case. It had been rattling around in his inner flak jacket pocket, along with the spare bullets for his Ed Brown. Appropriately enough, he decided, his mouth quirking. No nonsense mixed with the sublime.

Just like Emm. He waited for her response.

She stared at the ruby and diamond ring winking at her in the moonlight. Ross had had several nice rings left to him by his paternal grandmother, but this was his favorite. Three carats. The center Burmese ruby, virtually impossible to find today in this clarity, was as perfect as the woman he was gifting it to, and it was surrounded by brilliant white diamonds. When she still didn't answer, Ross pulled the ring out and lifted her finger.

"I know this is a bit sudden, but hell, it may ease the way with the Mexican authorities. We're in a very macho country." He began to get nervous when she still stared down, mute. "Besides, this is the best way I know of to hold you close, where I can keep an eye on you. Handcuffed to my bed . . . pregnant and barefoot in my kitchen." He was deliberately goading her, trying to get a rise out of her. But his fingers began to tremble a bit when she still sat there, on her heels, staring at the ring. Was she going to say no?

Dear lord, he'd never even considered that possibility. "Wow, if I'd known this was the way to shut you up, I'd have stolen the Hope Diamond," he joked. Still nothing.

Finally he added, "It's my sworn duty, too, in the interests of protecting my fellow law enforcement officers. Now you've helped catch one of the world's most dangerous drug dealers, you may tackle the Mafia next, God forbid."

To his huge relief, Emm finally stirred. She threw her arms around his neck and kissed him, hard.

He kissed her back, not even feeling the pain in his side. They were sweaty, dirty, blood streaked, sore, and Americans in a foreign country, but no kiss had ever satisfied either of them as much. When they drew apart, she looked at him seriously. "What about Elaine?"

"Who the hell is Elaine?" he said and slid the ring on her finger. "What about your career?"

She couldn't avoid a flicker of regret, but she said, "If I have to choose, I choose you."

"Maybe you don't have to choose. I'll have a heckuva wedding present for you." And to shut her up again in that most pleasurable of ways, he kissed her, sideways this time. Deeply.

As the medic clambered down the slope toward them, he found the couple entwined in a passionate embrace and slowed his pace a bit. Ross would obviously live.

Ross would. And, well . . .

And there, beneath a smiling half moon, Ross Sinclair pledged his troth in the age-old way, kissing Emm through blood and grit and grime, which somehow made the vow a bit more sacred. Even if it was on foreign soil. Literally.

CHAPTER 16

A few days later, Emm carried a big bouquet into Yancy's hospital room. Her sister was sitting up, a drip still attached to her arm, but color had begun to come back into her face. Emm had visited a few hours after the gunfight, relieved when the doctors told her they'd reached her in time, and that Yancy's wound had slowed to a trickle.

Emm and Ross had checked into the nicest hotel in Mexico City and cleaned themselves up, teasing each other about comparing scars. Then they'd been taken to police headquarters for a very long, tedious debrief that lasted almost two more days. Yancy had also been quizzed as soon as she was conscious, and her information, she'd learn later, would lead to the arrest of the major players in the Los Lobos cartel. As the general told her, she had suffered greatly, but her insight would save many innocent young women from the same fate.

Yancy had turned away, tears in her eyes, and the general had called for Emm. Emm did what she could to comfort her sister, but tears dripped from her own eyes because there was really nothing to say to assuage the horrific loss of a child, especially in such a brutal way. They had at least been able to recover Jennifer's body, and she'd be traveling home with them.

Now, a few days later, the entire team had been cleared to leave the country, including Yancy, and they were there to travel with her in the van to the DEA jet.

There was only one big question. . . .

"Where do you want to go, honey?" Emm asked, sitting next to her sister to hold her hand. "Ross has asked me to marry him, and he has several guest cabins behind his house, if you'd rather have your privacy, but we'd love for you to stay with us awhile in Amarillo.

And . . . there's a place for Jennifer, too, if you decide to stay, or we can transport her back to Baltimore."

Fully herself finally, Yancy turned her cool green gaze on Ross. "When Emm loves, she's Gibraltar. I can be a pain in the ass, and she's the only one on earth who never gave up on me."

He shifted his feet a bit, flushing, and said only, "I probably don't deserve her. But I love her and will spend the rest of my life trying to make her happy." He caught Emm's hand. "And we both want a family, so we can pass on what we've learned the hard way. We . . . hope you'll stay with us awhile so we can get to know one another."

She relaxed a bit, staring over Emm's head. "I . . . don't know. I don't know where I want to go, or what I want to do. Jennifer . . . we both believe in cremation, anyway."

Emm bit her lip, looked for Ross's approval. He nodded.

"Yancy," Emm said, "they've arrested Brett Umarov. Inside the compound, they found tons of evidence linking him to Los Lobos. Ross says they have enough to send him away for a very long time. And if he's an accessory to . . . murder . . ." She tailed off, hesitating to mention Jennifer's name.

Yancy looked at Emm. "And Curt? Was he involved, too?"

Ross nodded. "It seems Mr. Tupperman is the one who brought the Chechens to Umarov as possible business partners. The funds we found in his account were not from Los Lobos. They were from Eastern European mobsters interested in working with the cartels. Because of his travels and his exposés, plus his fluency in Spanish, he was able to broker the deal and help with money laundering. For a piece of the pie. That's why Cervantes didn't know him. Umarov was the contact; Curt was the facilitator."

"Abby—I mean, a colleague of Ross's," Emm said, "found a case of money in the back of the Jeep. Inside was Curt's Belize bank account and routing numbers. He tried to slip away after everything was over and had just about convinced the DEA he was innocent when Abby brought the case to them."

Ross finished simply, "The Mexican authorities requested and got the US attorney general's permission so that Curt can be tried in the Mexican courts. He won't do his time in a cushy federal pen. He'll be in a Mexican prison for a long time."

Yancy smiled, but it was still a wan one.

Emm swallowed. "If you want to go back to Baltimore, I'm okay with that, Yance. I'll even go with you for a while."

Ross glanced sharply at her, then away, when assessing green eyes turned in his direction.

Yancy smiled, really smiled, with a flicker of her old mischief, for the first time since coming to the hospital. "Bluffing again, sis? You still suck at it."

"Hey, I learned from the best . . . You should have seen my ante with that asshole drug dealer. It was a doozy. We're both still here, aren't we?" She carefully caught her sister's hand. "I'm sorry, Yance. . . . If only I could have come sooner."

Yancy turned her face away, her voice so soft Emm had to strain to hear her. "It was too late for Jennifer anyway. She never would have been the same. . . ."

Emm squeezed her hand harder. "At least you're safe."

Nothing for a long moment, and then a bleak little, "Yeah. Safe."

And Emm knew it would be a very long time before her sister felt either safe—or whole—again.

About a year later, Yancy, her hair cut fashionably short so it framed her beautiful face, walked into the Hoover building to meet her very pregnant, very busy sister. She'd lived on Ross's good graces for only a couple of months before she'd insisted on getting a job. She'd decided to give Texas a try because she really had nothing holding her in Baltimore.

She'd dusted off her clerical skills and gone to work for a local law firm, but after the wedding, when Emm had officially been added to the deeds of the Hoover and Draper buildings and started the redevelopment, Yancy had yielded to her pleas and helped her with all the legal and administrative tasks Emm despised.

Sometimes, she even talked a bit about Jennifer.

Emm knew her own pregnancy was a boon, not just to her and Ross, who could scarcely keep their hands off each other, but to Yancy as well. Babies meant a new beginning, even after terrible grief.

Yancy had watched Trey a few times after Emm introduced her to Jasmine, and the three women were now fast friends. Abby occasionally joined them when she came into town for business. She'd arrived today for her first tour of the buildings and had already made a very sensible, logical suggestion to fix one of Emm's design dilemmas.

Today, three months before her due date, Emm was giving Jasmine and Abby a tour of the upper-floor apartment she was having constructed for her and Ross as a place for them in town.

Yancy was following along with the plans on an iPad. She'd converted the document to digital herself after taking a CAD course, pointing at the area on the plans Emm was struggling with while Abby peered over her shoulder. All three women were discussing the issue when Chad and Ross entered the foyer.

Ross bellowed, "Where's my not so little woman?"

Emm yelled back, "And whose fault is that? Where's my dinner? I'm hungry." She grinned at Jasmine and Yaney. All four women went to the balcony, which overlooked the lobby.

"You're always hungry," Ross said, grinning foolishly up at his wife.

Chad and Ross bounded up the steps. "Jasmine, don't get any ideas," Chad warned, stopping two steps down when he saw Jasmine standing next to rounded Emm. Ross finished the climb, grinning as he watched the debate.

Blinking innocently, Jasmine looked at Chad. "What ideas?" She caressed Emm's stomach.

Emm held her hand there. "Feel him kick?" They knew it was a boy. Because Emm had turned thirty-nine during her pregnancy, they'd had all the latest tests.

Chad pretended horror. "Good grief, what if it's catching?"

Ross put his arm around his wife and grinned at her. "Yeah, what if it is? Three boys is better than two, I've heard. More compromise."

Chad pushed his hat back. "Yeah, not when they're led by a little terror who's too much like his namesake." Trey was entering his terrible twos, and Chad was still learning to be a father. He'd resisted Jasmine's efforts to talk him into another child. So far.

But he was wobbling.

Ross winked slyly at Jasmine. "You just need to whip up some more fried chicken. That'll soften him up."

Jasmine hooked her arm with Chad's. "Good idea. Would you all like to come out this weekend? I promise not to burn it this time."

Pulling her close, Chad drawled, "I know of something else that would work for sure."

"What's that?" Jasmine smiled up at him.

"A leather harness suspended from the beams."

Jasmine whacked him as the others laughed. Abby looked mystified, but her rare laugh made the others smile when Emm whispered in her ear.

Then all of them trailed after Emm as she continued the tour.

Emm was literally glowing, partly from the pregnancy but mostly from happiness.

Abby trailed behind, bringing up the rear, feeling a bit like an intruder.

And if somewhere, deep inside, she was both a bit envious and a bit melancholy at the sight of the happy couples, she didn't show it.

Yancy dropped back to join her. She saw the look on Abby's face and hooked arms with her. "All this domestic bliss makes me want to toss my cookies. Would you like to go with me to this cute little dive bar I've found?"

Abby wasn't precisely certain what a dive bar was, but she really liked Yancy, who in her own way was just as unconventional and secure in her own skin as she was. "I would enjoy that immensely."

And off the two women went.

The other four didn't even notice.

Read on for a glimpse of Colleen Shannon's first Texas Ranger, *Foster Justice,* available wherever ebooks are sold!

"Intense romantic suspense with a sexy edge."
—Tanya Anne Crosby
New York Times **best-selling author**

One Riot, One Ranger . . .

That's the Texas Ranger motto, but when Chad Foster's rebellious brother goes missing, it's time to put his elite training to use investigating a crime that strikes much closer to home. Turning Los Angeles inside out to retrieve Trey and save their ranch from a ruthless land grab is a no-brainer, even if it puts his badge at risk. His only lead is a heart-stoppingly sensuous exotic dancer with a very tempting butterfly tattoo, the woman who helped scam his brother out of their ranch. But staying on top of this redhead's every suggestive word and sensual move means putting his case— and his heart—right in the line of fire. . . .

A Texas Ranger, complete with quarter horse, is as out of place in downtown LA as a lawman is in the bed of a suspect, but with both their lives at risk, Chad has to put his trust in the one woman who could bring him down for good, and pray that somehow hard evidence is really just a pack of lies. . . .

A TEXAS RANGERS NOVEL

COLLEEN SHANNON

FOSTER JUSTICE

CHAPTER 1

As rustlers went, they were better'n most, Chad Foster decided, caressing his AR-15 rifle mounted with a night vision scope. The thieves, probably the same ones he'd been chasing all over the Panhandle, had herded his cattle up to this plateau far above the canyon floor, giving the Black Angus little room to escape being forced into the huge trailer. Still, pursuing lawbreakers as part of his job and finding them rustling his own private stock were two different things.

Keeping his spirited stallion, Chester, still with his knees, Chad peeked around the outcropping, gauging distance and angle. If he aimed just right, he should be able to take out enough tires on one side to cripple their rig. Then what? He was one man, on a horse, against three hardened criminals in a huge tractor trailer.

While he contemplated his options, a Texas sunset painted Palo Duro Canyon in golden and red hues of blood and glory. The rays winked off his distinctive Texas Ranger Lone Star badge like a warning light. But the scroungy wannabe cowboys were too busy to notice, zipping around on ATVs, corralling steers toward their cattle trailer. Chad's lip curled. No matter how fancy their rig, likely stolen, too, Chad viewed rustlers on a par with worms and strippers: the only critters too low to fall down.

Cattle prices had finally gone up enough to make it worthwhile for a part-time rancher. Should be just enough profit to catch up on those back taxes Trey had let slide. He wasn't about to lose the cattle now—even if he was outgunned and outnumbered. Hell's bells, the old Ranger motto was still as valid today as it had been when coined over a century ago: "One riot, one Ranger." His decision made, in his usual to-hell-with-the-consequences fashion, Chad eased out of hiding while the rustlers were busy with the trailer latch. He reined Chester around the outcropping to take careful aim at a huge rear tire.

A stray steer spooked Chester. The stallion whinnied and reared. Looking up, the rustlers spotted him. In his cowboy hat, chaps, and spurs, with the rearing sorrel quarter horse reddish against a violet sky, Chad was an image right out of the Old West, when retribution was more than a fancy word. Getting the message, they abandoned their ATVs for the truck.

Chad needed both hands to calm Chester, the rifle slung over his shoulder, and by the time he was able to take steady aim, the perps had fired up the huge diesel and stirred up a cloud of dust, leaving him choking in their wake. He squinted, his eyes tearing as he tried to sight, but the scope was useless in all this dust. He shouldered the rifle and kicked Chester into a gallop, moving at an angle that would cut them off at the dirt road leading off the plateau.

Then, to his shock, he realized the huge vehicle, with a screeching of brakes and spitting of dirt and rock, had done a one-eighty, driving back toward the canyon edge. Chad wheeled Chester around to keep pace. The truck's lights pierced the haze of dirt and dusk, blinding spooked and confused cattle. Behind them was the canyon rim; in front loomed that huge mechanical monster.

While Chad stared, trying to figure out what in tarnation the rustlers were trying, the truck lurched forward, Klaxon horn honking, lights blinking, rock chunks spitting as it came, startling several steers. The confused cattle took the path of least resistance and ran away—straight toward the canyon edge, less visible in the growing gloom.

God Almighty, they were forcing the steers over the edge just to spite him! Chad looked frantically around, but he had no backup and little inspiration, only hard choices.

Lose his herd, or risk his life to stop the stampede. On horseback.

In the end, the choice wasn't difficult. He had no wife, no kids, and no girlfriend. In fact, he only had three things he valued in life: one little brother who hated his guts, the fourth-generation Amarillo ranch that had bred them both, and The Job. And if he let these assholes buffalo him, he'd risk all three.

The truck gained speed, horn blaring, and the milling cattle went from a lope to a panicked stampede. At this rate they'd be over the rim in minutes. Spurring Chester into a flat-out gallop, Chad bent low over his stallion's neck, leaping over boulders, down a small gully, back up the other side. But the rough path allowed him to cut in front of the truck and ride alongside the herd, perilously close to the canyon edge.

However, Chester had been a cow pony all his life, and he'd herded panicked cattle before. They wove through the milling herd, slowing some of the laggards a bit more with their diagonal passage. Chad pulled his rifle and fired at boulders above the lead steer's head. Bits of rock sprayed the steer in the face, making him snort and slow a bit, but that damnable horn blared again.

Roaring, the engine revved into a higher gear, brights flashing, and the slowing stampede picked up speed. They were halfway to the edge now, a sheer drop two hundred feet to the canyon floor.

Chad sped up again. He could risk everything and try to get in front far enough to herd them around, or take on the truck now and to hell with the herd. Or he had one shot to do both. Urging Chester to the edge of the stampede again so he could gain speed on the outside, Chad guided Chester with his knees and sighted back over his shoulder as he rode, trusting his horse with his life.

Holding his breath and letting the rhythm take him, Chad became part of Chester, feeling the rise and fall of each step, his hands steady on his rifle. He sighted at the horn as it blew a fresh clarion. *Bam!* The shot landed dead center, killing the horn's bellow with a gush of air.

Next he aimed at the headlights. He hit one before Chester stumbled slightly, and Chad almost went flying. He had to let the rifle sling back over his shoulder while he grabbed the reins. They were galloping even with the lead cattle, and he urged Chester faster, putting distance between him and the head of the herd.

Ten feet, twenty, thirty, fifty . . .

Just before the canyon rim, Chad wheeled Chester like the quarter horse he was, damn near on a dime, sighting again before he stopped. Chester's hooves broke rock off the crumbling edge. One part of Chad registered the rockslide he'd started and how long it took the rocks to hit the canyon floor, but the coolest part of his brain calculated distance and angle.

The other headlight was smack dab in his crosshairs. *Pling!* The last light went out. The truck slowed, downshifting again. Taking advantage of that hesitation, Chad shot repeatedly now at the rocks littering the path of the stampede leader. The steer blinked and bawled as rocks scoured its face, slowing as it shook its head.

Chad shot a scrubby tree into bits, more litter blocking the lead steer's path. It slowed again. The cattle in back, now that they weren't blinded and spooked by the horn and lights, had also slowed. But the truck, idling for an ominous moment, began to speed up again, gears grinding. The cattle in back shied away.

Glad he'd put in his biggest clip, Chad fired at the lead cattle again, grazing hooves. They stumbled. A couple fell, slowing the ones behind.

But they were close, too close, a mere thirty feet away now.

He had one chance to avoid being swept over the canyon rim by his own herd, and he took it, firing at the rig's tires. One blew, two, three on one side, and the truck began to lurch, slowing as the front axle hit the ground.

Chad tried to fire in front of the lead cattle again and cursed when he heard an empty click. They'd slowed a lot, but were still coming. Using the only weapon he had left, Chad cued Chester into a rear and roared at the top of his lungs, wildly waving his rifle over his head, hoping he loomed large and terrifying against the dying sunlight.

Chester whinnied, pawing the air. Ten feet away, the lead steer veered to the side rather than face the angry quarter horse.

The rear cattle milled around again, confused.

Chad was able to whack the last few cattle away from the rim and make his way toward the rig. It lay skewed on one side as Chad quickly put in another loaded clip and reined Chester toward the driver-side door, rifle pointed.

He was expecting it, so when he saw movement in the gloom, he fired. Yelling in pain, the driver dropped the pistol he'd been aiming at Chad's head. Chad fired at the passenger-door side, too, and it slammed shut.

Holding the rifle steady on the driver, Chad appeared at the window, his angular, grimy face as hard as the landscape around them. "Haven't you heard, boys? Beef's bad for you. Especially when it isn't yours." He waved the rifle at them. "Out. This side, all of you."

The driver got out first, cursing a blue streak Chad ignored. His men followed. "Put your hands on the side of the truck." They did so.

Still seated on his horse, Chad ignored his handcuffs and pulled his lariat.

"Lean back away from the truck." When they obeyed, Chad neatly hooked the leader around the waist, and got down and tied the hands of the next two men with the same rope, turning them into a cowboy-style chain gang. He cinched the other end of the rope around Chester's saddle horn.

"Hey, mister, what you doing? You don't mean to walk us back all that long way! In the dark?" protested the lead rustler.

Chad kneed Chester, forcing them to stumble along behind. "You put me in a mind to herd something. It's only, say, twenty miles back to headquarters. We'll see how much piss and vinegar you have then." Settling back in his saddle, Chad ignored their bitching and walked them down the road, through peacefully grazing cattle.

He debated calling Trey to let him know he wouldn't be in until morning, but it was a useless courtesy since little brother was probably stone-cold drunk. Like usual. Over a woman not worth a hat tippin', as his daddy would say.

Colleen Shannon grew up in West Texas, where the skies are as limitless as the tales told by its many colorful residents. Surrounded by oil men, lawyers, and drillers in a community that has produced two presidents and many national leaders and businessmen, Colleen grew up reading and writing stories of every kind. After college, when she married and was expecting her first child, she used a scrap computer to write her first romance. She sold it herself in less than a year, and at the age of twenty-six began a new career and never looked back. The strength of her first book led to her nomination by Romantic Times as Best New Historical Author. She went on to win or be nominated for many other awards, and her fifteen single title releases have appeared on numerous bestseller lists. She has well over a million books in print.

Her newest release is from Kensington, a romantic suspense, her first published contemporary. It is planned as the first in a series about modern Texas Rangers, another interest of Colleen's because her ancestor, a Texas Ranger, was one of the first people buried in Brown County cemetery, Texas. Another one of her ancestors was a signatory to the Texas Declaration of Independence.

Visit her at:
www.colleenshannonauthor.com
Facebook: www.facebook.com/RomanceWriter?ref=h1
Twitter: Colleen Shannon@bookwriter2001

www.ingramcontent.com/pod-product-compliance
Lightning Source LLC
Chambersburg PA
CBHW031359250626
47155CB00004B/1333